It Had to Be You

Danielle Palli

IT HAD TO BE YOU

ISBN: 978-1-7367982-5-6 (Print)

It has brought me so much joy being able to write the third and final book in the Music Mystery Series. Like with my first trilogy, The Data Collectors, I love all my characters like they are dear friends (even the troublesome ones!). I half expect them to knock on the door one day and come for a visit. (Not really. But how cool would that be?)

I would like to thank my friends, family and fans for taking the time to read, review and share my works with others. Special thanks goes to my friend and colleague, Cindy Readnower of Skinny Leopard Media for her editing and publishing support. Thank you to Graham Mack for co-producing and narrating the audio version of my books with me. Thank you to my 'partner in crime' and the love of my life, John Palli, for his never-ending support.

A trip to Ireland inspired the location of this book, and I'd like to also send a heartfelt thanks to Mike Costello, a guide who regaled us with historical anecdotes about the Emerald Isle (most of which were true!) and left me with these wise words, "Never let the truth get in the way of a good story."

For all the people who have shown up in my life just when I needed them, I am grateful.

Prologue

Note: This section contains spoilers for Book 1 (***If I Didn't Care***) and Book 2 (***Pennies from Heaven***). If you're starting with Book 3 (***It Had to Be You***), or need a quick recap, this will get you caught up.

The year is 1999 and almost eleven months after the Troubles ended in Ireland.

Emma Post and her boyfriend, Officer Dennis McCleary, helped solve the murder of wealthy tycoon Erasmus Vandenberg, owner of Vandenberg Nutraceuticals, and were now settling into their new home in Florida.

But they had unearthed a can of worms, Vandenberg nutraceuticals was tied to the Church of Infinite Love, an organization well-regarded as a cult. Somehow, Erasmus Vandenberg had secured supreme control over both the church and the nutraceutical company, working alongside his daughter Edwina and other Elders of the church, selling faith-healing, miracle nutrition bars, and the security of a safe life on one of their many campuses worldwide. The only family members seemingly above suspicion were the socially awkward Elsbeth Ions (Edwina's daughter); hermit Edgar Vandenberg (Elsbeth's uncle); and distant cousin, the ever-charming playboy, Baxter Baker.

Officer Dennis sought the advice of his former boss, Detective Jose Ortega, who gathered a team comprised of his colleague and former love interest, forensic scientist Dr. Penelope Washburn; cybersecurity expert and private investigator, Darwin

Fennec; and his partner, Rue Brennan; and finally, an officer with the Tampa sheriff's department, Shep Stern.

The team had managed to shut down the church's operations in Florida, only to learn that the Vandenberg family was returning to their roots...that is, reopening their original factory in Ireland, one that had lain dormant for years. With the reemergence of the factory, the church was likely to resurface as well, rebranded and repackaged...but just as dangerous.

At the behest of Midge Pasternak, a woman Darwin and Rue had sent to prison nearly two years prior, Rue agreed to join Ortega, Penelope and Shep in Dublin. It was Midge whose meddling brought Rue and Darwin together in the first place, after they teamed up in New York to clear their names of a double-murder—one up-and-coming singer and one art model—in order to outsmart Midge's sociopathic partner in crime, Jax Liebling.

In an odd twist, Rue revealed she had been brought up in the Church of Infinite Love and would likely know how they operate. Therefore, her presence on this newest case was essential. Unfortunately, Darwin Fennec's ties with Ireland were not good ones, and he vowed never to set foot on the Emerald Isle ever again.

Chapter 1
Edwina

New York

Edwina was getting restless. Ever since Vandenberg Nutraceuticals shut down the Florida factory and word got out about the church's questionable practices; they were hounded by the police. And while they found enough evidence to link the company to at least five deaths at church campuses in the Northern United States, family lawyer, Mr. Lundy, and his team had done such a good job of covering their tracks that no one person could be blamed...except of course, one of their Ambassadors who died under suspicious circumstances while in prison. They took the fall for Erasmus's death, and the death of a Deaconess at one of the Pennsylvania church campuses. But the older cases went so far back that it would take many more years and cutting through lots of red tape and corruption to get to the bottom of it all.

Still, the damage had been done. In addition to Vandenberg Nutraceuticals facing bankruptcy, church membership had fallen by nearly 40%. Apparently, the faith-healing business was not what it used to be. Then, of course, there was the fact that Emma Post, a figure model who now controlled the bulk of the company, was planning to sell off both factory properties...one in Florida and the other in Dublin.

And, as if it couldn't get any worse for Edwina Vandenberg, daughter of Erasmus Vandenberg, Erasmus saw to it that Edwina got next to nothing in his will. The New York condo now belonged to her daughter, Elsbeth, and in another few months, Edwina would be tapped out and forced to sell her luxury estate in the Hamptons.

She had already laid off all of the housekeepers at both locations, with the exception of Ferdinand, Erasmus's personal assistant. Despite taking a considerable pay cut, Ferdinand remained a loyal member of the church and to Edwina.

Edwina sat on the couch of the home that now belonged to her daughter, recognizing that she had limited time left as Elsbeth's guardian. She flipped through a tabloid that unearthed a conspiracy theory that everyone on staff at the factory or at the Vandenberg residences were also secret Ambassadors and Elders of an underground cult. Unfortunately, the story was a little too on point.

Edwina let out a huff as she ripped the cover from the tabloid, crumpled it up in a fit of anger and launched it like a baseball into the fireplace. It hit the mantle and dropped, un-singed, in front of the hearth.

"Would you care for a sherry, Madame Edwina?" Ferdinand asked. "It might settle your nerves."

Edwina stiffened her shoulders for a moment before consciously relaxing them away from her ears and tilting her head from side to side to loosen her neck.

"I'm afraid I need more than sherry to settle my nerves tonight, Ferdinand. What I need is...a miracle."

Chapter 2
Midge and Jax (Not Jaks)

Dublin

"Okay, I'm here," Midge announced, dropping her carpet bag on the floor with a thud. She struggled to breathe. "Is it me?" she asked, looking around. "Or do you manage to suck the oxygen out of every room you enter?"

"Perhaps, I simply take your breath away," Jax answered, moving toward Midge. "I've missed you."

Midge stepped backward, holding her palms out as a barrier. "That's close enough, mister."

Jax paused, fighting back a smile. "So coy," he admired. "Alright," he agreed, "I'll play your little game."

Midge looked at the handwritten note he had left her. "This is signed Jax with an 'x' versus Jaks with a 'k' and an 's.' Did you forget how to spell your name?"

"I got tired of everyone mispronouncing it. Besides, I thought you'd find it sexy...'Jax.'" He fanned his hand out as if his name were appearing in lights.

"You realize that it's slang for 'toilet' here, right?" Midge slipped the note back into her coat pocket.

Jax frowned.

"And what about 'Liebling?'" she challenged. "Jaks with a 'k' was a problem, but not that unfortunate last name you settled on?"

"'Liebling' means 'darling,'" Jax, now with an 'x', explained.

"So you're a darling toilet?" Midge retorted.

Jax's steely eyes bored into Midge as he fought back anger. "I remember a time when you couldn't get enough of me, baby," he softened his voice. "What happened to us?"

"You know darn well what happened to us, darling!" Midge surveyed Jax from head to toe, along with the surroundings, ensuring that he wasn't armed and that she could make a hasty getaway if needed. She saw two escape routes...one was the door of his flat, through which she'd just entered, the other was a window behind the living room couch that may or may not open, with who knows what beneath it? She stepped backward, closer to the doorway, just in case.

"My goodness, are you planning your escape already?" Jax was surprised. "I thought you knew me better than that." He moved forward.

She jolted.

He stopped.

"Yeah, well, so did I," Midge answered flatly.

"I came home one day and you were gone. Why? What drove you away from me?" Jax appeared almost hurt...almost.

"That would be a series of 'whats', Jax," she answered. "Locking me in the bedroom while you set fire to the living room because you thought I was having an affair—"

"I didn't like the way that barista was looking at you—"

"So, suffocating me was the answer?!"

"I was outside the entire time. I wouldn't have let you die. It was just a—"

"A what, Jax? A warning?" Jax remained silent. "Then there were sex rituals—"

"I thought you liked those," Jax protested.

"Look, I may have my share of kinks, but you took things way too far. Feather tickling and fuzzy handcuffs are one thing. Almost choking me to death while sticking pins in me is something else."

"They were acupuncture needles," Jax explained. "If anything, they were supposed to help you relax."

"While you were choking me?!"

"So, you didn't like that?" Jax clarified.

"No, Jax!" Midge was astounded. "I didn't like that!" Without thinking, she began pacing the room, nervously. This was a challenge as she was limited to walking from the front door, past the small kitchen on one side, to the living room on the other, to the opposite wall. Behind it, was presumably the bedroom. "It was different when you took your vengeance out on people who deserved it, but not when you turned your violence on me."

"Baby," Jax carefully circled around Midge, his back toward the door. "I would never intentionally hurt you. How could I? I love you."

"I know I'm no expert on love, but I'd be willing to bet what you feel for me isn't love. It's obsession."

"Oh, really?" Jax grinned, taking a cautious step toward Midge, eyeing her from head to toe. Despite her protests and her obvious discomfort, she still craved his attention, and he knew it. "Can't my obsession be out of my overwhelming love and desire for you?" He took another step. "Why do you think I pushed for us to get a marriage license, a destination wedding as it were?"

Midge backed up, only to butt up against a long end table.

The side of it pressed into her back. It was then she realized that Jax was now blocking the front door and moving toward her. How could she have let her guard down? She was smarter than that. "Destination wedding, my ass! To you, it's a business opportunity and a chance to get me away from anyone or anyplace familiar to me. You take control by relieving me of mine, by any means possible."

"Maybe I just reel with jealousy at another man...or woman, for that matter...taking your attention away from me. Maybe I just want you all for myself...to possess you. I thought a change of scenery would be good for us."

"What are you talking about?" Midge questioned, uncomfortably. "What other man? And what other woman? I've never even dated a woman," she protested.

"I'm talking about Rue Brennan," he explained. By now, he had reached his target. Resting his left hand on the table, Jax kept his right arm at his side, leaving just enough room for Midge to slip past him and escape. Only, she didn't budge.

Jax was so close, she could feel his breath on the side of her face and the heat kicking off his body.

"Rue's my bestie, that's all," Midge explained.

"Thanks to your 'bestie,'" Jax whispered, "you ended up in a women's detention center, remember? She's the reason we both almost ended up spending the rest of our days behind bars."

"I thought you liked bars," Midge answered, recalling one of Jax more elaborate cages during a lovemaking session.

"Funny, baby," he smiled. "Last chance—"

"Last chance for what?" Midge choked out as Jax leaned in until his lips were a mere inch away from hers.

"I thought so," he smiled. She knew it too. Unless he planned to chase after her, there was nothing preventing Midge from bolting for the open door, other than perhaps fear or...something else.

Suddenly, Jax grabbed Midge by the hair with his right hand and dragged her lips to his as he kissed her, forcefully. Despite her better judgment, she kissed him back, leaning uncomfortably over the table. She put one hand behind her for support.

She broke her lips free for a moment, only to reaffirm, "Rue is just a friend. I have a friend code and all."

"Do you now?" Jax kissed her again, biting her lower lip, playfully. "Well, I don't like it when your 'friend code' gets in the way of us."

"There is no 'us' anymore, Jax," Midge explained.

"Think so?" he answered simply, as he grabbed her hips and lifted her onto the table until she was seated with her legs dangling off the edge. He separated her knees and moved his hips forward until he was firmly pressed against her belly, and wrapped his arms around her in an embrace, pulling her feverishly toward him. "Then why did you come back?"

"To tell you in person," Midge explained. Even she knew it sounded weak coming out of her mouth. She draped her arms over his shoulders as he nuzzled her neck.

"Tell me what?" Jax asked coyly, kissing her again.

"To stop calling, sending me messages, spying on me, sending me presents. It's over," she whispered as she somehow managed to pull him even closer, so that their bellies and chests were firmly pressed together.

"I can't stand all this space between us," Jax complained, breaking free long enough to unbutton her coat. She struggled to remove it, until it was finally laying behind her on the table with her still sitting on the edge of it. Jax eyed her black dress and matching stockings, noting that the hem only reached mid-thigh. "If I didn't know any better, Midge," Jax confessed, "I'd say you planned this."

"Don't be silly," she whispered, breathlessly, "you and I are finished."

"Are we?" Jax grinned, seductively moving toward her again. Only this time, he slid his hand on the inside of her thighs, moving upward as he used his other hand to press against her chest until she was lying with her back on the table, legs still dangling over the side. "Somehow, I don't think we are."

"The door is open," she reminded him, quietly. "Anyone could come by and see us."

"Well, then I hope they enjoy the show," Jax replied, seductively.

Midge stared at the ceiling momentarily, fighting back a moan. "Maybe once more, for old time's sake?" she offered, gasping at his touch.

Jax smiled, mischievously, before reaching for his belt buckle.

Chapter 3
Red Eye to Dublin

Dr. Penelope Washburn thumped her carry-on bag behind her as she followed Jose Ortega to their seats in TWA's First Class cabin. Never having traveled so well, she looked sheepishly toward Rue Brennan and Shep Stern as she boarded the plane. They were delegated to Coach. No one knew where Midge Pasternak was. Rue thought that this was probably for the best, at least until they had gotten settled in Dublin.

Penelope paused when she reached her seat, surveying the wide aisles and ample space with childlike wonder. "Wow," was all she could think to say, in her smooth Southern accent.

"Yes, well." Ortega relieved Penelope of her bag, sliding it in a storage unit under her chair. "Say what you will about Nancy, but she certainly knows how to travel in style."

Nancy Ortega was his soon-to-be ex-wife, after he'd discovered, quite recently, that she was having an affair. But she was gracious beyond measure and dipped into her family fortune to finance Jose's (or, Ortega, as he was most often called) tickets to Ireland, even calling to ensure the airline upgraded Penelope at the last minute. Nancy had her connections, and she had no trouble using them, particularly when inspired by guilt.

"I'll say," Penelope answered, uncomfortably, as she sat down and fastened her seatbelt. She was not a diamond and pearls kind of gal. Her definition of luxury was a Sunday afternoon nap on the couch with her cat curled up beside her, purring. And while it had been well over a decade since she and Ortega had been an item, before the breakup and his hasty marriage to Nancy, Penelope felt as if she were somehow stepping into the shoes of a woman of which she could not fill. She wasn't sure why it bothered her so much. It never had before. Yet somehow, she suddenly felt inferior. *Why?* She wondered to herself. She watched as Ortega dutifully procured himself a Jameson whiskey and a glass of Prosecco for her from the flight attendant. *There isn't anything still left between us anymore...is there?*

Penelope eyed Ortega's beverage curiously. She knew him to be more of a Kentucky bourbon sort of guy. Ortega pulled out a Cuban cigar and lit it. After taking a puff, he answered her knowing gaze with a, "Well, 'when in Rome,' as they say."

He sat back and took a sip of his whiskey and another puff of the cigar. Nancy would not approve. And, while the wound was still fresh, somehow he felt an odd feeling. *What was it? Relief?*

Finally, they were en route to Dublin, where the First Class cabin was treated to steak and potatoes delivered on a dining tray with a table cloth and utensils...not a boxed lunch sandwich typically reserved for economy. Penelope's eyes grew wide, but said nothing.

"Excuse me, sir," a flight attendant addressed him, uncomfortably, "but we don't allow cigars on the plane."

"Not even in First Class?" Ortega was surprised. He'd never flown First Class before, but he assumed that the rich could get away with anything. At least, that was his observation from his many years in law enforcement.

"Cigarettes are okay, though," she offered. "May I offer you a cigarette?"

"Oh, no," Ortega cringed. "Nasty stuff."

The flight attendant wasn't sure why the distinction, but smiled politely and extinguished the cigar for him.

Penelope couldn't understand how his palette couldn't be tainted by a cigar before dinner anyway, but she decided not to press the issue. After all, why spoil a good moment?

The attendant announced the in-flight movie, moments before a large screen at the front of the plane lit up. They were screening, *When Harry Met Sally*, one of Penelope's favorites. She plugged her earbuds into the port in the arm of her chair and giggled pleasantly. Ortega glanced her way and smiled, opting to watch the screen in silence with passing interest.

"Aww," she grabbed Ortega's arm, reminiscing, as Harry Connick Jr., launched into *It Had to Be You* from the soundtrack. "They're playing our song," she laughed. She remembered a slow dance one night at a friend's wedding where Ortega had been her *plus one*. The singer was actually a recording by Frank Sinatra, but the song was the same. She removed an ear bud and pressed it into Ortega's left ear. He leaned in, uncomfortably.

"Some others I've seen," Penelope sang quietly to Ortega. "Might never be mean. Might never be cross or try to be boss, but they'd never do—" She smiled up at him. Ortega peered back at her as if he were dreaming and might wake up at any moment. The last 48 hours had been surreal.

"Another drink, sir?" A flight attendant interrupted their revery.

Penelope released Ortega's arm, and slunk back into her seat, the sudden movement pulling the bud from Ortega's ear canal and sailing through the air and landing in her lap. *How embar-*

rassing. She was behaving like a schoolgirl. She knew it, and she didn't like it.

"No, thank you." Ortega replied, turning to Penelope, motioning to her beverage. "And you?"

"No," Penelope smiled pleasantly at the attendant. "Nothing more for me, thanks."

After dinner, the lights in the cabin were further dimmed and the movie came to an end. Penelope reclined in her chair, slid an eye mask on and turned blindly toward Ortega before putting in ear plugs. "Goodnight, Jose," she whispered quietly.

Ortega, who had decided on another whiskey night cap after all, swirled the ice cubes in his glass and whispered back, "Goodnight, Penelope."

While Penelope and Ortega were enjoying dinner and a movie with ample leg space, Rue and Shep were sandwiched in the cheap seats between the smoking and non-smoking sections of the plane. Rue coughed and wrinkled her nose, distastefully. Shep's oversized frame seemed to take up more than his share of space and Rue was certain he was hogging all the extra oxygen too. Despite shrinking into her seat, Shep's elbow seemed to keep digging into her ribs.

Rue was stuck in the middle seat. To her left, at the window, was a small woman who had padded herself up with an oversized pillow and a comforter that she had wrapped around her like bubble wrap. It wasn't long before a gentle snore could be heard from deep within the folds of the blanket.

Rue folded her arms and closed her eyes in a vain attempt to fall asleep, but Shep was having none of it. With case files strewn across his tray table, he sifted through them obsessively, trying to connect the dots.

"Help me make sense of this," his voice boomed in Rue's ear just as she began dosing off. She sat up abruptly, startled. Shep didn't seem to notice.

"Wha?" Rue yawned, rubbing her eyes in an attempt to focus.

"You were a member of the Church of Infinite Love, correct?"

"Yup," Rue answered, groggily. "Born into it. Took far too long to get away."

"And you didn't know anything about Vandenberg Nutraceuticals selling drug-laced products to the church as part of a faith-healing racket...and to control the masses...not even an inkling?" Shep seemed doubtful. "Where did you grow up, under a rock or something?"

"That's one way of describing it," Rue answered flatly. "You've clearly never experienced brainwashing or led a sheltered life. You do what you're told and don't ask a lot of questions."

"What happened if you asked questions," Shep persisted. "You'd think they'd appreciate an inquisitive mind." *For a generally smart man, Shep said a lot of dumb things.*

"More like an obedient one." Rue attempted to roll to one side, turning her back toward Shep. "Could we discuss this in the morning? I'm exhausted."

"Yeah, sure." Shep was visibly disappointed. He took solace in a bag of peanuts offered by the flight attendant. Rue cringed. Somehow, Shep managed to make as much noise as humanly possible trying to open the tiny bag with his thick fingers.

Rue closed her eyes and willed herself to mentally block out the sound of Shep's crunching, which was somehow *not* drowned out by the white noise from the plane.

"But can you just answer one more question?" he tried again, moments later.

Rue flopped on her back in a huff, hunched in her seat as if she would melt into the floor at any moment. "What?" she asked, agitated.

"How'd you get out? I mean, couldn't you just leave?"

Rue wondered that very same thing. It wasn't as if there were armed guards at every campus or even gates that locked at night. So, why did it take her several attempts to get free? And why, once she'd gotten out, had she gone back?

"Well, it's like this, Shep," Rue tried her best, "get a bunch of insecure people down on their luck, like my parents. Tell 'em how special they are, that they're the 'chosen ones' with a reward in heaven. This life doesn't matter, cuz there's a better one, one that will treat 'em like they deserve to be treated."

"So far, that sounds like most religions," Shep offered.

Rue ignored him, she was on a roll. "Feed 'em a nugget of truth that they can bite into so they develop trust. Then, little by little, start manipulating that truth. Do it well enough and no one questions it. Start meeting at out-of-the-way, secret places because non-believers just wouldn't understand and might even try to sabotage the church. Begin cutting off outside influences that might conflict with church doctrine. After all, the Devil hates the chosen ones and the church, and would do anything to destroy them. It's okay if people ridicule you. That's a sign you're doing the right thing in God's eyes. Persecution becomes a badge of honor."

"Wow," Shep replied, "your parents must have been really gullible."

Rue's face felt flushed. "And what about your beliefs, Shep? Last I checked, you have a pretty strict religious code of ethics, to include your wardrobe and your diet...not that anyone could tell, as much as you eat."

"Hey," Shep whined, "I have low blood sugar." After a few

minutes of silence, he tried again. "Sorry, didn't mean to strike a chord there—"

"Trigger," Rue corrected.

"What?" Shep asked.

"I think you meant, a 'trigger.'"

"Not sure there's a difference—" Shep stopped mid-sentence at Rue's death glare. "Never mind. But that still doesn't answer the question. Why didn't *you* leave?"

"Why?" Rue bounced the idea around for a moment.

"Stop overthinking and just answer the question," Shep prodded, impatiently.

"Fine," Rue agreed, blurting out, "I didn't leave because I was born into the cult that told me how and what to think from day one. You only got to learn what they thought was important for you to know, and that created a reliance on them for safety and security. They get you believing that the real world is a scary place and that if people don't get you, the Devil will. And if you leave? Well then, now you've pissed off God too." Rue folded her arms, angrily. "Why didn't I leave? Because I had no idea how to take care of myself or think for myself, and the only people I had to ask were telling me that everything would be just fine if I just listened to them and behaved."

"But, somehow you got out," Shep pointed out.

"Yes," she answered. "I did."

"What changed?"

Rue thought a moment. "I was all set to be married off to an Elder in the church." She sifted through the memory in her mind. "Since I was already considered too old by the church's standards, that meant they'd expect me to get pregnant right away. If that happened, then like it as not, I would have been stuck in that life forever. And the thought of that was scarier to me than anything I could expect to experience in the outside world."

"You got out," Shep nodded approvingly. "Against the odds, you got out...good going."

"Yeah, but I didn't know anyone. Midge was the first person I met when I reached Manhattan, and she helped me get settled into my apartment and find a job."

"Your first friend was a psychopath...nice."

"Say what you will about her, but she kinda helped save my life."

"Hmm," Shep answered, nodding his head and grinning. "The Lord works in—"

"Don't!" Rue cut him off.

"Sorry," Shep replied. "Bad joke." He collected his files, folded up his tray table, and stuffed his paperwork in a duffle bag under his seat. "But hey, you said you wanted to get some sleep. We can talk more later." He leaned back and closed his eyes. In a moment, the sound of a small kazoo could be heard as he inhaled and exhaled. Finally, his mouth dropped open and a bit of drool landed on his shirt.

Rue cringed distastefully and turned her back on him for a second time, shifting in her seat, trying in vain to get comfortable. *Great,* she thought, shutting her eyes. *Now, I'm wide awake.*

The blanket-wrapped woman sitting next to her peeked a head out from her cocoon. She touched Rue carefully on the shoulder. Rue opened her eyes to see a cherub-faced woman with bright blue eyes looking at her with deep sympathy.

"I'm sorry, sweetie," she cooed, "I couldn't help overhearing your story. That must have been awful."

"Well," Rue answered, "life is a lot better now." She thought about Darwin and how they'd left things when she'd gotten on a plane to Ireland. "Still got a few things to work out, though."

"Well," the woman answered softly, "if it would help, I can pray for you. Would you like that? Can I pray for you?"

Rue felt her jaw clench, before answering calmly. "Please don't."

The four arrived at Dublin Airport mid-morning, and by the time they'd reached their short-term rental in Swords, they were dead on their feet. It had been years since Ortega had been to Ireland. The last time was when he was investigating a high-profile case involving one of the longest-running feuds on the Emerald Isle, but Ortega didn't want to revisit that story, even in his mind. Fortunately, some of his old connections were still good, and he was able to line up temporary housing just outside of Dublin. It was a two-bedroom rental with a single bathroom and efficiency kitchen. It wasn't glamorous, but it was functional.

They knew they weren't going to accomplish much that day, so they agreed on a quick trip to the local Tesco for a few groceries to prepare a light meal followed by an early night.

The team had all jumped on a plane to Ireland on short notice and without a plan, a sad reality that only hit them as jet lag set in.

Rue rationalized that she wanted to help make sure the church didn't face a resurrection in Ireland. Yet, in the back of her mind, she wondered if what she really needed was space to process past traumas and work through her relationship with Darwin. Nothing was really wrong, per say, except that she had been pulling away from him and he knew it. Something about the situation, as happy as it was, left her feeling trapped. It's not as if she couldn't leave any time she wanted to, not that she did, but old wounds were surfacing, reminding her of a time where she was stuck in a life she couldn't get away from. And of course, there was the guilt over the death of her mother, a Deaconess who died after trying to help her. And finally, there was that nagging feeling about Midge. Despite all the havoc her friend unleashed in her life, what she told Shep was true. She didn't know anyone when she escaped to New York, and for a long time Midge was the only person she could count on. A small part of her felt like she owed her something, despite everything.

Ortega was itching for a case he could sink his teeth into, and was dying to know why the church had shut its factory down in the first place. Nancy had given him an ultimatum once, and he gave in, retiring from work that he loved in an effort to save their marriage. But now that Nancy was no longer in the picture, there was a part of him that relished an adventure, a complex case spanning two countries.

Shep, as we would come to learn, disliked injustice of any kind, along with puzzles he couldn't solve. If there were other motives, no one really understood what they were. Something about his personality caused him to somehow fall into strange situations, getting wrapped up in everyone else's drama while lacking the ability to say, "No."

Meanwhile, Penelope tried to convince herself that she was doing the right thing by helping the team. And since she was now out of a job, why not take an exciting trip overseas? If she were being honest with herself, she would have admitted that what she was really hoping for was a do-over. What if she and Ortega could go back to the way things were? Minus the fighting and breaking up, of course. They had this electricity between them when they worked together.

While Ortega would have much rather had Penelope stay in his room, he didn't want to make assumptions. And, he was fairly confident that Rue and Shep had no interest in being roommates. So Shep and Ortega took the small room, equipped with bunk beds and a small dresser and chair that sat next to a clothing rack, while Penelope and Rue made do in the slightly larger room with one single bed and a fold-out cot from the closet.

"You want the top bunk?" Shep asked when they had settled into their rooms.

Ortega eyed the oversized man, annoyed. "What do you think?"

"Right," Shep said. "Probably best if I take the top, even though I'm heavier than you, cause your knees probably couldn't handle climbing up and down the ladder."

"Why would you assume that? Just because I'm older? My knees are just fine," Ortega complained.

"So—"

"Go," Ortega motioned. He removed his sweater and pants, draping them across the chair, but left his undershirt and boxers on. He sank into the bottom bunk, uncomfortably. The mattress had little shape left to it, and he could feel the springs beneath it on his spine. *It's like I'm back in college,* he thought. Ortega waiting impatiently as Shep tossed and turned, trying to get comfortable, his mattress sagging so much that Ortega was concerned the bed wouldn't hold his weight. The frame was too short for the tall man, so Shep settled on curling up in a fetal position. It was the best he could do.

Just as Ortega was about to nod off, Shep spoke up. "So, are you an Dr. Washburn an item?" Shep had a knack for asking inappropriate questions at the worst possible times.

Ortega sighed. "Not for a long time," he answered.

"What went wrong?" Shep asked, inquisitively.

"Goodnight, Shep," Ortega answered, abruptly ending the conversation.

Chapter 4
The Plan (According to Midge)

"Why did you drag us all the way to Ireland, Midge?" Rue asked, sliding into a chair across from her former friend. Shep, Penelope and Ortega followed suit.

Midge, still a fugitive after having escaped a women's detention center in New York, returned long enough to convince Rue that she needed to help her take down the church, and Jax Liebling, for good. It was she who convinced them to fly to Ireland in a rush, only to promptly disappear and then resurface three days later. A note was left taped to their flat instructing them when and where to meet her later that day—a bar and restaurant not far from where they were staying.

"Correction," Midge eyed Penelope, Shep and Ortega, as the five of them sat gathered around a table in the Old Schoolhouse to talk. "I dragged *you* to Ireland. I wanted your string-bean boyfriend Darwin Fennec along and encouraged your buddy

Elsbeth to pay a visit to her dear Uncle Edgar. The rest of youse guys were unexpected."

During the early hours of the day, the restaurant was nearly empty, and the only one planning on eating was Shep who let his stomach override his principles. He ordered the fish and chips even though he was fairly convinced it wasn't kosher. And the only one drinking was Midge who was now on her second Jameson double-shot.

"I swear," she complained, "they water this down."

"You ordered it straight up," Rue reminded her.

"That don't mean they don't fill the bottle with a few parts wuh-ter, if you know what I mean." Midge leaned in and whispered loudly, her Tri-state Philly-New York-Jersey accent becoming thicker the more she drank.

A server shot Midge an annoyed look, but said nothing. As long as they were paying customers, she was going to be polite to the rude American.

"Can I get anything for the rest of you?" the server asked. Penelope, who felt bad about taking up space and not ordering anything, asked for a cup of tea. "Biscuit with that?" the server asked.

After a long pause, Penelope added, "Sure."

Ortega and Rue waved off anything. For once, they were of the same mindset—get what information you needed from Midge, and get out. After all, neither of them trusted Midge, and for good reason. It just so happened that they had no authority to do anything but report her to the New York police department, and they hesitated to do that while she was useful to them. And furthermore, they shouldn't even be here in the first place. Ortega had retired. Penelope was fired. Rue was too close to the case to be objective and Shep was, well, Shep. He was still gainfully employed back home, but if his supervisors got wind of what he was up to, he likely wouldn't be for long.

This plagued the former detective immensely. He had always been on the straight and narrow, but ever since he met Rue Brennan and her cyber forensic investigator boyfriend, Darwin, bending the rules was becoming increasingly easier. He justified it in his mind because it was all in order to bring down the 'bad guy,' but if he sat alone with his thoughts for a little too long, he might have come to the conclusion that one of the 'bad guys' was him. He put it out of his mind.

"I assumed you'd want the help of Ortega and Shep if you had any intention of taking down the church," Rue defended. "And Penelope—"

"Rookie mistake," Midge chastised. "But it's okay. Despite your gross error in judgment, I can work with this."

"What exactly is going on here, Miss Pasternak?" Ortega demanded.

"Calm down, Fuzz," Midge answered. Ortega lurched forward and opened his mouth with a retort but Penelope grabbed his arm before he could answer. Instead, he sucked in his breath "In my revised plan, as of two minutes ago, *you* get to take down the entire Church of Infinite Love operation and the Vandenberg Nutraceuticals empire to boot. Darwin and Rue were supposed to get that honor, but whatevs." She rolled her eyes casually, as if they were discussing what movie to see that weekend, not a murderous cult.

"Kinda thought we already had done that," Ortega answered, feigning ignorance.

"Please," she waved a hand at him. "I know your reputation. You're not *that* dumb."

Ortega balled a fist. Penelope tapped his arm, supportively, glaring at Midge. *She's just trying to bait him,* Penelope thought.

Moments later, the server returned with Shep's meal. She eyed Penelope. "Ah, sorry. Tea will be right up..." The group fell silent until she had scurried off to the kitchen, remembering Penelope's tea.

"You know as well as I do they are rebranding their efforts by selling off the Florida factory and giving the Dublin factory and the church a facelift," Midge explained, leaning forward and watching as the server walked away.

"So, business as usual?" Shep used his fingers to break off a piece of the crispy fish, dipping it into tartar sauce and popping it into his large mouth. He then proceeded to wipe his fingers on a napkin, a touch of the tartar sauce still sticking to his chin.

"Not hardly, Beefcake," she answered, amused. Shep furrowed his brows, taken aback. He wasn't entirely sure how to take that comment. "They may give the illusion of change, getting out of the faith-healing business even, but if Jax Liebling is involved, there's something else going on."

"What?" Shep demanded.

"I don't know yet," Midge answered.

Ortega let out a deflated sigh. He suspected Midge *did* know but she sure as hell wasn't telling.

"Listen, F—" she was about to use her new nickname for Ortega, saw his expression, and thought better of it. Midge wasn't always keenly observant, but Ortega's expressions weren't exactly subtle. "Ortega," she finished. "The one thing I know for certain is that if Jax is involved, it's bad. And he's not one for sharing. He may have put that lemming, Baxter Baker, as the front man at the nutraceutical company, but make no mistake, Jax is the one in charge. And, I know him, give 'em enough time and he'll have both Baxter's job and Bernie's too."

"Who's Bernie?" Ortega questioned.

"You mean you don't know?" Midge was incredulous. To Rue she asked, "Can you believe this guy?"

"Ms. Pasternak—" Ortega tried again.

"Fine, fine fine..." Midge relented. "Following Erasmus Vandenberg's untimely death, the reins of the church fell to his daughter, Edwina Vandenberg. Except, according to church law, a woman can't be in charge, so Bernie stepped in. As I said, Jax doesn't play well with others. Given enough time, he's gonna want both operations."

"And what's it to you?" Penelope chimed in as the server set down her tea and biscuits. Penelope mouthed a 'thank you' and the woman nodded before retreating to the kitchen.

"The church ruined my bestie's life," Midge punched Rue in the arm.

"Ou!" Rue rubbed her arm. "And I wouldn't say 'ruined.'"

"Not to mention what she did to that gal, Elsbeth," she added.

"Why do you care about Elsbeth?" Rue asked. "You barely know her."

"That's not what's important," Midge answered. "What is important is that these gents can go down in history as shutting down the largest global grift of the century, and you can get revenge on the people who screwed up your life."

"Again, I wouldn't go so far as to say—" Rue tried again.

"Fine, revenge on the people who—" Midge began.

"I wouldn't say revenge—" Rue interrupted.

Midge punched the table with a fist, angrily. "Sorry!" She eyed Rue. "You're lucky you're my best friend," she acknowledged, "cuz you sure are a piece of work. Alls I'm sayin' is you can ensure that future generations won't have to go through what you did in your wackadoo upbringing."

Rue caved, "Fine, I can get behind that reason. But the larger question still remains, why would you help us?"

"Like I've told you before, Jax is obsessed with me. The only way to get him off my case is if he's behind bars for a very long time."

"And yet, you came to Ireland seeking him out, not the other way around," Shep pointed out.

Midge smiled and winked at Shep, reaching over the table and dabbing the tartar sauce on his chin with a spare napkin. He blushed, rubbing his chin as if there were still something on his face. "Good observation, Beefcake," she answered. "But Jax has been following me all over the States and parts of Europe for the past year. I even tried escaping to Japan for a bit, but he found me there too. So when I heard what he was up to in Ireland, I knew this was my chance to head him off at the pass."

"Hang on, Midge," Rue interjected. "You told me that after all this was over, you were going to turn yourself in. Why not do that now and return safely behind bars where he can't reach you."

"Where he can't—" Midge shook her head. "Oh you poor, naive little thing. There's no where I can go where Jax couldn't find me. At least if he's under lock and key, I'll know where he is at all times."

"Wait a moment." Penelope asked, "If you're that afraid of him, why are you here in the middle of the day? Does he know you're in Ireland?"

"Of course, he knows it." Midge grabbed the third and final whiskey that the server placed in front of her and stood. She sucked it down and plunked the glass next to the other two. "I'm staying at his flat...ta-ta, my friends. I will be in touch. But don't try to reach me. Jax can't know I'm talking to youse guys."

"What are we supposed to do in the meantime?" Shep whined. "Take in the sights and wait for your call?"

"No, Beefcake," she answered, "you and Fuzz...sorry...Detective Ortega, geez, so sensitive," she eyed Ortega's expression, this time, noticing a few imaginary daggers flying from Penelope's eyes as well. "You can check out the Vandenberg factory and interview Jax and Baxter, maybe do a little snooping. But again, you haven't seen me since Rue visited me at the woman's detention center in New York over a year ago. Capisce?"

"Wait," Rue remembered. "Why is Elsbeth here? Isn't she safer back home?"

"With her nutball mother, Edwina? Not even. As far as I can tell, her uncle Edgar is the only one in her family not mixed up in this business. When you take the family down, she'll be protected."

"Why the sudden interest in Elsbeth, Midge?" Rue wasn't sure what Midge's angle was, but she knew it wasn't empathy.

Midge's eyes bore into Rue's momentarily, the side of her jaw twitching slightly. "As I said," Midge answered, measuring her words carefully, "you and she were innocent victims of the Church of Infinite Love. I don't like seeing the innocent get hurt."

"Then we should probably check on Elsbeth," Shep called out. "Just to make sure she's safe."

Midge had already reached the front door, tugging it open as a gust of wind tore through her hair as it funneled into the room. "You can if you want, Beefcake," she called, "but I think the Westports have already got that covered."

Chapter 5
Bernie, Mr. Lundy and Jax

Two Months Ago, Dublin

Bernie Forger wasn't very happy when he arrived by the Oscar Wilde Statue at Merriam Square. If he had his way, he wouldn't be in Dublin at all, but in his high-rise condo in Manhattan. He was just settling into his new role as the ordained leader of the Church of Infinite Love following the death of his predecessor Erasmus Vandenberg when the church came under close scrutiny of the police and the media. He wasn't a bit concerned about the police. Mr. Lundy's team could take care of that. And, he was fairly certain the Vandenbergs had a large number of the police force in their back pocket. The press, on the other hand, were a different story. Even when you did them favors, offered them exclusive interviews and fancy hotel stays, they still found ways to discretely leak information about the church's questionable practices.

They called the Church of Infinite Love a cult. *How dare*

they? Bernie thought to himself. Unlike Edwina Vandenberg who very well knew that at the end of the day, it was all just business, Bernie bought into his own hype. He believed himself to the be chosen one to lead his small, elite flock to glory in the afterlife. That's what made Bernie so dangerous. Like Jax, both men had an overwhelming sense of self-importance coupled with a healthy dose of delusion. Perhaps that's why Bernie took an instant dislike to Jax Liebling, who, from his perspective, seemed to appear out of nowhere. He slithered in when no one was looking, and now he was on the verge of taking over Vandenberg Nutraceuticals at the behest of Mr. Lundy.

Jax arrived moments later, gnawing on what appeared to be a piece of freshly-baked soda bread wrapped in white paper. Jax finished chewing as he crumpled the paper and surveyed the area for, presumably, a trash receptacle. Finding none, he tucked the paper discreetly in the ivy vines at the base of the monument, below Oscar's foot—thereby making it someone else's problem.

Bernie eyed Jax, distastefully, but merely nodded a head, acknowledging his presence.

"Gentlemen," Mr. Lundy arrived moments later, briefcase in tow. He never seemed to go anywhere without it. "Thank you for meeting me here. Let's take a walk." He motioned for them to follow. The three men began a slow stroll down the short meandering path around the square.

Jax grinned and silently padded along behind him, while Bernie fell into step beside Lundy. "Lundy, what's going on here?" Bernie whispered. "Do we really need *him* here?" Make no mistake, Bernie wasn't even trying to be subtle.

"I know you don't like me, Mr. Forger," Jax addressed the man from behind. "But you should. I'm about to make life a hell of a lot easier for you."

"How do you figure?" Bernie spat back.

"Ahem," Mr. Lundy cleared his throat. Lundy had the two

qualities that Jax and Bernie lacked. First, he never, absolutely never, lost his temper or control over the situation—any situation. Second, his mind wasn't clouded by delusions of grandeur. He was manipulative when it suited his best interests, and he was exceptionally good at it. "You know I'm here only to serve," he said with false humility. "I had the honor of serving Erasmus Vandenberg and his family for nearly two decades, and I know the inner workings of both the church and Vandenberg Nutraceuticals. Trust me when I tell you that it is refreshing to see both organizations fall into the hands of such worthy men as yourselves."

Jax puffed his chest out a little. Bernie lifted his chin with pride. Both were oblivious that Mr. Lundy was merely stroking their egos. And it worked.

"Bernie, Jax has a plan that can help clear the good name of the Church of Infinite Love and help you turn a profit. That's good business all around. I think you should hear him out."

Bernie bit his lip. The men paused as a few teenagers moseyed past them hooting and laughing loudly at nothing in particular. Finally, he said to Jax, "Well, go on then."

Jax unbuttoned the top collar of his shirt. The tightness around his neck felt suffocating. He sniffed a moment and answered. "I think we should convince the Vandenberg family to name Baxter Baker CEO of Vandenberg Nutraceuticals."

"What?" Bernie was incredulous. "Baxter Baker? Out of everyone in the family, he's not only the least competent man for the task, but he was the one who tried to sell out his family, the business and the church in the first place!"

Jax paused. He knew the strength of a silent pause and used it to frame his thoughts very carefully. Finally, he replied, "And that's exactly why you need to put him in charge and encourage the family to divorce themselves of the company and sell the outstanding shares to me."

"How does this help me and my calling, exactly?"

Jax chewed on his inner cheek to cause enough discomfort that he didn't give anything away in his facial expressions. What Bernie referred to as a 'calling,' Jax would have named it an 'opportunity' or a 'mission.'

"What he means to say," Mr. Lundy intervened, "is that with the rest of the family being out of the nutraceutical business, media attention will turn its attention away from them and the church."

Bernie was struggling to put the pieces together. "But giving up the factory will cut into the church's bottom line," Bernie protested.

"I promise you, it won't," Mr. Lundy encouraged. "My team has been over the contracts with a fine-tooth comb and met with your accountants for countless hours. The only way for the Church of Infinite Love to survive and to keep you out of bankruptcy and out of prison is if you have—"

"A scapegoat," Jax finished, grinning so wide you could see both his upper and lower teeth.

"You mean…" Bernie connected the dots. "Sell out Baxter."

"Your words, not mine," Jax answered in a sing-song voice. "But it would be poetic justice, wouldn't it?"

"That might keep the media and the law off our backs, but I'm in the business of selling miracles. The church has always relied on those health bars to encourage compliance. What will we do without them?"

Mr. Lundy wanted to cringe at the word 'compliance' when talking about members of the church, but he kept his expression neutral.

"What I'm suggesting," Jax finished, "is a rebrand. Let Baxter take the fall, and then I'll step in and help resolve this. By the time I'm done, the church will have seen the light and people will be buying up Vandenberg health snacks like Girl Scout cookies if it means continuing the Word of God."

"So, you'll be in charge," Bernie confirmed. "What happens to the rest of the Vandenberg Elders?"

"Does it matter?" Jax argued. "They'll get a nice chunk of change, and you can encourage them to donate it to the church's mission. They still see you as their new leader. Why not capitalize on that?"

"I don't capitalize, Mr. Liebling." Bernie's face grew red. "My only interest is God's great work," he finished.

"Of course, it is," Jax gloated, condescendingly. Bernie lurched forward and reached for Jax's collar as if to shove him off the path and onto the well-manicured lawn.

Mr. Lundy, being a large man, sandwiched himself between the two. "Would you mind not causing a scene?" he asked calmly. Bernie backed down. To Jax, he said, "You are a real piece of work, you know that?" Lundy shook his head while Jax adjusted his shirt and swept back his hair with his hands.

"Do you really think I should go along with this?" Bernie asked Lundy.

"Yes, Mr. Forger, I do," Lundy nodded. "And I think if you look at this from a clearer perspective you'll realize that no matter the motive, this is in everyone's best interest."

Jax snorted, "Except for Mr. Baker's!"

For once, Bernie couldn't help himself, a deeply-rooted laugh bubbled up from his chest as he joined Jax in uncontrollable laughter at the thought of poor Baxter being the fall guy.

The only one not laughing was Mr. Lundy. He knew better than to let emotions interfere.

Chapter 6
Emma's Decision

Florida

"Emma Post, how delightful it is to hear the sound of your voice," Baxter's voice crackled across the phone lines.

Despite her long-standing relationship with Dennis, and her dislike for Baxter's overinflated ego, she had to admit that the sound of his voice gave her the chills...just for the moment. She quickly dismissed them.

"What can I do for you, Mr. Baker?" she asked, flatly.

"Emma, how disappointing," Baxter chastised. "No pleasantries? Cut to the chase? Is that it? After I—"

"After you saved my life," Emma finished. "I am truly grateful for that, Mr. Baker. But it also has not escaped my attention that you bring it up every time you need a favor. What is it this time?"

Behind her, Dennis could be heard rifling through the closet in the hallway of their St. Petersburg home. Once he heard who was on the other end of the line, he made an extra effort to make as much noise as possible, even slamming the closet door closed using much more force than was necessary.

Emma shot him a look. He rolled his eyes, held his hands up in surrender and then retreated to the living room.

"Emma, I'm hurt," Baxter sulked, ignoring the clatter he heard across the line. "By the way, what's all that racket?"

"None of your—" Emma caught herself. Dennis had pointed out to her that sarcasm was her default mode. She was trying to be better. "Nothing for you to worry about, Mr. Baker."

After an awkward pause, Baxter asked tentatively, "I know you already have a sale pending on the Florida factory," he began.

Good news travels fast, Emma thought. But then again, Baxter had been an executive of Vandenberg Nutraceuticals for years. It made sense that he would know about the sale.

"Yes, that's right," she admitted. "I'm sorry, Mr. Baker. I know that must be a financial blow, but I am talking with my accountant and lawyer so that I can offer nice severance packages to all employees of the company, including yourself." Emma couldn't believe what she was saying. *My accountant and lawyer?* This time last year she was barely making ends meet and living in a drab apartment in the lower West side of Manhattan. Now, she and Dennis had waterfront property, premium gym memberships, a property manager and even their own financial and legal team. The thought of it gave her a headache. While life was simpler before, she didn't miss stressing over paying her rent and how to afford the rising price of groceries.

"That's very thoughtful of you, Miss Post, but money is not what I'm concerned about," Baxter answered with false bravado. In truth, he cared quite a lot about money, particularly if he didn't have to work to have it.

"Then, why are you calling?" Emma was confused.

Baxter cleared his throat and sucked in a deep breath. "I want to buy the Dublin factory. Er, I mean, I want to buy you out as primary shareholder."

"You want to buy me out?" Emma was surprised. "With what?" She was under the impression that with the only working factory out of commission, that Baxter's financial resources would have dried up with it.

"Really, Emma. I'm not as bad with money as you seem to think. Besides, I have financial investors."

"Really? Who?" Emma was curious.

"Does it matter?" Baxter become defensive.

"Of course it matters," her voice went up in pitch. "I planned on shutting down Vandenberg Nutraceuticals completely, cutting all ties with the Church of Infinite Love, and selling both properties to ensure this sort of thing never happens again."

Emma was referring to the fact that Vandenberg Nutraceuticals had been owned by her deceased friend, wealthy philanthropist Erasmus Vandenberg, who also headed up a cult that controlled its members through mind-altering products created at the factory. In addition to the psychological harm it caused many members of the church, it also resulted in the death of several women. Emma still hadn't come to terms with the fact that Erasmus turned a blind eye to much of it, convincing herself that he, himself, planned to shut down operations as soon as he found out. His murder cemented this belief. Because anything other than this would mean that a man who was like a kind grandfather to her was a complicit liar.

Baxter tried a different tac. "Okay, okay," he relented. "The truth is, Elsbeth plans to sell the Manhattan condo as soon as Edwina has to legally turn it over to her. She and I will work together to make sure Vandenberg Nutraceuticals returns to what dear old Erasmus wanted...to make the world a healthier place with his nutrition bars."

"Elsbeth?" While Emma had no doubt as to Elsbeth's intellect, she wasn't convinced she had the knowledge to run an operation that large.

Baxter, reading her mind, added, "I also have a silent partner willing to invest. He's apparently pretty well known in certain social circles, so I can't say more than that. But what I can promise you is no more ties to the church and no illegal products."

Emma paused. Baxter knew her weaknesses: Elsbeth and Erasmus. Even knowing that she was being played still didn't completely rule out the possibility of selling her shares, and releasing control of what remained of the company to Baxter. She could be rid of the whole lot of them for good...the Vandenberg family, the church, her old nemesis, Rue Brennan, and that cyber forensic boyfriend of hers, Darwin Fennec...all of them. She could settle down in their little house in Florida, just she and Dennis, with Detective Ortega as a crotchety neighbor who joined them for dinner once in a while to talk about the good old days when he and Dennis worked together on the force.

"May I ask why the Dublin factory is of such interest to you?" Emma pressed him. "It's been shut down for years. Wouldn't it be easier to re-brand and start fresh in the States?"

"Well, it should come as no surprise to you that I don't exactly fit in with my family there. In fact, I think it's a safer bet for me to remain in Ireland. I know my way around and have my own security team."

"Security team?" Emma was curious.

"Tell you about it some other time. The point is, the factory, while in need of some retrofitting, was set up to specs for product production. It doesn't make sense for me to reinvent the wheel when I have a ready-made location right here, does it?"

Emma had to admit that he had a point. And, truth be told, she did feel guilty about Baxter taking a bullet for her. Not to mention that he was one of the only members of the Vandenberg family who had been honest with her from the beginning.

"Give me a couple of days to mull it over, Mr. Baker," she finally answered.

"Thank you, Miss Post. That's all I ask."

Baxter hung up the phone, sat back in his chair and eyed the weasel-like man who was sitting on a leather sofa across from him in a small office in Dublin.

"What happened?" Jax Liebling's eyes bore into Baxter's skull.

"She said she'd think about it," he answered. Jax's fists balled up as he forced in a breath.

"I see," was all Jax said.

"Why are you so interested in the company, anyway?" Baxter asked. "And why is it so critical to keep your name out of it?" He was growing very suspicious of his new business partner.

"Let's just say, Emma Post and I have a past, and leave it at that."

Baxter eyed Jax, curiously. He doubted it was of the romantic nature, as Jax wasn't much to look at and gave off this weird predator vibe. Truth be told, Baxter didn't much like his company, but thus far, Jax was doing what he promised: he protected Baxter from the police, shielding him from his involvement in Vandenberg Nutraceutical's shady dealings. Jax even convinced the remaining shareholders—family members who, quite possibly, wanted to see Baxter dead, to name him CEO of the company, and now he promised to help him take over the company entirely. And while he was suspicious of Jax Liebling's motives, Baxter was always pretty good at looking the other way when the truth became inconvenient.

Baxter nodded at Jax and quickly changed the subject.

"What was that about?" Dennis asked, struggling to hide his annoyance at learning it was Baxter Baker on the other end of the phone line—the same man who managed to skirt questioning by the police about what he knew about Vandenberg Nutraceuticals selling drug-laced nutrition bars to the Church of Infinite Love as part of their faith-healing scheme. He was also highly aware of Baxter's fondness of Emma. And despite the fact that Baxter was in Ireland, while he and Emma were living together in their home in Florida, Dennis still didn't appreciate Baxter's phone call.

"He wants me to sell him my shares of the company and turn the Dublin factory over to him," Emma answered, surprised.

"After everything that's happened?" Dennis was incredulous. "Rather brazen of him. And does he actually have that kind of cash?"

"Says he has a private investor, not to mention the support of his cousin Elsbeth."

"Hmmm," Dennis thought a moment. "We should probably run this by Jo." Jo was Dennis's nickname for his now-retired boss, Detective Jose Ortega, a name that Ortega hated, but learned to live with.

As if he heard his name from across the pond, Dennis's cell phone rang. "Jo!" Dennis answered cheerfully. "What's up? Aren't you supposed to be in Dublin by now?"

"We are," Ortega answered. "Penelope...er, Dr. Washburn and I arrived a coupla days ago. Still fighting off jet lag. Hey listen, my international cell plan is a joke, so I've got to make it quick."

"No problem, Jo. What do you need?"

"It just so happened that I got wind of some activity at the

Vandenberg factory today. It's been dormant for years, and I was curious if you'd heard anything?"

"Actually, it's funny you ask. Emma just took a call from Baxter Baker. Maybe you should talk to her. Hang on."

Emma took the phone and quickly filled Ortega in on her conversation with Baxter, ending with, "What do you think I should do?"

"I think you should take the money and run," Ortega answered, bluntly.

"What?!" Emma was surprised.

"Look, Miss Post. I've seen this sort of thing a million times. Some wealthy family gets caught with their hands in the cookie jar, manages to skirt the law and then rebrand their business in a more wholesome way. They know it's not wise to continue their business dealings in the US, so they've set their sights on Ireland."

"If that's the case, shouldn't I sell off the property to someone else, like I'm doing in Florida?"

"What do you mean, 'like you're doing in Florida?'" Ortega's reaction seemed borderline aggressive. This was news to him.

"Yeah," Emma confirmed. "A nonprofit that sells healthy snacks to raise money to support young women and babies said the set up was perfect for their needs."

"Does this company have a name, by chance?" Ortega was suspicious.

"Honestly, I didn't think to ask," Emma confessed. "My lawyer handled all of it so I didn't have to deal with Mr. Lundy and the Vandenbergs." Mr. Lundy was the Vandenberg's primary attorney, and as such, Emma didn't trust him.

Dennis eyed Emma, questioningly. Emma covered the phone and said, "He's asking if we knew who wants to take over the Florida factory." Dennis motioned for Emma to hand him the phone. She obliged, keeping an ear close as Dennis spoke with Ortega.

"Jo," Dennis began, "want me to see what I can find out?"

"No!" Ortega all but yelled into the phone. "The family is dangerous. Just connect me with your lawyer so I can ask him some questions, and I'll have Shep do some digging. Outside of that, I want the two of you to stay out of it entirely."

Dennis cringed. He wanted to help, but not only did he have no jurisdiction and wasn't in the position to legally do anything, but he dared not risk putting Emma in harm's way again, particularly given the fact they recently learned she was expecting a baby—their baby.

"So what can we do?" Dennis asked.

"Put Emma back on the phone," Ortega ordered. Then, catching himself, he added, "Please."

Emma took the cell phone.

"Listen Miss Post, my cell phone is about to die, and I just want to be sure to tell you one thing...I think you should take Baxter Baker's offer. It's the only way you'll get out from under that family's influence unscathed. Let me worry what happens after that, okay?"

Emma touched her belly, instinctively. "Okay," she answered. For once, not arguing just for the sake of it. "I'll let Mr. Baker know my decision."

Chapter 7
The Westport Grifters

Dublin

The Westport family resented being lumped into the 'Irish mob' category, when, in point of fact, they were neither mafia-related nor Irish. Their family fled to County Mayo sometime during the Russian Revolution, but conveniently, no one can find records of their original surnames. They became the Westports, and managed enough under-the-radar grifts to amass a small fortune. So while they may have been 'mob adjacent' they had a racket all their own. They even set up a side family jewelry business, selling gold-plated watches, manufactured gemstones and the like, careful to not overinflate the value of the items...just enough to turn a profit that would go unnoticed by tax collectors.

But they didn't take kindly to Vandenberg Nutraceuticals setting up a factory in Dublin—not because they were against big business coming to town—but because the Vandenberg's selling drug-laced nutrition bars to members of the Church of Infinite Love under the guise of 'faith healing' was too attention-grabbing a grift. The Westports were successful because they were largely unknown. Therefore, when the Vandenberg factory came to town, they resorted to doing a very mob-like thing...they began demanding money from the late founder and CEO, Erasmus Vandenberg, and his executives for personal and property protection...to the tune of 10% of the executives' annual salaries, along with 10% of the net profits of anything shipped out of the Dublin factory. They called it a 'tithe.' The irony was not lost on the Vandenberg family, though they didn't find it amusing.

Once the Florida factory began thriving, however, the Vandenberg's claimed the Dublin factory was no longer in service and shut it down. So the space sat there, dormant, and the Westports stopped demanding money. After all, if Vandenberg Nutraceuticals and the Church of Infinite Love were no longer drawing unwanted attention to Dublin by the authorities and the global media, then the Westports could safely manage their smaller business ventures without suspicion...until today.

"Mr. Westport," a young man dressed in street clothes and a ball cap cautiously approached the older man who was busy adding butter to the top of a blood pudding muffin before popping the entire pastry into his mouth. His dining habits didn't quite fit the sophisticated image the Westport family was going for, but none dared correct him.

Constantine Westport's throne-like chair had a personal dining table in front of it, both of which were on a raised platform that overlooked the main room of his mansion where he could see all corners of the space clearly. This large sitting area appeared more like one would find when visiting a castle and museum of some indeterminate past. As such, Constantine had all manner of 'historic-like' things, such as a metal suit of armor in one corner, a totem-like pole in the other, and a variety of tribal masks along the central wall. It was a beautiful room that echoed from the high ceilings…but one that really made no aesthetic sense.

"What is it, Scratch?" Constantine Westport asked, licking butter off of his thumb.

"I have some…troubling news." Scratch adjusted his cap, nervously.

"What news?" Constantine's deep blue eyes bore into Scratch's as if trying to read his thoughts. He shifted his large frame in his chair which squeezed beneath his weight as if in pain.

"Well, sir," Scratch continued. He knew that his boss hated small talk and word mincing. He got right to the point. "We have it on good authority that the Vandenberg Nutraceutical factory has resumed their operations as of this week." He paused, waiting for a reaction. He didn't have to wait long.

"What?!" Constantine slammed a meaty fist on the table, sending a cup of tea, along with an open bottle of Jameson sitting next to it, toppling clumsily to the floor, splattering tea and whiskey everywhere. Constantine paused to eye the hot liquid spilling down his hand before shaking it, angrily. Liquid dripped of his hand and onto his pants, the side of the table, and finally, the floor.

Within seconds, the housekeeper was there, mopping his hand off for him with a kitchen towel before she and another servant cleaned up the mess. The Jameson bottle remained unbroken. The same was not true of the shattered tea cup.

"Is Erasmus with them?" he asked.

"No, sir," Scratch answered. "Erasmus Vandenberg is dead."

"Well," Constantine reasoned, "he was pretty old."

"Actually, he was murdered…by one of his own, sir."

Constantine paused for a moment before a hearty laugh bubbled up from his belly. "Hah, well, I can't say as I'm surprised. Nice guy, but didn't understand the rules of the game."

A servant brought the large man a fresh cup of tea, her older hands shaking clumsily.

"Thank you, Iris," he acknowledged, taking the cup before she accidentally spilled it. Iris was getting on in years and could no longer handle many of the household chores she used to tend to, but Constantine valued loyalty above all else, and prided himself on adjusting her work to suit her aging body, making her in charge of hiring and training the younger staff. Iris was also tight-lipped, and that was a good quality to have among your staff when you're a grifter.

Iris nodded, seeming to vanish into the background, silently.

Constantine returned his attention to Scratch who was now busy plucking a bit of leftover breakfast from his teeth with a toothpick and wiping it on his jeans.

"So, who's heading up the operations now? Mordecai? Victor?"

"From what I hear, Baxter Baker, sir."

"Baxter?" Constantine let out a laugh. "That lazy, good-for-nothing playboy? Since when has he taken an interest in the family business?"

"Well, since Erasmus's untimely death, and with the Florida factory being shut down, seems it was in his financial best interest to resume operations here. He's also hired on a consultant."

"A consultant? What consultant?" Constantine demanded.

"Some guy named Jax," Scratch answered.

"Jacks, like a toilet?" Constantine snorted.

"His name is Jax Liebling, and he was involved in the Florida factory, but I don't know in what capacity."

"Who hires a guy who's named after a toilet?" Constantine couldn't let it go. He giggled and shot a glance toward a young servant whose name he hadn't learned yet. She giggled along, supportively, abruptly stopping as soon as her boss did. The room fell silent. "Well, whatever his name is, I'm none too fond of them drawing attention to Dublin again, particularly if, as you say, there were troubles in Florida," Constantine continued, "Are they aware of our rules?"

"Yes, sir," Scratch nodded. "In point of fact, Mr. Baker reached out to me."

"Really?" Constantine was surprised.

"Yeah." The young boy put his hands on his hips and shrugged his shoulders. "It seems Baxter has got a target on his back because he may have been the one who ratted out the family business."

"Why am I not surprised?" Constantine forcefully slapped the table. This time, the young attendant was ready, grabbing the tea cup and Jameson bottle before they could get knocked to the floor a second time.

"He's offering to pay you 15% of all net profits and 20% of his salary."

"Why so much?" Constantine was suspicious. "We were only charging 10% before."

"Because he doesn't just want your blessing to work in your territory," Scratch answered. "He wants your protection against his family. Says he'll cook the books so no one questions the 5% increase on the profit side."

Constantine let out a bellow, grabbing his cup of tea, cradling it in one large palm before taking a sip. After a long pause, he commented, "Cook the books." He laughed. "That's funny." After a long pause he offered, "Tell him we'll accept his deal...but I want 40% of his salary. I won't put my guys at risk for anything less."

Chapter 8
The Proposal

"**Y**ou're still frightened of me," Jax stated. It was not a question. He and Midge were reclined on each end of the couch sipping cocktails in the middle of the weekday with their legs intertwined.

"Don't be silly, I'm not—" Midge stammered. She was not easily intimidated, nor flustered. And yet, around Jax, she seemed to be both.

"And you like it." He put his feet on the floor and slid over to her side of the couch, reaching past her to set his drink on the end table. A chill went up Midge's spine. He leaned in to whisper in her ear, "Admit it."

"A little," she confessed, tilting her head sideways as he kissed the side of her neck.

"You came all the way to Ireland to find me." He was so close to her that his torso rubbed against the side of her hip, erotically.

"Correction," Midge sucked in a breath, "you summoned me."

"And you came," he reminded her. "And then, you stayed. Why?"

"I don't know if you've noticed this or not Jax," Midge explained, leaning back to sip her beverage. "But bad things seem to happen to me and the people I know when you don't get your way."

"Whatever do you mean?" he asked, innocently, eyeing her lip as she wiped the bottom of it with her fingertips, holding her cocktail out to avoid spilling it.

"Really?" Midge replied. "I thought we already had this conversation. Remember this?" She pulled the strap of her dress off her shoulder, revealing a scar. "When you burned me with a cigarette because you thought I was hitting on a waitress...who later ended up mysteriously run over by a 'drunk driver' that night?"

Jax leaned in and kissed the scar. "Well, I'm sorry about that. But I had nothing to do with that slut you were flirting with."

"Bullshit." Midge stood, setting her cocktail on the end table by his and taking a step away from Jax, creating some distance between the two of them.

"You don't believe me?" Jax asked, innocently, standing.

Midge softened her voice, somewhat defeated, "I never believe you." She took another step back.

Jax looked pained. "That hurts." He grabbed his chest with one hand as if wounded in the heart. "So when I tell you that I love you and that you're the only woman for me, you don't believe that, either?"

"Not the way you show love, no," Midge answered.

A flicker of something that appeared like anger crossed Jax's eyes quickly and then disappeared, and yet, Midge could have sworn she saw actual flames of fire in them.

"Well," Jax backed away, tapping the fleshy part of his fist on his thigh as if tenderizing a steak. "What would I need to do to prove my love to you? Enough so that you stop running away from me?"

"Marry me," Midge answered.

"What?" Jax was surprised.

"You don't love me enough to marry me?" Midge challenged.

"I do," Jax tilted his head sideways. "I'm just very confused. One minute you're running away from me and telling me you never want to see me again. The next you ask me to marry you, after turning down multiple marriage proposals prior. I'm not sure you even know what you want!"

Midge took a tentative step toward Jax, shyly. "Maybe I'm partly to blame," Midge admitted.

"For what?" Jax grew suspicious. "You've never taken responsibility for anything in your life!" he laughed.

"Hey!" Midge whined, the New York in her accent growing stronger the more agitated she became. "A person can grow, alright?!"

Jax found this amusing and curious. While Midge's actions always seemed reckless to those around her, for him, they were crystal clear...until now. She agreed to marry him once before. They had gone as far as to apply for a license. Then she ran away, and now she was back again. Still, he was confident he would come to understand this supposed 'growth' phase soon enough. *Maybe she is just afraid of her feelings for me,* Jax told himself.

"And what have you discovered, baby," Jax encouraged, "that's causing this recognition that you might be partially to blame?"

Midge bit her tongue for a moment at Jax's all-too-willingness for him to let her cast blame on herself. It was fine when she did it, but she didn't need encouragement.

"I recognize that my friendliness might be construed by some as...encouragement."

"You mean the way you flirted with that waitress," he confirmed.

"Not flirting," Midge wagged a finger at him. "Friendliness."

"I see," Jax chuckled a little.

"But perhaps my friendliness has, in the past, been taken to mean a sexual or personal interest of which I did not intend."

"I hope you're not talking about you and me?" Jax leaned in again and nibbled her ear.

Midge shrank a little at his mouth on her neck. She knew she had a terrible weakness for him, and while she recognized that it made little sense to anyone else, for her, it felt insurmountable. And that was the problem, Jax was her Achilles heel. When she was around him for too long, it not only hurt her, physically, but she made big mistakes, far bigger than ones she'd ever have made on her own.

"Of course not," she whispered, leaning in and stealing a kiss. "I just mean that by marrying you and being a little more conscious of my interactions with other people, perhaps I can prove to you that I'm serious about us. I've had time to think it over and...I'm ready."

"So, no more running away?" Jax set down his drink and relieved her of her empty glass and set them on the coffee table. He took her face in his hands and put his forehead against hers in a mix of hope and disbelief.

"I promise to be loyal, but I need you to stop hurting me." Midge held her breath a moment, not entirely certain how this accusation would land.

"I promise to do my best," he finally agreed. "You know, I never mean to hurt you. I'm just so passionate about you, that when other people get in the way of us, it makes me furious."

"That brings me to another topic," Midge said.

"Really?" Jax moved back, still holding her face in his hands.

"Are we almost done talking, so I can have my way with you again?"

"Almost," Midge agreed. "There's just one more thing."

"And what's that?" Jax asked.

"A wedding present."

"A wedding present," Jax repeated. "What exactly did you have in mind?"

"Rue Brennan," Midge answered. Jax tightened the grip on her face angrily digging his thumbs into her cheeks deeply enough to leave marks. "Ow! What did we just talk about?" Midge reminded him.

Jax released his grip and leapt to his feet. Once he'd reached the kitchen counter across the room, he slammed it with the side of his fist. "How am I supposed to keep my wits about me when you rile me up so easily. What about Rue Brennan?" he spat.

"She's in Ireland," Midge answered.

"What? Why? How?" Jax was confused.

"Apparently, she and Detective Ortega, the guy who grilled you after those models died, remember?" Midge paused for confirmation.

"Of course, I remember," Jax's face took on a crimson and purple hue. He couldn't mask how enraged he felt.

"Well, somehow Ortega got tangled up in the Vandenberg case, and since Rue Brennan was a former member of the Church of Infinite Love, she's here to help him shut down the church's operations, for good."

"Does she know you're here?" Jax asked.

"What? No! How could she?" Midge played innocent, leaving out the minor detail that she was the very reason Rue discovered that the church and Vandenberg Nutraceuticals was planning to rebrand and set up shop in Ireland instead of the States, at least until the scandal had blown over and the cops lost interest.

"She followed you," Jax nodded. "Did you lead her to me? Or even worse, did you lead her on?" Jax stood over Midge with an angry expression that she'd come to know all too well. It took every ounce of courage to remain calm.

"No, my husband-to-be," Midge batted her eyes at him. "I have nothing to do with her being here, but I can get rid of her."

"How?" Jax asked. "Are you finally going to shoot her, like we should have done back in her apartment two years ago when we had the chance?"

"Something like that," Midge grinned at him.

"Is she supposed to be my wedding present?" Jax eyed her with sudden interest.

Midge smiled at him seductively. "Now you're catching on." She slid up to his chest and touched a hand lightly just below his collar bone. "While there isn't much I can do when Ortega invariably comes knocking at the factory door looking for you, I can at least provide a distraction. I'm sure Rue's disappearance will rattle his nerves a bit."

"Disappearance?" Jax asked. "Do I get to watch?"

"No, my dear hubby," Midge answered, kissing him on his chin. "If I've learned anything from hanging around with you is that it's much cleaner covering your tracks when there's no body and no weapon to be found."

"Then how will I know when you've done it? A picture?" Jax asked.

"A picture that I'd have to take to a Fotomat to have developed?!" Midge was incredulous. "No, too risky. But don't worry," she assured him, "I have something much better in mind."

Chapter 9
Moira Dodd

Dublin

People either liked Baxter Baker or they hated him. There was never any in between. He could usually tell within thirty seconds into which camp a person fell. Baxter didn't care either way. He knew he was, by most people's standards, handsome, charming and quick-witted. It didn't hurt that his family came from money and that he successfully maintained his role as regional manager at Vandenberg Nutraceuticals for nearly a decade. Therefore, if someone didn't like him, they were simply *wrong*. The fact that he was now assuming the role of Chief Executive Officer further solidified his feelings of self-worth, not that they were ever in question.

There were exceptions to this rule, of course. Namely that most of the Vandenberg family got wind that Baxter was likely responsible for procuring incriminating evidence against both

Vandenberg Nutraceuticals and the Church of Infinite Love who, as it turned out, were both led by the late great business tycoon Erasmus Vandenberg. Both the Elders of the church and the executives of Vandenberg Nutraceuticals had it in for Baxter. Were it not for the intervention of opportunist Jax Liebling and Erasmus's personal lawyer and as-needed 'remover of obstacles,' Mr. Lundy, they would have made sure that Baxter Baker disappeared, permanently.

Instead, Jax convinced the family to lay low during police investigations in the States, letting Baxter, and Baxter alone, assume the role as the new CEO and 'face' of the Church of Infinite Love, while the Elders carefully remained in the shadows. Jax was to become a silent partner who served in an 'advisory' capacity to Vandenberg Nutraceuticals. Meanwhile, he also suggested that Vandenberg executives promptly resign from their positions and disavow knowing about any wrong-doing that led to the death of several members of the church over the years—not to mention the long-running faith healing scam that made them millions. Well, everyone but Baxter.

And so, Baxter took over the one remaining factory, located in Dublin, where he now resided. Mr. Lundy saw to it that Baxter was released from police custody and anything tying Baxter to the case surrounding Erasmus Vandenberg was conveniently wiped clean. And after all of Baxter's proclamations of having a change of heart, the money and the title were too good to pass up. What he didn't realize, however, was that he wasn't merely putting up a good front for the family...he was being set up as scapegoat.

And yet, Baxter strolled into the Dublin office at 10:15 a.m. midweek with all the swagger of someone who didn't have multiple people who wanted to kill him, along with his usual clear sense of entitlement, yet no sense of responsibility. He prided himself on being proactive in buying out the remaining shares from Emma Post with the help of Jax Liebling and, eventually, his cousin Elsbeth, of course. And whether warranted or not, he felt confident that being under the wing of the Westports would afford him protection...well, mostly confident.

He brushed a lock of blonde hair away from one eye and winced a little. The gunshot wound he'd received recently still stung on occasion, causing his gate to be a little wider and more awkward when he was walking. Yet somehow, this only served to make him more attractive to women...well, most women.

"Good morning, Mr. Baker," a lilting voice greeted him.

Surprised, he turned to eye the strange woman sitting behind the reception desk. She had a small frame and the desk seemed to all but swallow her whole. She had a round face with even rounder black-rimmed glasses that made her green eyes shine larger than life. Her fiery red hair was tied back in a tight bun.

"I'm sorry, but who are you?" Baxter asked.

"Your associate, Mr. Liebling, hired me as your new assistant," she explained. "I'm Moira Dodd. It's a pleasure to meet you." She stretched a long arm across the desk, but remained seated.

"I see," Baxter answered. (He really didn't.)

Baxter eyed the Moira curiously. She wasn't entirely unpleasant to look at, he decided. Perhaps if she let her hair down? Wore contacts? Perhaps traded in that awful rose-colored blouse that she was wearing for something a little less matronly?

Baxter walked over to the desk, taking her hand and cradling it between his palms. "It's a pleasure to meet you, too, Moira." He held her gaze longer than necessary and flashed a devilish grin. "Perhaps you and I should become more acquainted if we're going to be working together."

"How so?" Moira asked.

"Well, maybe I could take you to dinner at the Mulberry Garden, followed by a stroll through the Temple Bar? A drive to the Cliffs of Moher for a hike, if you're feeling adventurous?"

Moira paused for an inordinately long time before answering. "Not sure I'm up for a stroll nor a hike, Mr. Baker."

Moira's torso moved backward as she wheeled her way around the desk. It was only then that Baxter realized that Moira was sitting in a wheelchair. The corner of her mouth turned up in a grin. And, while she never lost that sparkle in her eyes, one thing was very clear to Baxter. *She did not like him.*

Baxter was quick on his feet. "My apologies, Miss Dodd...or is it Mrs. Dodd?" He glanced down at her left hand, but she had inconveniently covered it by laying her right palm across it and resting them in her lap.

"You might have thought to ask that before you began hitting on me," she replied curtly.

Baxter was confused. Her voice was songlike, but he couldn't quite place her accent...Irish...Scottish...Welsh? Perhaps it would have been easier had he spent more time in Ireland prior to his recent relocation. But that wasn't the confusing part. What had him stumped was that although her words dripped of sarcasm, her voice was ever sweet, as was the expression on her face.

"I beg your pardon," Baxter defended, lifting his nose as if offended. "I most certainly was not hitting on you. I was merely being cordial. If we are to work together, we should get to know one another." This was uncharacteristic of Baxter who prided himself on being true to his nature and making no apologies for it.

"With all due respect, Mr. Baker, that's a load of crap and we both know it," Moira said, as gentle as ever, peering up at him. "Now, if you're any sort of a gentleman, you'll take a seat, so I don't have to get a neck cramp staring up at you and so that you don't appear so domineering."

Baxter opened his mouth to speak, but closed it again. He'd never had anyone, particularly not an employee, talk back to him. The closest he'd come to that was Emma Post, the woman who inherited the bulk of Erasmus's fortune, and one of the few he'd actually started developing feelings for. But whereas Emma was brazen, fiery and fierce, Moira's wit was like a well-sharpened blade, the kind that took a moment before you'd even realized you'd been cut.

Baxter merely smiled, and rolled his office chair from behind his desk, and stationed it in front of Moira, where he took a seat in front of her so they could meet eye-to-eye.

"That's better," Moira nodded. "Now before you go talking about getting to know one another...which, you'll agree, would be highly inappropriate, anyway, seeing as how I'm working for you, and that automatically puts you in a position of authority—" Baxter opened his mouth to speak, but Moira held up a delicate hand to silence him. "Don't you think we should talk about my responsibilities here?"

For the second time, Baxter was confused. Never having taken much responsibility at his work prior, he wasn't entirely certain what to expect from Moira. People who worked for him previously just sort of...knew what they were supposed to do without being asked.

"Didn't Mr. Liebling explain the role, seeing as he hired you?" Baxter asked.

Moira let out a songlike chuckle. "The only thing he explained to me, Mr. Baker, is that he point-blank hired me because I was just pretty and professional enough to make a good impression with the media and potential investors, but not so attractive that you'd be distracted by me."

"How on earth could I not be distracted by you?" Baxter questioned softly with a genuineness that surprised even himself.

"Em," Moira rolled back and forth in her chair. "Not exactly your type, am I? I mean, Mr. Liebling seems to think you only have eyes for saucy athletic girls and skinny, long legged super-model types. And, as you can see, Mr. Baker, I'm am neither of those."

"Well, Moira," Baxter said calmly. "It seems to me that Mr. Liebling doesn't know me very well at all."

Chapter 10
Shooting Lesson

Edgar's Leitrim Estate

Shots rang out in the air as Elsbeth downed a clay pigeon. It shattered mercilessly, landing in pieces on the ground.

"Great going!" Isaac yelled. Isaac was her Uncle Edgar's personal assistant. He smiled at Elsbeth, and then, realizing that she couldn't possibly hear him with her protective headgear, gave her a thumbs up. She smiled back, momentarily lowering her semi-automatic target shotgun before he quickly pointed to the ground.

Isaac then unleashed a clay rabbit, nearly catching the girl off guard. She hoisted her gun back up and quickly took aim. It took her several rounds, but she finally hit it, its head flying off in a large chunk.

The clay rabbits, Elsbeth decided, were not as fun as flying clay pigeons. For one thing, they were slightly easier for her to hit and they didn't splinter into a thousand pieces in midair and spray every which way, which is how Elsbeth preferred it.

Uncle Edgar signaled for her to lower her weapon, which she did. He followed suit, setting his gun on a long table from which the two were safely stationed behind, away from the field. He removed his safety goggles and earmuffs and motioned for her to do the same.

"Well done, my dear," he praised. "Just give me a moment, won't you?" Edgar unloaded his shotgun before doing the same with Elsbeth's. When he was confident all safety precautions were taken, he called out to Isaac, "All clear!" He waved his arms in the air. Isaac waved back, his sign that it was safe to clear the field, which really meant nothing more than for Isaac to gather the non-used targets and gently rake the field to spread the clay remains around evenly. Since they were biodegradable, he only wanted to encourage them to decompose faster by ensuring there were no unnecessary piles in one particular area of the field.

Edgar turned to Elsbeth. "I must say, you're far better at this than Baxter. I wouldn't have expected it from—"

"A girl?" Elsbeth finished, saltily.

"I was going to say, for someone who hasn't been shooting for very long." Edgar winked at his niece. "Your mother, Edwina, was pretty good at it, but too impatient to really develop the skills. And then," he sighed, "she got so wrapped up in the church that she stopped visiting altogether...pity."

Elsbeth nodded, "W-w-w-ell," she stammered. "E-enough about her." Elsbeth furrowed her eyes, confused. She had faked the stutter for so long out of fear, that the mere mention of her mother actually set her off again.

"Let's talk about something else," Edgar answered, gently, wrapping an arm around her.

Moments later, Isaac joined them as they walked back toward the house.

"Did you show her your venomous snake room yet?" Baxter called from the house as he made his way toward them.

"Back again?" Edgar was surprised. "Aren't you supposed to be under cover or something?"

"Protection," Baxter answered, after catching up with the trio. "The Westport goons are surveying the property as we speak."

One such 'goon' overheard Baxter, tilting his head and muttering, "What an arse," before promptly returning to his routine.

"Sorry," Baxter cringed. "I was just kidding, of course."

"Feck off," the guard answered, flicking Baxter the finger.

"You make friends everywhere you go, it seems," Edgar laughed. "But how did we not notice them. Isaac?" he questioned.

Isaac shrugged. "Not used to anyone caring too much about the likes of us," he replied. "I barely remember ta lock the house at night, half ta time."

"Hmmm," Edgar thought, rubbing a tired eye. "We should probably make it a point to start doing that."

"Aye," Isaac nodded. "Particularly with this mug around." He shot a glance at Baxter who merely smiled as if he had just been given a compliment.

Baxter sidled up next to Elsbeth and asked, "When did you get here?"

"A couple days ago," she answered.

"Does your mother know you're here?" he wondered.

"What do you think?" She frowned. "I can't even go to the bathroom without her asking about my bowel movements."

Baxter snorted. "Well then, I should probably be sure to head out soon. If I have a target on my back, I don't want to put you in danger."

"What makes you think mother wants to hurt you?" Elsbeth was surprised.

"After the evidence I supplied to the cops about Vandenberg Nutraceuticals and the church?" His voice rose in pitch. "Let's just say, I'm glad it was you on the field today and not Edwina."

Elsbeth thought back to why she was there. It had been Rue Brennan's friend, Midge, who convinced her that she'd be safer in Ireland with Uncle Edgar while the dust settled on the home front. She'd only met Midge once in Rue and Darwin's condo, and yet, the woman's energy made an impression on her, somehow.

"Will ya be wantin' dinner, Baxter?" Isaac finally asked as the four made their way indoors. "Gonna begin preppin' shortly."

"No, thank you, Isaac," Baxter answered, touched that he even had an invitation. Although, he typically just showed up while an angry Isaac plopped food on his plate and complained about not making enough. Therefore, Baxter reasoned, perhaps Edgar's personal servant was just being proactive.

Issac nodded and peeled away from the group, heading toward the kitchen.

"I'm heading this way," Baxter pointed toward the study. "Won't you join me, Elsbeth?"

"Can't," Elsbeth answered. "Edgar is showing me his body collection."

"I'm sorry...what?" Baxter was certain he'd misheard his cousin.

"The bodies," she repeated, a little louder this time.

"She's exaggerating just a little bit," Edgar answered, uncomfortably. "I happened to have attended an exhibit on the ancient Jivaro of Ecuador and was able to procure a few historic remains for my collection. Different from my usual, I know, but just as fascinating."

"You mean like shrunken heads, and such?" Baxter asked, surprised.

"Heads, teeth, some clothing and weapon samples, basic stuff, really," Edgar explained, leaning in as if sharing a secret. "Except for a couple of fairly well-preserved corpses...mums the word," he whispered.

"But I thought you only collected reptiles and poisonous bugs and things?"

"Well," Edgar explained, chuckling, "this is a bit of a departure from my usual, but curiosity got the better of me."

Baxter swallowed with some difficulty. With the threat of violence looming over his head, he found Edgar's recent collection to be somewhat unsettling. Baxter couldn't understand it. Edgar was so against killing anything that he insisted on clay pigeons and rabbits instead of hunting and made it a habit of saying a Native American prayer over dinner anytime Isaac prepared meat. Yet, he was fascinated by deadly plants, animals and insects that killed other things...now, add humans to that list.

"Would you like to join us?" Edgar asked.

"Pass," Baxter held up a hand. "But you two go ahead." He touched Elsbeth on the shoulder. "Er, but stop in for a chat once you're done, won't you?" he asked.

"Sure, Baxter," Elsbeth nodded before heading off to view Edgar's newest additions to his collection.

Baxter shuddered, wondering how exactly he ended up with such a strange family.

Chapter 11
Not What He Seemed

Edgar's Leitrim Estate

"You shouldn't be here, Elsbeth," Baxter chastised his younger cousin after they found a moment to themselves.

"Nice to see you too, Baxter," Elsbeth answered flatly, walking over to the whiskey decanter sitting atop the mini bar in the corner of Edgar's study. She picked up a tumbler and splashed a hearty pour into it.

"Since when do you drink?" Baxter was surprised, glancing down at his own pint of Guinness and wishing he could chase it down with a shot of Jameson, but he dared not. He had to keep his wits about him these days.

"Since the moment I realized how nutty our family was," she plopped down on a leather chair across from her cousin and crossed her legs, one bouncing nervously as she sat.

"So...age three?" Baxter joked.

Elsbeth smiled. There was a glimmer of the care-free Baxter she used to know and sometimes even liked.

Ever since Baxter agreed to help Elsbeth's grandfather Erasmus gather evidence against the church and the family, he had become slightly more serious, more...*what was the word?* Elsbeth thought to herself. *Hesitant. That was it.* Frankly, she missed the more annoying, cavalier Baxter. It was a fun departure from the household her mother Edwina ran.

Elsbeth, herself, not wanting to grow up in the family business and being too afraid to stand up to them, feigned a learning disability and incurable stutter. An embarrassment to the church, Edwina did her best to keep Elsbeth out of the public eye as having an 'abnormal' daughter flew in the face of the church's claims to faith healing.

Elsbeth took a sip of her whiskey, trying not to sneeze as the aroma tickled her nose. Baxter stifled a laugh.

"I miss Grandfather Erasmus," Elsbeth lamented. "He was a good deal better than the lot of 'em." Baxter let out a snort. "What's so funny?" she demanded.

"Dear old Erasmus may have developed a conscience in his old age, maybe even bought into his own hype and had the fear of God and eternal damnation on the brain, but he wasn't at all the man you thought he was." Baxter stretched an arm out over one side of the couch and thumped his fingers on the back of it.

"How dare you say that!" Elsbeth's face turned beet red. "He was the only one who was kind to me, even when everyone else treated me as if there was something wrong with me! He loved me."

"While that may be true, though I take slight offense that you don't think I care about you, did it never occur to you that perhaps he felt guilty that his healthy snack bars may have permanently damaged you?" Baxter pointed out.

"Are you implying that my grandfather Erasmus was only

nice to me because he felt sorry for me?" Elsbeth blinked, fighting back tears that were stinging her eyes. It was true that at a young age, Edwina filled her up on those 'healthy' church-branded bars as a way to control her. This caused abnormal side effects that she only discovered after innocently swapping lunch snacks with a young girl in grade school. The girl had a seizure. Elsbeth got better. From then on, Elsbeth only pretended to eat her snacks and kept the illusion of having a disorder out of concern over what might happen if her mother learned the truth.

"I'm merely pointing out that you are lionizing a man who wasn't as nice as you seem to think he was."

Elsbeth all but dropped her glass on the end table with a thud and crossed her arms like an angry child. "Well, he was a good deal better than you," she pouted.

Baxter sighed. He had bigger things to worry about than placating his cousin. "I'm sure he was," he conceded. "But I've never pretended to be anything other than exactly who I am."

Elsbeth slunk back and sank into the couch. "A jerk," she blurted out.

Baxter took another sip of Guinness and nodded in agreement. "Can't argue with that."

That broke Elsbeth, who covered her mouth so he couldn't see her stifling a laugh. Her shoulders and belly quivered a little. It was contagious, and moments later, Baxter let out a boisterous laugh, and for the next several minutes, he couldn't stop. It had been quite some time since he'd laughed and he needed it.

Finally, Elsbeth asked, "Okay, I'll bite. What do you know about our late Erasmus that I don't know?"

At that moment, Baxter heard the sound of a motor car and jumped uneasily. He glanced out the window and breathed a sigh of relief as he watched a black Mini Cooper purposefully meandering up the driveway.

"What's that all about?" Elsbeth asked.

"Protection," Baxter explained. "They'll be popping in to check on me in just a moment, so let me make this brief."

"I'm listening," Elsbeth answered.

"You weren't even born when most of this was happening," Baxter began, draining his beverage and placing it on the coffee table without a coaster. As if the sound of a water ring staining the furniture could be heard like an emergency siren, Isaac appeared out of nowhere, grabbed the glass and wiped the table off with a white towel. He paused to grimace at Baxter before leaving the room as soundlessly as he'd entered.

Baxter continued, "Didn't you ever find it odd how Erasmus Vandenberg, business mogul and multimillionaire, could suddenly take charge of the Church of Infinite Love *and* ensure that our family ran both companies simultaneously?"

"You just said it, yourself, Erasmus was a business mogul."

"Three decades ago, Vandenberg Nutraceuticals was on the verge of bankruptcy." Elsbeth sat up, surprised, but said nothing. "Dear Erasmus was approached by then church Elder, Herman Armory, a longtime resident of the Emerald Isle. The church was having trouble selling faith healing and Armory had an idea."

"The birth of the 'healing' nutrition bars," Elsbeth answered, putting 'healing' in air quotes.

"Exactly, snacks to treat everything from pain, anxiety, fatigue, depression and insomnia all specially branded for the church to be used in its healing ceremonies. Suddenly, Vandenberg Nutraceuticals is back in business and the church is raking in a fortune off of those who are desperate enough to try anything to ease their suffering." Baxter saw Elsbeth's expression change. "I know what you're thinking."

"Do you?" Elsbeth asked.

"You're wondering what happened to Armory."

"That's right," Elsbeth admitted. She may have thought

Baxter was a louse sometimes, but he was a good deal smarter than most gave him credit for.

"He died under mysterious circumstances, along with several others among the Elders of the church, all within a one-year period."

"And no one became suspicious?" Elsbeth was dumbfounded.

"Of course people became suspicious...particularly when Vandenberg Nutraceuticals set up a second location in Dublin." Baxter lowered his voice to a whisper. "The Westports weren't too keen on having Erasmus encroach on their territory."

"The Westports?" Elsbeth asked. "You mean the grift—"

"Ahem," Baxter cleared his throat as a young security officer, dressed all in black, stepped soundlessly into the room. Baxter looked up at the man, shooting Elsbeth a sideways glance.

"The perimeter is secure, Mr. Baker," the man announced. "But we should get you back to Clontarf before dark."

"Of course, Scratch. Give me ten minutes?"

"Aye," Scratch answered, eyeing Elsbeth with considerable interest.

"My cousin, Elsbeth," Baxter explained, before adding quickly, "she's under the Westport protection as well. Constantine is sending Dough to look after her." The corner of Scratch's mouth turned up in a sly grin. "So, don't get any funny ideas!"

"Hmph," Scratch scowled. "What d'ya take me fer, anyhow?"

"Ten minutes," Baxter repeated.

Scratch nodded. "I'll jest be in the cahr then, yeah?" The young man retreated.

"What the hell was that all about?" Elsbeth asked.

"The long and short of it?" Baxter finished. "Rumor has it that dear old Erasmus teamed up with Lundy, your mother, Bernie, Mordecai, Victor, and the rest of the Elders to take the original leaders out, one at a time."

"You mean murder?!" Elsbeth's eyes grew wide. "Not dear Erasmus! I don't believe it!" Elsbeth stood, folded her arms and stamped her foot like a small child.

Baxter looked up at her. "And they tried to pin the murders on the Westports."

"I assume you have proof of all this?" Elsbeth was incredulous. And yet, deep down, she knew Baxter was telling the truth. At least, he was telling the truth as far as he saw it. Perhaps her fear of telling Erasmus and Edwina her secret 'miracle' return to health was because a part of her knew that it was the safest option.

"Not really," Baxter answered. "I was working on it before all at the shit hit the fan when Erasmus died and left his money to Emma Post."

"But how come that goon—" Elsbeth motioned toward the driveway, "is looking after you? Isn't he a Westport henchman?"

"He is," Baxter nodded. "But the Westports aren't typically in the murder game. They didn't like being framed any more than they liked Vandenberg Nutraceuticals and the Church of Infinite Love encroaching on their territory—and being obvious about it in the process."

"So, what did they do?" Elsbeth asked.

"They demanded money for 'renting' space in their territory."

"How were they planning to enforce that if they aren't in the murder business?" Elsbeth wanted to know.

"I didn't say they *wouldn't* resort to murder, just that they might try other painful and persuasive methods first."

"Hmmm," Elsbeth thought a moment. "Is that why Erasmus eventually closed the Dublin factory and moved to Florida?"

"Bingo," Baxter confirmed. "He used to joke that in Florida, you could get away with just about anything...and get people to pay you to do it!"

The lights on the Mini flickered through the window.

"Listen, I gotta go." Baxter stood.

"Where are you going? Clontarf, did he say?"

"Better if you don't know, exactly. I'll contact you again when I can, or you can come by the factory during business hours. It's a public place and I don't think anyone would risk harming me there."

"Hmmm, not so sure about that." Elsbeth was uncertain.

"Let's hope you're wrong," Baxter answered, his voice cracking a little. "In the meantime, Dough should be arriving soon. He's a tall, overweight leprechaun with a curly ginger beard and mustache. I've already let Edgar and Isaac know."

"What is this Dough supposed to do for me, exactly?"

"Protect you," Baxter answered. "After all, you were responsible for helping the police uncover the truth about the Vandenberg family the moment you stepped into the Florida factory." Elsbeth cringed. *How'd he know about that?* In the recent past, Elsbeth aided Emma Post in sneaking into the factory to investigate. The family may not have known that at the time, but by now, they may have figured it out.

Chills went up Elsbeth's spine. Desperate to get away from Edwina, she was hoping that Midge was right, and that hiding out at Uncle Edgar's estate in Leitrim for a while would be safety enough. She was wrong.

Chapter 12
Gaslighting

Dublin

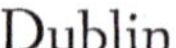

Bernie Forger met with a small ensemble of church Elders in a reserved conference room at the Alexander Hotel in Dublin. Notably absent were members from the Vandenberg lineage, and a few Ambassadors unable or unwilling to make the trip to the Emerald Isle. There were, of course, a handful of Elders whose whereabouts were a mystery, but Bernie dismissed any concern about them.

No matter, Bernie thought. He was just being tested by God. He knew it.

He stood at a podium wearing a blue suit and matching tie. His crisp white shirt had been starched so severely that you could hear it crackle as he moved.

"How long before we go live?" he asked, wiping beads of sweat from his brow with a handkerchief.

"Five minutes," Mr. Lundy answered, sitting beside Jax

Liebling at a long conference table. Meanwhile, one of the church Ambassadors dotted Bernie's face with powder until he grew frustrated and shooed the man away. "I'm certain it's fine," he muttered.

A hired videographer and IT specialist announced, "Places!" His sound technician nodded, making minor adjustments to a large soundboard sitting on the table in front of him. Meanwhile, a backup cameraman stood at the ready, there to capture the side angles of Bernie as he spoke, and to prepare for scene changes when they transitioned in and out of commercial breaks.

Finally, the moment arrived, and Bernie's Ambassador, a make-up artist who doubled as a show runner, announced with mounting excitement, "We are live in 5-4-3-2-1..." He gave Bernie the thumbs up.

"Ladies and gentlemen," Bernie addressed the camera, squinting at the bright lights that were stationed in front of him and flanked him on each side. He did his best to ignore them and focus on the message.

Just then, the sound of a wailing child could be heard outside the conference room door, followed by a mother shushing the child as they hurried past the room. A flash of anger crossed Bernie's face before he regained composure, joking to the camera, "Blessed are the children, for they shall lead the way."

An amen erupted from a non-existent crowd, manufactured by the audio engineer.

Bernie scanned the room, as if addressing thousands. In truth, he may have been, as this live broadcast was being aired at the Church of Infinite Love locations throughout parts of Europe and the United States. However, he couldn't see the crowds that had gathered. In point of fact, he couldn't even be sure that many crowds *were* gathered. The media attention had not been good for the church and membership had been suffering. And while he tried to give the illusion that he was addressing many, there were fewer than a dozen people in the room during his speech, himself included.

"It is written that the closer we become to the Almighty, the more the Devil will try and smite us down. The recent persecution of the church by the media and those who claim to be of 'the law' is a clear indication that the End Times are near." He paused for dramatic effect. "Now," he continued, "you, the faithful, bear witness to this pivotal moment in history when nearly half of the flock has fallen away. This is not due to the failings of the church. This is not even due to the false claims that the church was responsible for the deaths of a few members who turned their backs on God." Bernie paused again, scanning the fake audience before looking directly into the camera. "No, this is because our God continually sets the bar higher and higher, and only the chosen ones, his most righteous, will ever join him as great leaders in the Kingdom of Heaven."

"Amen," Jax, the make-up artist, and Mr. Lundy said from the audience. The sound technician strategically added a few shuffles and ambient noise from the fake audience, along with a few 'amens' and 'yes's' from the audio mixer.

"For that reason," Bernie continued, "we have to be diligent in our understanding of Him." He looked toward the heavens. "We need to be spending less time watching television and reading newspapers and more time studying and understanding his word."

Jax bristled a little. *This isn't part of the script. What is Bernie up to?* He eyed Lundy who sat there, expressionless. They had gone over the speech just that morning.

Bernie held up a small book. "The Church of Infinite Love is proud to announce that it is starting its very own publishing house. Beginning in the new year, we will be selling—at a nominal fee to members, of course—a series of educational materials meant to simplify the Bible and distill the wisdom of God into a message that is digestible to all ages, particularly our youth."

The cameraman held up his hand, indicating that Bernie had less than thirty seconds to finish his message before they had to switch to a commercial.

"That's not all," Bernie announced, a gleam in his eyes. "As we know, the children are our future. Therefore, I'm also excited to share that the church is breaking ground on a new facility in Belfast that will serve as an educational school for our youth. Tell you more about it after the break."

The cameraman indicated that Bernie was off air, and quickly switched to footage to some generic instrumental music and a backdrop of what appeared to be a large audience. The stock footage was meant to convince viewers that this, in fact, was the crowd in which Bernie had been speaking. It was a delicate balance, the messaging they were going for. The crowds had to appear just large enough to feel as if the message were worthwhile and important, but not so many that people no longer felt special and unique.

"You've got about five minutes, Mr. Forger," the show runner announced before pouncing to add more powder to Bernie's brow as a few beads of perspiration were forming across his forehead.

"A towel might be better, don't you think?" Bernie complained. "These lights are hotter than Hades!"

"Interesting choice of words," Jax sneered at him. "And by the way, where *did* those words come from?" he challenged. "You were supposed to discuss the rebranding of Vandenberg Nutraceuticals and how support of the company's new direction will directly impact the work of the church."

"And that's exactly what I'm doing," Bernie defended. "After the break, I fully intend to share how the sale of our refined snack bars will help feed the kids in Kenya and poorer populations, etc. etc., and how a portion of the proceeds will also go toward educational materials and the new publishing house."

"What publishing house?" Jax challenged. "What new school? This is all news to me!" Jax didn't like being kept in the dark about such things where money and power were concerned.

"We're back in thirty seconds," the show runner alerted.

Bernie took his place at the podium and said, "You're in charge of overseeing the factory, and that's all! You have no say whatsoever in the direction of the church."

Jax's face turned an odd shade of red mixed with a little purple as a vein stood out on the side of his temple. He moved toward the podium, arm raised, when Mr. Lundy intercepted. Lundy, being a large man, had no trouble body-blocking Jax. "Let's step outside," he whispered, just as the camera's started rolling again.

Once they were a safe distance from the room, Lundy offered, "Join me for a drink." He motioned toward the hotel bar and restaurant, empty at this time of morning, save for a few jet-lagged travelers having coffee and pastries in one corner of the room. To the bartender he asked, "Can I get a drink for my associate?" To Jax, he asked, "What'll you have?"

"Midleton," Jax spat out. "If you have it."

The bartender eyed Lundy for confirmation. "We have it, but er—"

"It's fine," Lundy replied, reaching into his suit pocket and pulling out a large wad of bills and laying several on the counter.

"Make it a double," Jax sneered, knowing full well how expensive a pour was, given that the distillery had been closed for more than two decades, making what was left a rare find. "Neat."

"Is there any other way?" the bartender nodded, smiling. "What about you?" he asked Lundy. "The same?"

"Oh no," Lundy answered. "Never touch the stuff. Just a club soda with lime, thanks."

The bartender set two coasters down and placed their drinks on them. Jax took a moment to swirl the glass in his palm, sniffing the whiskey's aroma appreciatively before taking a sip. His mood lifted slightly.

"Better?" Lundy asked.

"Only a little," Jax answered, still fuming. "Why the hell wasn't I let in on these new developments? I thought I was part of this operation?"

"You are," Lundy confirmed, "but there's a reason you were kept in the dark."

"What reason might that be?" Jax questioned, taking another sip.

"Bernie's a hot head," Lundy reasoned. "Not rational like you and I."

The irony was lost on Jax, who merely nodded.

"The point is, I had to make it look like he had a leg up on you, so he could feel more in control. And I needed you to be convincingly surprised. Which, you were. Well done."

"What are you up to?" Jax asked, suspiciously.

"Bernie's a loose cannon," Lundy answered. "If he had his way, he'd take his whole 'armor of God' speech and start his own army—literally. No, you're the one I see running the school as president. That is, if you want it. After all, you are an educator."

Jax thought back to his days as an in-house artist and instructor at the Atelier in New York. He'd never gotten the recognition he deserved back then, but maybe now?

"Bernie will never go for that," Jax complained. "How are you going to convince him?"

"I like to think of it more as a 'we,'" Lundy pointed at the space between he and Jax. "I've got an idea. Meet me back here after Bernie and his crew have wrapped up for the day. For now —" Lundy took a sip of his previously untouched club soda before plunking the glass back on the bar. "We should get back in there. Bernie will wonder where we've gone."

Lundy slipped out of the taping a few minutes early and had a double-shot of whiskey awaiting Jax's arrival. Given that Jax's favorite was no longer in production, it cost a pretty penny. Even the bartender was befuddled, but Lundy tipped well, so he didn't ask any questions.

"Do you have a menu?" Lundy asked quietly. He was surprisingly meek for such a looming man with an imposing presence.

"Certainly," the bartender reached behind the counter and drew a small, laminated page filled with bar bites and handed it to Lundy. There was nothing on there that would suit Jax's expensive taste, so Lundy improvised. "What can you get me from the main dining room that will look like a modest bar menu item but will satisfy someone who likes to think he has a refined pallet?" The bartender chortled, until he saw that Lundy wasn't laughing. "I'll make it worth your while," Lundy promised. "I just don't have time to waste on a four-course dinner."

"Hmm," the bartender thought a moment. "I might be able to rustle up a few lamb chops a la carte."

"Excellent," Lundy nodded. "Any foie gras or pâté?"

"I've got a chicken liver pâté."

"Can you smear it on a small burger and set it on a bed of lettuce and call it a foie gras and sirloin small plate?" Lundy slipped him a few bills.

The bartender nodded. "For that price, I'll call it anything you like. I'll even throw in a jig if you want." He danced a moment from side to side, bending his arms in the process.

"That won't be necessary," he answered, just as Jax made his appearance. Jax had an odd expression on his face, and his lips twitched as if he were having a conversation with someone who wasn't there. His mood lifted when he saw the beverage. *Finally, someone treating him the way he deserved to be treated.*

"Hope you don't mind," Lundy explained. "But I've put in an order for few small plates while we chat."

Jax nodded and reached for his beverage. Meanwhile, Lundy sat with his usual club soda and lime.

"How did the rest of the taping go?" Lundy asked. "Sorry I had to miss it, but I had other family matters to attend to."

"It was Bernie being Bernie," Jax lamented. "He all but incited his audience to violence in defense of maintaining the 'old ways.'"

"Well, the man is steadfast in his beliefs, I'll give him that," Lundy acknowledged.

"He's got a God complex, if you ask me," Jax complained, sucking down his whiskey and motioning for another.

"I'm afraid you've polished off our only bottle of Midleton," the bartender explained. Before Jax could express his discontent, the server offered, "I've got a small batch, 25-year-old Teeling though?"

"Fine," Jax blurted out, as if he shouldn't have to use his energy to answer questions from a mere bartender.

Several other hotel guests began to wander into the bar area. Lundy stared at them intently, making them just uncomfortable enough to choose seats at tables on the opposite side of the bar from where they sat.

The server returned a few minutes later with the Teeling, setting it before Jax and quickly removing his hand as if Jax were a dog and he was afraid he might suddenly get bitten. He retreated, silently.

"So, what's your great idea?" Jax asked. It sounded more like an accusation than a question.

Lundy paused, weighing and measuring his words carefully.

"Bernie may be a great spokesman for the church, but he lacks your business acumen," Lundy complimented. "I would rather have him stick to what he does best and have you focus on what it is *you* do best."

The bartender returned with a small plate in hand, a white linen towel draping his arm, ceremoniously. "Petite lamb chops with a raspberry reduction sauce and mint glaze with a hint of our signature seasonings."

Lundy looked at the bartender, surprised. The man winked at him, as if in on a joke, and set down two small plates in front of each of the men.

Jax pinched one of the chops between his fingers and nibbled at it like a mouse nibbling on a piece of cheese. He nodded, approvingly.

"So, what is it that I do best?" Jax asked, between bites.

"Well, you have been a successful businessman and investor in many industries. I heard your scholarship program alone drew hundreds of students to the Atelier school in New York, not to mention that you yourself are a skilled artist and teacher."

"Flattery will get you everywhere," Jax grinned.

"But it's true," Lundy paused to take a bite of his own lamb. Somehow, he was such a pristine eater that his face and hands remained immaculate, even while eating with his fingers. "I would like to see you more involved in the Church of Infinite Love's budding publishing house, COIL Publishing, for short, and be a key investor and partner in the COIL Young Ambassador's School."

"Bernie will never go for that," Jax lamented.

"You let me deal with Bernie," Lundy answered. "What I need to know from you is your level of interest. I can share the financials and business plans for each, but I'd hate to waste your time, or mine, if you've got your hands full with your rebrand of the factory...or should I say, factories, plural?" Lundy eyed Jax for confirmation.

"Oh, you figured that out, did you?" Jax smiled.

"I'm a pretty smart guy," Lundy smiled back. Lundy didn't smile often, but when he did, it appeared mostly genuine.

"Yes, I managed to convince Erasmus's little benefactor, Emma Post, to sell the Florida factory to me, but did my best to keep my name out of it."

"I suspected who the silent partner might be. But that subtle switch from Jaks with a 'K' to Jax with an 'X' might have been a brilliant legal maneuver. It's amazing how a letter change can screw up title and other searches."

"But you still figured it out," Jax sipped his whiskey before polishing off his remaining lamb chop.

"Of course, I did," Lundy answered. "My associate, Mr. Adani, may have handled most of the arrangements on my behalf, but I'm still the one who has to oversee everything in the end."

The bartender returned again. He stood silently with two more small plates in his hand. "I have another small plate of morsels for you," he announced. If Lundy didn't know any better, he could have sworn the man's voice went from a heavy Irish brogue to British, as if he were trying to sound posh. Lundy was not easily amused, and yet he had to chuckle momentarily to himself as the bartender set the plates on their table. "A petite filet of beef topped with a duck pâté on a freshly baked brioche bun," he finished, quickly clearing the soiled plates. As he leaned over Lundy's shoulder, the lawyer slipped yet another bill into the server's pocket. The server nodded, gratefully. Without asking, he returned moments later with a fresh whiskey for Jax, and while he didn't request it, a glass of water.

As Jax bit into his petite burger, Lundy continued. "A small-print production of 'never seen by the public before' church doctrine and 'mystery knowledge' is already underway, but in order for the academy and the publishing house to reach its potential, we would need a sizable investment."

"And there it is," Jax sat back, wiping his mouth with a napkin. "I knew there had to be a reason you were schmoozing me with expensive food and liquor. You want money."

"You're not wrong," Lundy confessed. "But even more than that, I need people at the helm who, shall we say, are not emotionally invested in the teachings of the church."

"You mean a practical man, like me," Jax answered. "Someone who is interested in the bottom line and not dogma."

"Exactly," Lundy nodded. "Let's be honest, Mr. Liebling. I have lots of connections thanks to my long-standing ties with the Vandenberg family. But you can see how Erasmus Vandenberg's conscious got him killed and nearly wiped out the Vandenberg family fortune in the process."

"Good thing I don't have a conscious," Jax observed. "But I'd have some say over how the academy and the publishing house were run, yes? Bernie as much as told me to keep my nose out of church affairs and focus on healthy snacks and the factory side of things."

Lundy knew his opportunity had arrived. He leaned in as if sharing a secret. Jax did the same. "Between you and I, Bernie is not likely to be at the helm for long. I've already got his replacement in mind."

"Really? Who?" Jax demanded.

"All in good time," Lundy answered. "But I need more of a commitment from you before I divulge too much."

"Okay, you show me your plans, minus this mystery leader, and I'll consider making an investment. How much are we talking, anyhow?" Jax waved his fingers as if money were no object.

"An even million should get us through the door," Lundy threw out the number, casually.

Jax's face dropped for a microsecond before recovering. "What makes you so sure I have that kind of money?"

"Oh, I know all about your accounts in the Caymans, Mr. Liebling. As I said, I'm a pretty smart guy. And what you don't have, I know you have creative ways of procuring."

"You just show me the plans and I'll decide then," Jax answered.

"Of course, and I'm happy to discuss it with your lawyers as well," Lundy offered.

Jax sneered. "Lawyers? Don't need 'em and don't trust 'em," he answered blatantly. "Present company excluded, of course."

"Of course," Lundy answered. Lundy took a dramatic pause, as if once again making mental calculations in his head.

"What is it?" Jax asked. "I can see the wheels in your head turning so fast there's smoke coming out of your ears."

Lundy forced a practiced chuckle. "Once again, you are not wrong, Jax. Forgive my impertinence, but if we are going to do business together, I have to ask...you're an independent guy, right? From what I've heard, you have no wife and kids, and no family to speak of."

Jax smiled as his gaze floated away for just a moment. He was thinking about Midge, and her recent proposal. Still, it was too soon to count those proverbial chickens and all. "I am currently unmarried," he answered. "And you are correct that I am a lone wolf, so to speak."

Lundy sighed. "Well, that puts an added stress on this arrangement."

"What stress?" Jax asked. "I haven't even agreed to anything yet."

"I've been in this business a long time," Lundy shook his head, mournfully. "Years go by, and a board member or key company figure dies with no will to speak of, and their estate becomes escheated."

"Ah," Jax nodded, knowingly. Lundy could tell from Jax's blank expression that he was bluffing. Lundy played along.

"And you know what happens from there." Lundy nodded and gestured as if Jax were following along. "The state takes over if there is no heir, and those of us who were counting on investment funds lose our shirts. We have no access to the money promised, unless...well, unless the investor creates a will and leaves his money to a charitable cause—"

"Like a church or nonprofit academy," Jax finished for him.

"Exactly," Lundy answered. "I know it's an uncomfortable topic, and I look forward to many years of working together, but if I'm going to get buy-in from the Elders of the church who are still very much involved in the church behind the scenes, they need to feel confident."

Jax drained his glass, his water still untouched. "I'll tell you what, Mr. Lundy." He stood. "You get me your proposal and I'll consider my options."

Chapter 13
Lundy and Bernie

"Where did you run off to today, anyway?" Bernie Forger asked Mr. Lundy, when they met for breakfast the morning following his first televised broadcast since Erasmus Vandenberg's death.

"I had to soothe someone's nerves," Lundy answered calmly, taking a sip of his decaffeinated tea. Meanwhile, Bernie downed his second cup of coffee that morning and flagged down the waitress for a refill.

"Lemmee guess, Jax Liebling?" Bernie answered as the server refilled his cup. "Bless you," he said to her and smiled. She flashed a smile back, baring a set of yellowing teeth that were not nearly as pristinely polished as Bernie's manufactured pearly whites.

"The same." Lundy nodded.

"I think bringing him in was a mistake," Bernie answered. "He's got a screw loose, somewhere."

"Yeah, but he's a screwball with a lot of money," Lundy answered.

"Is he that good of a businessman?" Bernie seemed surprised. "How does that little scamp of a man have that kind of money? He's not good looking. He's not well-connected, and he doesn't seem all that bright."

"He's smarter than he looks," Lundy admitted. "But not by much. From what I can tell he gained his fortune flying under the radar and swindling unsuspecting billionaires out of their money. Then, he did the genius thing of dumping his money into publicity and managed to make a name for himself as an up-and-coming artist back in the late 70s, selling his works to some of the same people he swindled."

"Heck of a guy," Bernie answered. "Are you sure the church should be involved with him? If he's that shady? Aren't we trying to repair our reputation?"

"Of the church, yes. Vandenberg Nutraceuticals, not so much," Lundy replied.

"I don't follow," Bernie answered. "The Vandenberg name IS the church."

"Not anymore," Lundy replied. "The more we can separate ourselves from the nutraceutical business and funnel our efforts into the academy and the publishing house, the greater our chances of rebuilding our reputation and our wealth."

"For the good of the church, of course," Bernie answered.

"Obviously," Lundy agreed. "But you know as well as I do that the Lord works in mysterious ways. If he brought us Jax Liebling to launch us into a new era, then why not let him use his dirty money for good?"

"But he's expecting the church to retain partnerships with Vandenberg Nutraceuticals. Heck, many of the Elders are still heavily invested."

"About that," Lundy said.

"What about that?"

"I think that once we've secured Jax Liebling's seed money for the academy and COIL Publishing House, I think we should convince the Vandenberg family to re-invest elsewhere and get out of the nutraceutical business altogether."

"But Jax purchased with the idea that we'd be a partnership. A large portion of the factory's money came from church members who wanted healing from their ailments, or from non-believers who were out of options and willing to try anything."

"After we get what we need, I say we abandon a sinking ship," Lundy suggested. "Let he and Mr. Baxter Baker go down, while we walk away."

Bernie smiled. "All for God's work," he reaffirmed. "It's just too bad that the Vandenberg name is still attached to the factory."

A lightbulb went off in Lundy's head. "Good thinking," he replied. "Perhaps I should put it Jax's head to rename the company as part of the rebrand."

Bernie's hand began trembling as a result of too much caffeine. He set his coffee cup down and wiped his brow with a napkin. "But won't Jax retaliate after we've ripped the rug out from under his feet?"

"You just keep doing what you do best and lead the church," Lundy answered. "Let me worry about Jax Liebling."

Bernie nodded. "I trust you, Lundy. We couldn't have gotten this far without you."

Chapter 14
The Vandenberg Factory

"Detective Ortega, how nice to see you again," Jax oozed friendliness when Ortega dropped by the Dublin factory, seemingly out of the blue. Friendliness was out of character for him; therefore, it merely came across as slithery and condescending.

"You don't seem surprised to see me, Mr. Liebling," Ortega observed. "I'm going to assume you got an inkling that I might be popping by?"

"A small inkling." Jax set the book he was leafing through onto his desk, remembering Midge's warning about his potential visit. "But perhaps you can let me in on what brings you all the way from New York to Dublin? Or should I say, Florida? I heard a rumor that you retired."

"Well, you have me at a disadvantage, Mr. Liebling," Ortega confessed. "As I am having trouble connecting the dots between our last conversation, where you got away with murder and now seem to be running a million-dollar nutraceutical factory."

"We prefer to think of it as healthy lifestyle products these days," Jax corrected. "And if you'll recall, I was never convicted of anything."

"Oh, that's right," Ortega answered. "You managed to pin the blame on your girlfriend, Midge Pasternak, and then leave her in jail to rot."

Jax's expression dropped. Ortega remained silent and waited for his response.

"The actions of my ex-girlfriend have nothing to do with me," Jax answered simply.

"Don't suppose you've been in touch with Ms. Pasternak lately, have you?"

"What? In prison?" Jax feigned ignorance of her escape, the one that he initiated. "Needless to say, I was disappointed to learn that my former love interest would do such horrible things and ended things immediately."

"I see," Ortega played along, tugging at his ear, thoughtfully. "I do find it a little strange that your name crossed my path once again, though, Mr. Liebling."

"Likewise," Jax answered. "I'll share if you will."

"Well, that's just fine," Ortega agreed. "I'll go first if you don't mind." Jax turned a palm up and motioned for Ortega to continue. "You see, while in Florida...you were right, by the way, I am semi-retired...but again, while in Florida, my services were enlisted to research the untimely death of Erasmus Vandenberg, which led me, as I'm sure you know, down a deep rabbit hole that ultimately led me here...to you, Mr. Liebling." Ortega paused for Jax's reaction.

Jax stared directly into Ortega's eyes for an uncomfortable few moments in which neither man blinked. "Yes," Jax finally spoke. "Nasty business. Mr. Baker, our new CEO, enlisted my help after the police unveiled a crude faith-healing and drug-using scheme that left people dead. Tragic really."

"You seem really broken up about it," Ortega noticed.

"We've been down this road before, Detective," Jax reminded him. "Just because I don't buy into the media hype and get all emotional over people who mean nothing to me, doesn't make me a criminal."

"Don't suppose you'd mind sharing with me how it is that you and Mr. Baker found one another?" Ortega asked.

"If you must know, I have many business dealings in Florida. I'm a wealthy man, Detective Ortega. I got that way by diversifying, and coming in to save sinking ships like the Vandenberg empire. It happens to be what I'm good at."

"I see," Ortega answered. "So, the rumor that you're simply going to pick up where the late Erasmus Vandenberg left off is just that—a rumor? No more weird cult practices and bogus faith healings?"

"I don't like to speak ill of the dead, Detective," Jax replied. "But with my influence, the products of this factory will all be legal and in compliance with all food and drug safety rules. In fact, you're welcome to take a tour of the facility if you like. We're rolling out a new natural food bar line with all organic ingredients. I recommend you try the Calm bar for stress reduction... made with valerian root and chamomile leaves. See? Nothing secret about any of the ingredients."

"Well, thank you for the recommendation," Ortega agreed. "I am feeling a little stressed, and might just take you up on that."

Jax smiled, feeling self-satisfied as if he'd won the argument.

"And, two of my people are already touring the factory downstairs, thanks to Mr. Baxter Baker...very helpful, cooperative young man," Ortega finished.

Jax's face dropped for a microsecond before his practiced smile returned. "Of course, I'm glad to hear it. According to what I've read, it was Mr. Baker who led the police to learn about dear old Erasmus's underhanded dealings to begin with."

"Yes, he's been most helpful," Ortega concurred. "Think I will join them and see what Mr. Baker and my team are up to if you don't mind. Thank you for your time." Ortega tipped a hat to Jax.

"That's it?" Jax called after him.

Ortega spun on his heals. "What else would there be?"

"It's just that," Jax answered. "I really shouldn't be saying anything seeing as how I'm invested in the company and all...but you might have a longer conversation with Mr. Baker to find out what more he's not telling you about the factory operations back in Florida."

"Oh really?"

"Yes," Jax lowered his voice. "But you didn't hear it from me. If it's all just horrid rumors, then so be it. But if he was in some way responsible for the scheme that led to many premature deaths, then I'd rather know before I get in too deep...business-wise."

"Seems like that might have been something to consider before investing?" Ortega pointed out.

"Indeed," Jax grit his teeth. "It's just that I recently learned some news that had me grow suspicious of the young man and the church."

"Thought the church was dead?" Ortega asked, doing a fair job of feigning surprise.

"No, you didn't," Jax shook his head, unconvinced. "But what you may not know is that Bernie Forger, the man who took Erasmus's place as head of the Church of Infinite Love, plans to open up an academy to 'spread the word,'" Jax used air quotes. "There's also talk of a small publishing house."

"So, you're not convinced that the church is turning a new leaf?" Ortega confirmed.

"I am not," Jax answered. "Don't get me wrong, I'll happily

sell them products from our healthy food line, but I'd rather not be involved with people who have questionable practices."

"Hmmm," Ortega smiled insincerely. "Seems to be the exact people you like to be involved with."

Jax sat on the edge of his desk and picked up his book, pretending to leaf through it. "Just be sure to have a talk with Mr. Baker. And when you're done, you might want to look up Bernie Forger."

While Ortega was busy in his talks with Jax Liebling, Shep and Penelope were busy touring the factory with Baxter Baker and his assistant, Moira Dodd. Unlike past interactions with Vandenberg Nutraceuticals, where the only way to get into designated areas was undercover, Baxter seemed as welcoming as a tour guide at a history museum. If one didn't know any better, they might assume that Baxter had pretended to be in charge for so long, that now, he was actually happy to be *doing* something.

"Nice of you to take time out of your schedule to show us around Mr. Baker," Shep commented. Shep, being a bit taller and heavier than Baxter, slunk with his shoulders hunched, like an oversized monster from a B-movie. Meanwhile, Baxter kept his pace slow and measured with Moira rolling in her wheelchair at his side. He seemed to intentionally ensure that he didn't step in front of her. Meanwhile, Moira buzzed along in a hybrid electric chair with manual options. Every once in a while, she underestimated the space between two workstations and got stuck on the edge of a bench and had to manually reverse and move forward by grabbing the wheels. When that happened, Baxter always tried to intervene. And every time, Moira slapped his hands away in defiance.

This interaction did not go unnoticed by Dr. Penelope Washburn who smiled to herself, but said nothing.

"Of course," Baxter answered. "We're always happy to show members of the US police force around. I know we've had our... differences...in the past. But I can assure you that under my direction, Vandenberg Nutraceuticals is fully transparent, an open book, if you will." Baxter smiled and raised his arms wide, like Willy Wonka giving a grand tour of the chocolate factory. It was, admittedly, a little over the top.

On the inside, Baxter was a bundle of nerves. It was no secret who tipped the police off as to Erasmus Vandenberg and the family's underhanded dealings with the church. And he was well aware that he didn't have many friends left, but he decided it was better for both him and the reputation of the company if he were as compliant as possible with the authorities—even ones who, technically, had no jurisdiction in Ireland.

"Correct me if I'm wrong," Shep began, "but in the Florida factory, you had the main production area and one for research and development. Is that still the case?"

Baxter didn't know the answer to this. He looked to Moira for support.

"Ah, you did your homework, lad," Moira chimed in, pausing as she spoke. She had trouble rolling and talking at the same time...another thing that Penelope couldn't help but notice. "Aye, we do have an R&D department, but we're so new that it's more, as you would say, a work in progress. We're happy to show it to ya, though," she offered.

"That would be great," Shep responded. "I guess I'm curious how your products have changed, given—" Shep scratched his chin, not really sure how to be delicate about it.

"That the last ones were laced with illegal drugs?" Moira finished.

Baxter was surprised by Moira's candor, but relieved that she took the initiative all the same. While most bosses might have taken offense to their assistant speaking out of turn, Baxter found it refreshing. Not only did it take the pressure off him, but Moira had this uncanny knack for knowing what to say and what not to, something he had never mastered.

"Well...yes," Shep admitted.

"The health bars general ingredients are the same with ones for energy, sleep and mood-boosting, only our new line uses all natural ingredients: cocoa, valerian, lemon balm and the like. And all are clearly labeled on the package to account for allergies."

"So, no funny business," Penelope offered.

"No funny business," Moira confirmed.

The factory was much smaller than the old one in Florida with fewer workers on the floor. Shep also noticed that in Florida, women and young boys made up the workforce, but here in Ireland, it seemed quite a mix of men and women of all ages.

"I don't mean to be rude," Penelope began, embarrassed, "but I don't suppose you'd be okay with us taking a few samples of your product line? It's just that it would go a long way to proving to the authorities that Vandenberg Nutraceuticals has turned a new leaf."

"By all means," Baxter smiled. "Moira? Could you see to it that they have an ample collection of all our products? Enough for lab testing and a few extra should they get snacky later in the day?"

"Of course, Mr. Baker," Moira smiled. To Shep and Penelope she said, "If you would accompany Mr. Baker back to his office, I can see to it that supplies are sent up over the next few minutes."

"Thank you," Penelope replied.

Moira lagged behind as Baxter, Shep, and Penelope made their way to the elevator leading to the executive suite. Once inside, Baxter suddenly hit the emergency stop button on the lift. Shep eyed him, confused.

"Okay," Baxter whispered. "This may be the only chance I've got to speak in confidence, so listen up." Shep nodded, but said nothing. "It's true that the factory appears on the up and up, and my family won't come near this company with a ten-foot pole with its reputation, but I wouldn't trust any of 'em as far as I could throw 'em. If you have further questions, I suggest you contact me through Moira. Above all, I'd appreciate if you'd conduct as much of your business as possible off property, understand? One visit is quite enough. Any more than that, and Jax Liebling and my family will be breathing down my neck."

Before Shep could respond, Baxter hit the button and the lift resumed its route to the main offices. The doors of the lift opened, where Baxter nearly collided with Ortega, just having finished his talk with Jax. Ortega put his arm out, planting a hand on Baxter's shoulder to steady himself and avoid running into one another.

"Er, sorry," Ortega said, awkwardly.

"No problem," Baxter sidestepped, giving Ortega room to pass and Shep and Penelope to get out of the lift.

"Actually," Penelope intervened. "I don't believe you've met Detective Ortega in person, have you, Mr. Baker?"

Baxter looked up in surprise. "No, we haven't." He offered a hand to Ortega. "But your reputation precedes you."

Ortega shook Baxter's hand...decent grip, not wishy-washy. Ortega felt you could tell a lot about a person from their handshake. "Not sure what that reputation might be," he admitted. "But you're just the man I want to see. Mind if we chat for a moment?"

"Not at all," Baxter agreed. "Your colleagues are welcome to join us as well. As I've been telling them, I have no secrets."

As Ortega followed Baxter into the main office, he asked. "So, where is it that you're staying while in Ireland?"

"Okay," Baxter laughed nervously. "Maybe one secret. Given the sensitive state in which I left Florida, I do have to be careful who knows my whereabouts."

"Fair enough," Ortega nodded as the four of them piled into the office.

As expected, within minutes of their arrival, Moira resurfaced with a collection of healthy snacks boxed up and sitting in her lap.

"There ya go." She pushed the box across her knees. Shep took the cue and lifted the box from her lap. "Service with a smile," Moira laughed.

Jax, who hadn't yet left the office, had no intention of sticking around for any more questions. "Moira," he asked abruptly. "Call downstairs for my driver. I'll be dining out for lunch."

Moira bit her lip. Jax never requested anything; he just barked orders.

"Of course, Mr. Liebling," she agreed, rolling over to her desk and picking up the phone.

"It's a shame I can't stay," Jax answered with all the emotion of an android.

"No problem, Jax," Baxter smiled uneasily. "I can see to our guests from here."

Chapter 15
Just "Derry"

Last Night

"**R**eally, Midge," Rue slid into a booth at Beckett's Bar on a weekday evening when not much was happening. She dropped her small backpack beside her and pulled back the hood of her sweatshirt, letting her tousled hair fall down around her shoulders. "You had me rent a car and drive two-and-a-half hours to Londonderry to meet...on the wrong side of the road, I might add. You couldn't have picked a place near Dublin? Hell, even Belfast would have been quicker."

Midge took a long sip from a tiny straw that dipped into a nearly-finished Bramble cocktail. After a long slurping sound, she used the straw to stab a loose blackberry huddling at the bottom of the glass as if hiding behind several blocks of melting ice.

"Derry," she corrected. "I believe it's just 'Derry' now."

"Whatever, the point is—" Rue huffed.

"The point is, I'm trying to save your life," Midge finished. "Isn't that what best friends do? Look after one another?"

"What are you talking about?" Rue asked loudly, before Midge put a finger to her lips, reminding her to keep her voice down. Rue lowered her voice to a whisper. "You were the one who brought me to Ireland in the first place!"

Just then, a server stopped by their booth. "Any 'ting I can get for ya?" the server asked.

"Yeah," Midge answered, "Another Bramble for me and a—" Midge motioned to Rue.

"Uh, the same... I guess?" Rue finished. The server nodded and quickly moved on. "What exactly did I just order?" Rue questioned.

"Gin and blackberry... you'll like it, trust me. Now, about me saving your life—" Midge continued. Rue crossed her arms and rolled her eyes. "Would you look at you?" Midge sat back in the booth, exasperated. "No gratitude!"

"Explain!" Rue commanded, simply.

"Okay, fine." Midge leaned in. "You've been walking with a target on your back since you left New York, see?" She twirled her curly green hair anxiously, looked down at her beverage and swirled the remaining ice as if there were some small sips of gin left in the glass...there wasn't. "I brought you here to help bring down the Vandenberg family business at its core, only—" Midge paused uncomfortably.

"Only...what?" Rue asked.

"I didn't realize that the turbulence spanned this wide and far," Midge finished.

"Meaning, what, exactly? That you made a mistake?"

"What?" Midge stumbled. "A mistake? Bite your tongue. Midge Pasternak does not make mistakes." She continued the back and forth routine of twirling the ice in her glass with the small sip stirrer, and twirling an unruly piece of her hair, impatiently. Rue could almost count the rhythm...twirl, twirl...five twirls of the ice followed by seven twirls of her hair. One could write a haiku to the rhythm.

The server returned a few minutes later with two beverages. Midge breathed a sigh of relief as she retrieved hers and she relinquished her near-empty glass. She pushed Rue's beverage across the table toward her, encouraging her to drink.

Rue eyed the beverage, cautiously, looking at it and then Midge, and back again, as if Midge's touching it could have led to something sinister. It was a subtle reminder that this wouldn't have been the first time that Midge had poisoned someone.

"Are you kidding me!?" Midge all but yelled before collecting herself and lowering her voice. A few bar goers glanced in their direction with a mix of annoyance and amusement. "After everything we've been through together?"

"You don't exactly have the greatest of track records," Rue reminded her, before conceding to take a small sip of her beverage. "I'd hate to wake up tomorrow dead on account of you poisoning me," Rue finished, smiling.

"Em," Midge laughed. "You know that what you said is impossible, right?"

"My attempt at a joke," Rue added.

"Oh," Midge thought on this a moment before nodding. "Funny!" She nodded, supportively.

"Okay, so why am I a target all of a sudden?" Rue asked. "They caught the person responsible for my mother's death, and the death of Erasmus Vandenberg."

"My sweet, naive, Rue," Midge reached her hand across the table and rested it overtop of Rue's. Rue quickly withdrew her hand. Midge sat back, nonplussed. Rue's mother, a Deaconess in the Church of Infinite Love, and Erasmus Vandenberg, wealthy businessman turned artist in retirement, were murdered by a member of the church. It was regarded as a religiously-motivated killing and that they had been working alone.

After a long sip of her drink, Midge continued, "Their Ambassador was just a convenient scapegoat who happened to go unhinged at the perfect time. It's a shame that more people don't know how to control their anger and emotions, like me."

Rue framed her words carefully, before continuing, "You do remember that you killed two innocent women, not to mention a busload of convicts from a women's detention center in New York, not to mention—"

"That was Jax!" Midge protested. "The first gal, I never meant to kill. The second one had it coming, and I had nothing to do with any of those gals from prison! I'm telling you, that man is crazy!" Midge crossed her arms and looked around the bar nervously, as if by saying his name would cause him to appear. Rue thought Midge to be unflappable and was surprised by what appeared to be an unusual emotion for Midge...fear. "What?" Midge finally asked after a long moment of silence where Rue eyed her friend, curiously.

"You really are afraid of him, aren't you?"

"Who, Jax?" Midge waved a hand nonchalantly, but refused to make eye contact. "Please. I just said that to Fuzz and Beefcake so they would help me. Do I want Jax to leave me alone, absolutely. Am I riddled with fear—"

"Let's try this again," Rue folded her hands and placed them purposefully on the table. "If you were worried Jax was after me, why bring me here and put me in the line of fire?"

"Because I thought you were in greater danger back home. At least here, I can keep an eye on you."

"So, *you're* going to protect me?" Rue shook her head. "I don't buy it."

"Well, it's true," Midge insisted before rolling her eyes to the ceiling.

"You're lying to me, Midge," Rue accused her former friend. "I've learned how to tell when you're lying."

After what seemed like an eternity, Midge let out a sigh and chuckled a little. "You got me," she threw her hands up in the air. "While I do intend to protect you, I need you for another purpose," Midge confessed.

"What purpose?" Rue narrowed her eyes.

After another long pause, Midge answered simply, "Bait...I need you as bait."

"Bait," Rue confirmed. "And what makes you think I'll go along with whatever crazy scheme you're cooking up?"

"Because it's a win-win for everybody, and I mean *everybody*." Midge sucked down the rest of her beverage and motioned for another. "Can I get something salty over here? Maybe some peanuts or crackers or something?"

The server was attentive, plunking down a menu. "Fraid we're fresh outa nuts," the young woman eyed the menu. "But the stew and boxties are pretty good."

"A boxty," Midge smiled. "That sounds fun, like me." She winked at the waitress who merely smiled back and nodded politely as she walked away.

"You were saying," Rue reminded her. "How is this a win-win for everybody?"

"Easy, Ortega and Shep get to bust up the biggest con of the century, I get Jax off my case and yours, and—"

"And?"

"I can help resolve the bad blood between that tall drink of wat-uh boyfriend of yours and Constantine Westport."

"Darwin?" Rue sat up. "What does Darwin have to do with any of this?" She knew he said he couldn't set foot in Ireland again, but she refused to believe that after all this time, Constantine Westport would still blame Darwin Fennec and his sidekick

Bristol for his own daughter's choice in lifestyle and accidental drug overdose.

Midge read her thoughts. "It sometimes takes people an awful long time to forget," she said. "Not only did Westport lose a daughter, but his son and your precious Mr. Fennec tried to con the conner. That don't typically go over too big according to the Westport code."

The color started to drain from Rue's face. "Please tell me you're not planning to hand me over to Constantine Westport to appease his need for revenge?"

"Of course not," Midge defended. "I would never put you in harm's way like that. That's just irresponsible!"

Rue cleared her throat and shot a wide-eyed look. "Really? It sure seems like that's exactly what you're doing, putting me on the radar of both Jax Liebling and Constantine Westport. And what's all this bait shit, anyway?"

The waitress dropped off a small plate of cheesy potato pancakes with an extra plate and two forks. "In case ye wanna share, yeah?" she offered, winking at Midge before walking away.

"Eat up," Midge encouraged. "You're too skinny as it is, and who knows when your next meal will be."

"Well, that's encouraging," Rue retorted, but relented and took a small bite of the boxty. She was hungrier than she realized.

Midge leaned in and whispered. "I'm gonna let you in on a little secret, but just one." She paused while Rue leaned over the table. "Jax thinks he's clever enough to move into the Westport territory and not have to pay Westport's, shall we say, 'residence fee.' Once Constantine realizes that you and your team are here to move the Vandenberg operation out, it will go a long way to clearing the bad blood between Constantine and Darwin."

"Does Constantine even know who I am?" Rue asked.

"Between you and Darwin's entanglement in SpencerTech and B.A. Ellis Industry face-off, and your help in uncovering the church's and the Vandenberg's shady dealings, I'm pretty sure he knows all about the crime-stopping dynamic duo."

Rue cringed at the reference to SpencerTech. Its founder, Spencer Hargrove, had been her first boyfriend in New York and it was his underhanded dealings that brought she and Darwin Fennec together in the first place.

"Won't Constantine be worried that we'll turn the attention of the authorities onto the Westport empire?"

"You sure ask a heap-load of questions, Bestie." Midge took a bite of food, decided it needed salt, and sprinkled a hearty dose on the entire dish, including Rue's portion. "Not after we convince him that you're on his side...code of ethics, honor among thieves and all—"

"And how are we going to do that?" Rue asked, suspiciously.

"Ah, that's the million-dollar question, my friend. But that's for me to know, and you to find out."

Rue was a mix of horrified, fascinated, skeptical and fearful of Midge's plan...what little of it she knew. She was ready to tell Midge 'thanks, but no thanks' and hightail it back to the safe house where Ortega, Shep and Penelope were holing up, were it not for one problem.

All of a sudden her eyes began to feel a little sore. She gazed at Midge who now appeared as a hazy blob.

Midge smiled, "That's enough for you, my friend," she joked loudly. "Waiter. Check please!"

"No," Rue protested. "I'm not okay with this. I need to get back home. Darwin was right, I should have never come here."

Midge wrapped Rue's arm around her and helped her to her feet. A few bystanders at the bar stood to offer assistance.

"Be a doll, and help me get my friend into my car," Midge

said to a middle-aged man who wiped the beer mustache from his lips and set down his pint.

"Happy to oblige," he answered.

"No, I'm fine," Rue protested. "My rental's just outside."

"Don't think it's safe for you to be drivin' anywhere, lass. Yer friend is right."

It was only after Midge and Rue were safely in Midge's compact Opel Astra heading to who knows where, that their main server stepped outside to see what the fuss was about. A few gathered at the doorway, laughing.

"A young maiden jest couldn't hold her liquor is all...Americans!"

"The green-haired one?" the server nodded. "Aye, she downed at least four Brambles in under an hour."

"Nah," one of the bar goers answered. "Nah her. De other normal-lookin' one wit the brown hair. Could barely stand, that one!"

The group laughed.

"That one?" The server shook her head. "Barely touched her drink, she did." She watched as the car faded into the distance.

The bartender rested a hand on her shoulder. "Don't be getten' yer funny conspiracy ideas, Lil," he cautioned.

Lil nodded, but paused to eye the only rental car parked on the street outside. "Hmm, I wonder," she said, and went back to work.

From the passenger's side, Rue whined in an uncharacteristically infantile manner. "What did you give me?" Rue asked, leaning her cheek against the side of the window. It felt pleasantly cool while the rest of her skin felt as if it were somehow on fire.

"Don't worry about it," Midge answered. "You'll sleep it off in about eight hours." Then, after noticing how affected Rue seemed to be, she added, "Maybe twelve hours."

"If I'm going to die, can I at least call Darwin and say goodbye?"

"You're not gonna—" Suddenly, Midge got an idea. "Sure, call Darwin. But *don't* tell him where you are, understood?"

"No," Rue shook her head fervently, like a small child. "I wouldn't want him to get hurt."

"That's right," Midge answered. "Tell you what. You just dial and let him know you're fine. Okay?"

Rue nodded. It took her three attempts to focus enough to hit the correct numbers on the keypad.

"Rue?" Darwin picked up the phone on the first ring. "I've been so worried about you. I know I shouldn't be, but I haven't heard from you all day so—"

Rue breathed heavily into the phone.

"Rue?" Darwin was concerned. "What is it? Are you hurt?"

"No, I'm okay," Rue struggled to form her words. "I just called to tell you something."

"Yes, of course," he answered. "What it is, darling?"

"I want you to know that I love you."

Midge pulled the phone from Rue's grasp and hit the red button to end the call. She then rolled down the driver's side window and tossed the cell phone into traffic, glancing in the rear view mirror as it went skipping along the road, smashing to pieces before several cars ran over it. Midge then grabbed Rue's backpack with one hand, pulling it roughly from Rue's shoulders with her other hand still on the wheel. At the next red light, Midge quickly unzipped it and rifled through the contents.

Rue drifted off to sleep, only to awaken some time later. It was dark out, and the temperature had dropped considerably. Rue shivered, having suddenly gone from feeling very hot to very, very cold.

Midge pulled off the main road into a wooded area. On her lap, she couldn't help but notice a small, compact Swiss army knife...one that Rue carried with her when she traveled. She tried to move toward it, but Midge put a hand out and shoved Rue back into her seat with a little more force than was necessary for someone who had been drugged.

"Ow," Rue winced as the side of her head hit the window.

"Serves you right," Midge chastised. "Don't be so grabby."

"Where are we?" Rue asked, rubbing her head, fear mounting as she watched her friend, suspiciously. Chills danced up and down her spine. When Midge didn't answer, she added, "So it comes down to this, does it?" Rue slurred her words. "Is this the moment where you finally decide I'm no longer your 'bestie' and kill me?"

Midge winced, an annoyed twitch on her lips. She finally answered, "Just making a little pitstop."

Chapter 16
Disappearing Act

Leaving the Factory

"You get shotgun," Shep insisted, opening the door of their rental car so Penelope could climb in. "Unless you prefer to drive?"

"No, thanks," Penelope answered. "I don't even drive in Manhattan. Probably best to leave it to Jose...I mean, Detective Ortega."

Shep nodded and closed the door. Ortega waited while the Tampa Sheriff stuffed himself in the back seat, folding his knees into his chest. Penelope tried her best to pull her seat all the way forward to give him more room, but it was a tight fit any way you looked at it. Beside him, they had placed the 'evidence' collected from their factory visit. While they were fairly convinced Baxter wouldn't freely give them health bars to test if he didn't believe they were clean, they still wanted to check in with Ortega's connections at the local Guard to ensure everything was on the up and up. For whatever reason, Ortega's spidey sense didn't get triggered by Baxter. But Jax Liebling, on the other hand, was another story.

Ortega and Penelope chatted pleasantly from the front seat, replaying their meeting with Baxter Baker and Moira Dodd. It was quite a bit different from Ortega's previous visit to a Vandenberg Nutraceuticals factory. The last time was in Florida, and it was more an undercover stakeout with his soon-to-be ex-wife, Nancy; former crime suspect turned amateur detective, Emma Post; and her overly-enthusiastic assistant, Sprightly. Not to mention that Erasmus Vandenberg's own granddaughter, Elsbeth Ions, was on the scene helping the ragtag group gain access.

Today, however, was different. They were greeted with open arms after boldly walking through the front doors.

"What are you thinking?" Penelope asked when Ortega fell silent.

"Oh, I'm just wondering if they are playing nice for the time being, but plan on returning to their old tricks in a few months when the spotlight is off of them."

"Baxter Baker seemed on the up and up," Penelope answered.

"Baxter Baker has to be," Ortega offered. "He barely skirted getting arrested himself on manslaughter and racketeering thanks to a combination of him feeding info to the police and the Vandenberg lawyer, Mr. Lundy, working whatever underhanded deals he needed to cover up the boy's tracks."

"Not sure why," Penelope reasoned. "Why try to clear Baxter Baker's name, and then put him front and center here?"

"So, you think his comeuppance is more a 'not now' versus a 'not ever?'" Ortega offered.

"Exactly!" Penelope confirmed. "I guess we'll know more when we follow your lead to talk with the new head of the church, Bernie Forger."

"Right," Ortega confirmed. "For now, we settle in for a meal of whatever it is Ms. Brennan scrounged up for us and head to Belfast in the morning."

"Guys!" Shep groaned, grabbing his side. "I don't mean to put a damper on your plans, but I think maybe you should get me to a hospital first."

Penelope twisted in her seat, witnessing several health bar wrappers on the seat next to Shep, crumbs sprinkled down his shirt and a pained look on his face.

"What did you do?!" Penelope cried out. "Not only is that evidence, but we have no idea what's in those things!"

"Well," Shep defended, clenching his teeth. "You said yourself that they were likely clean. And I was hungry...low blood sugar and all."

"Right," Ortega wrenched the steering wheel and redirected them to the nearest hospital. "St. James is just a few minutes from here." He swerved in and out of traffic, taking turns that were a little harder than necessary, and not particularly safe.

"What's hurting?" Penelope asked, trying to get the rundown from Shep on the symptoms.

"A stabbing pain in my side," Shep groaned, holding his belly. "Not to mention some really unpleasant digestive issues...and nausea...are we there yet?"

"Almost," Penelope answered, not really sure. She did her best to keep him calm.

Ortega pulled into the emergency entrance as a triage nurse ran out to attend to them.

"My friend is not doing well," Ortega told her, flustered. "We think he may have been poisoned, but we can't be certain."

Within moments, Shep was whisked away on a stretcher while Ortega and Penelope were left in the ER waiting room. Ortega paced back and forth while Penelope just sat in one place with her knee bouncing nervously up and down.

"I tried phoning Rue," Ortega informed Penelope. "But she's not picking up at the house."

"Maybe she's out shopping?" Penelope offered.

Ortega looked at his watch. "Maybe," he concurred. "But my spidey sense is telling me something is wrong."

"You wanna take the car home and check on her while I wait here for news on Shep?"

"That might not be a bad idea," Ortega agreed. "Thank you, Penelope."

"Just be careful, Jose!" she called after him.

He smiled, despite the situation. It wasn't often she called him by his first name, given their sometimes-professional relationship, but he liked when she did. Ortega reached the parking area, climbed into their rental, and headed back to Swords.

"Ms. Brennan!" Ortega called out, cautiously, when he'd reached the small apartment they were renting. "Are you home?"

There was no answer. Ortega wasn't fond of carrying a weapon, but secretly wished he had his gun at this moment. Unfortunately, it was back in the States. He looked around for a suitable weapon, settling on a small Ogham stone statuette sitting on the end table by the front door. He held the weighted piece in his hand as he cautiously walked from room to room—which didn't take long, considering how small the place was. Windows were locked, and nothing appeared out of the ordinary.

Just then, the phone rang.

"Rue, is that you?" Ortega asked, concerned.

"Aww, so sweet that you care...but no!" A mouthy voice with a New York and Jersey hybrid accent replied.

"Miss Pasternak," Ortega caught his breath, agitated. "Mind

telling me where Ms. Brennan is? I'm assuming if you're calling, you've got something to do with it."

"Gee," Midge was offended. "Thanks for asking how I am. Not that you care."

"I don't," Ortega answered, gruffly. "Why are you calling? Where's Rue?"

"She's safe, let's start there," Midge answered, calmly. "Look Fuzz, I only got a minute, so stop yapping and listen."

"Go on."

"All you need to know is that she has willfully chosen to help me. She's safe for now, but in order to stay that way, you have to do exactly what I tell you."

Midge's orders were pretty straightforward. Ortega was supposed to wait twenty-four hours and file a missing person's report, and nothing else. "No snooping, no investigating, no checking in with your buddies at the Guard. And above all, don't tell Darwin Fennec nothin'."

"What am I supposed to do if he calls?" Ortega protested.

"Ignore his calls. He can't know anything."

"I don't think that's gonna fly. He loves—"

"I don't care what you think!" Midge yelled into the receiver. "Missing person's report, and that's all! Forget she even came with you to Ireland until further notice."

"How am I supposed to trust you?"

"You don't have a choice," Midge threatened. "If you don't follow my instructions, she dies." With that, Midge slammed the phone down.

Ortega stared numbly at the receiver, now buzzing a dial tone. Just then, his mobile phone rang. He set the house phone back in its cradle and pulled his cell phone from his pocket.

"Penelope," he answered.

"Good news," Penelope answered. "Well, sorta."

"What is it?" Ortega asked. He was due for some good news...ish.

"Shep wasn't poisoned," Penelope paused and added quietly, "too bad they didn't figure that out before they had his stomach pumped."

"Ooh," Ortega asked. "Is he okay?"

"He will be. Turns out he had a ruptured appendix. By the time you make it back here, he should be out of surgery. After he's assigned a room, we should be able to see him," Penelope said.

"Sucky timing," Ortega admitted. "But I'm glad he's okay. Sit tight and I'll be there to pick you up as soon as I can."

"Is Rue with you?" Penelope asked.

"That's another story," Ortega answered. "Can't say more by phone. Talk to you in a bit. Just do me a favor?"

"Of course," Penelope answered.

"Don't leave the hospital and just stay where people can see you, okay?"

"Uh, okay," she said.

Ortega had just finished his call with Penelope when his cell phone rang once again...it was Darwin. Ortega sighed and let it go to voicemail.

It was nearly midnight when they finally returned from the hospital with Shep left to sleep and recover from surgery. Darwin had called two more times, one with a voicemail message, "Ortega, what's going on over there? I got a cryptic call from Rue. She sounded as if something was wrong, told me she loved me, and hung up. Call me back, man!"

Ortega fumbled with the cell phone for several minutes. Penelope eyed him, but said nothing. She knew what he was thinking. He didn't trust Midge, but he also didn't want to do anything that might put Rue's life in danger. And he certainly didn't like this feeling of helplessness, not one bit.

She put a hand on his shoulder. Ortega glanced over at her before hanging his head in shame. "I let my ego get the better of me, Penelope...once again."

"And once again, you're being too hard on yourself," Penelope tried to console him.

"Not this time," he began pacing the floor which was difficult to do in the hovel that they had been sharing with two other people.

Knowingly, Penelope reached under the kitchen counter and pulled out a bottle of Jameson whiskey and fumbled through the cabinets until she'd found a small juice glass. She poured a healthy shot before reaching into the icebox for a cube. She swirled the cube as well as possible in the tiny glass and offered it to him just as he'd spun around and circled back.

"Thanks," he accepted it, surprised. "But where did this come from?"

"A gal has to have some secrets," she batted her eyes at him, her Southern drawl a little affected for emphasis. "I figured it might come in handy on a day when you needed...reinforcements."

Ortega smiled and took a sip.

"Alright, I'll bite," Penelope asked. "How is your ego to blame?"

"I was so set on bringing down the Vandenberg family, their cult, their shady company, and their empire that I put several civilians in harm's way by dragging you to Ireland."

"Hang on," Penelope corrected him. "Shep and I are far from 'civilians' and Rue Brennan is now an honest-to-goodness private investigator. We all knew what we were getting into. Or, at the very least, what we didn't know, we accepted and assumed the risks."

"But now I've got a mentally ill escaped con out there with Rue, and who the hell knows what her plan is? All I know is that it somehow involves that murderer Jax Liebling, and whatever it is, it isn't good!" Ortega raised his voice before downing his drink. "Sorry," he slammed the juice glass on the kitchen table. "I didn't mean to yell...or slam the glass down just then." He rubbed his forehead and resumed pacing.

Penelope fell in step behind him, expertly pivoting as he did, so that she followed, but never got in his way.

"Well, let's think about this a minute," Penelope reasoned. "Why did Midge kill in the first place?"

"What? Why—" Ortega thought a moment. "Because she thought she was helping Rue."

"By creating a dramatic scene to push Darwin and Rue together," Penelope held her palms up, "And—"

"And when someone threatened to try to pin it on Rue—"

"Midge stepped in."

"Yes," Ortega answered. "But why put her in danger again now?"

"So Midge could rescue her?" Penelope offered. "She does seem awfully concerned about what her 'bestie' is up to."

"Hmmm, maybe," Ortega answered. "You don't think she'd actually harm Rue, do you?"

"No, not intentionally," Penelope offered. "She might be putting her in danger, but there's more we're just not seeing."

"Damn, this is frustrating. Being outsmarted by a young hooligan."

"Hooligan?" Penelope laughed. "Listen to you." She abruptly stopped in front of him as he turned. Ortega bumped into her before catching himself.

"Sorry," he said, as he stood, his body only an inch from hers. He didn't back up.

"Neither one of us have had a decent night's sleep in days; we're in the wrong time zone, and it's late," Penelope reasoned, touching his arm.

"But if we don't report it—"

"We could report it and get her killed," Penelope said.

"We could not report it and get her killed," Ortega reasoned.

"And what will the police do with what little we have to go on?"

Ortega glanced off into space for a minute. "Rue said she was going to get us groceries," he peered into the distance.

"Yes? What of it?" Penelope asked.

"We had our rental car. There's nothing within walking distance."

"Maybe she called a cab?"

"Maybe. Or—"

"Or what?" Penelope asked.

"Maybe she called Midge?" Ortega suggested.

"Why would she do that without telling us?"

"Because they were friends from a long time ago," Ortega answered. "And you said it yourself, Rue is a bona fide investigator."

"I don't think we're going to make any wise decisions tonight," Penelope yawned. "I'm exhausted and so are you. For just this once, what if we sleep on it and file a missing person report in the morning, just as Midge said."

After a dramatic pause, Ortega put his hands on Penelope's waist. She glanced down at them in surprise and then lifted her chin to meet his gaze. "You're right about one thing, Penelope."

"What's that?" she whispered. There was apprehension in her eyes, and something else. Ortega hadn't seen that look from her in a long time.

"I don't think we're going to make any wise decisions tonight," he whispered back.

Ortega pulled Penelope in close and kissed her, the way someone kisses the one they love when they haven't seen them in a very long time. And it did go on...for a very long time. Finally, Ortega led her back to his room.

"Just one question?" Penelope gasped, breaking free from his lips.

"What's that?" He nuzzled her ear.

"Top bunk or bottom?" she snorted.

Ortega laughed, and then pulled her to the floor alongside him, rolling over her and pinning her arms over her head.

"Just like old times," she giggled. "Such a gentleman."

"Gentleman, my ass." He held her arms down and kissed her fervently on her lips. She lifted her hips slightly and moaned. "Are you trying to get away?" he joked.

Penelope shook her head. "No, never," she kissed him back. He released her arms and she circled them around his neck, hugging him to her with her back on the floor. He put the weight of his body on top of her, bracing himself with his hands, worried he might be too heavy for her small frame. She didn't seem to mind. She wrapped her legs around his legs, as if trapping him on top of her. "Never again."

Chapter 17
The Temple Bar

"It's just up here," Baxter pushed Moira's wheelchair along the cobblestone street with some difficulty. "Sorry," he apologized as the chair made jerky movements from side to side and back and forth, leaving Moira to hang onto the arm rests and brace herself.

"Where is it we're going again?" Moira asked.

"I'm told there's a little speak-easy-type pub up this way. It's supposed to be fun...very hush-hush and not too many people know about it."

"Really?" Moira was interested. "What's so special about it?"

"Don't know," Baxter confessed. "Just that it's so little known?" he suggested.

Against her better judgment, she finally agreed to a date with Baxter Baker on the condition that he knew there would be 'no funny business.' He agreed, wholeheartedly. After weeks of asking, she finally said, 'yes,' and he was not going to mess this up. She knew it was a bad idea, given that he was her boss and all, but she reminded herself that she was actually the one doing Baxter's job. So, that made it okay, didn't it?

Moira wore a bright red dress that evening, one with large ruffled sleeves that fanned out as if she were flamenco dancer. On her feet were small red ballet-type flats. An odd choice from a woman who was bound to a wheelchair and couldn't dance. Still, she wore one side of her hair down, letting it fall gracefully around her shoulder, the other side pinned back with a flower clip. Her lips, Baxter notice, had just a hint of a pink gloss. He tried not to look at them for too long because he found them distracting. Finally, he turned down an alley in the Temple Bar district.

"Should be around here somewhere," Baxter ran his hand through his hair, flustered. He was never flustered, always self-assured. And yet, for reasons which he could not explain, he felt the need to impress Moira. He wondered, *was it because she was one of the few women who seemed immune to his charms?* He found Emma Post alluring, too, and she couldn't be bothered with him. Did he only crave women who played hard-to-get? *No,* he thought to himself, *that can't be it. What was it?* While Baxter pondered to himself, Moira waited patiently for as long as she could before suggesting, "Em, could that be it?" She pointed to a black door that somehow blended nicely with the brick buildings that seemed to swallow it. It sat a few inches back from the building itself, making it easy to pass without seeing it.

"No, I don't think so," Baxter shook his head. "Should be up this way, I think."

Moira hung her head and pinched her lips together as if stifling a laugh. "I really think you might give it a knock and see," Moira suggested. "I mean, seeing as we're here already and all. What have we got to lose?"

Baxter relented and rapped on the door with two knuckles on the back of his fist. No one answered.

"See?" Baxter walked toward Moira, arms spread wide.

Just then, a small window in the door opened. It wasn't much larger than an index card. Eyes could be seen on the other side of the door, but they said nothing, merely staring. "That you, Moira?" a muffled voice finally asked.

"It is, Skinny," Moira answered. "Fancy meeting you here."

The door flung open and a very rotund man with a bald head and a graying beard greeted her. "As I live and breathe!" He smiled. "Moira Dodd, I haven't seen you in ages! Best come inside. Can't have the door open too long." He eyed Baxter up and down suspiciously. "This bloke with you?"

"I'm afraid so," Moira laughed.

"You've been here before?" Baxter was surprised.

"Eh, no." Moira winked at Skinny. "Skinny and I just go way back." Skinny tipped his head in return. He made his way over to the street where Moira sat.

"Didja injure yourself, then, Moira?" Skinny stood beside Moira, peering down at her in the chair. She grabbed the wheels and took a hard rotation to the left, leaving Skinny just at her right. While Baxter was momentarily distracted by the noise coming from the inside of the venue, Moira grabbed the moment. She elbowed Skinny in the side of his gut. He sucked in his breath.

"Well, get on in," Skinny urged, lowering his voice and wincing. "We're almost at capacity tonight."

Baxter took the handles on the back of Moira's wheelchair and rolled her through the door, only to be greeted by a narrow set of stairs. At the top, music and the loud voices of people laughing and carousing could be heard. Baxter's face dropped.

"Hmmm," Moira answered. "Sorry, Mr. Baker. But it looks like this might not work out as we'd hoped."

"Nonsense," Baxter answered. "I can carry you."

"Up those stairs!" Moira laughed. "You'll break your back, and likely drop me on my arse! No, thanks."

Baxter took Skinny aside and slipped him a few bills. "Anything we can do?" he whispered. Moira pretended not to notice.

"Not to worry," Skinny was confident. "Give me a tick and I'll be right back." Skinny bounded the steps two at a time. Moira eyed the stairs, reluctantly. Minutes later, Skinny returned with three other men. Before she could protest, they grabbed her chair, with her still in it, two in the front and two in the back and bounded up the steps. Moira's single hair clip came loose and bounced down the steps while her red locks flew haphazardly down her back. She struggled to keep her head and neck upright at the angle at which she ascended. She gripped the arm rest, half exhilarated, and half terrified at the threat of them accidentally dropping her, sending them all crashing onto the concrete below.

Baxter followed behind, occasionally putting his hand out as if there were any way he could protect her if she *did* take a spill. He spotted the flower clip and grabbed it on its descent, stuffing it in his jacket pocket.

At the landing, Moira breathed a sigh of relief as the men set her down. "Thank you, boys," she laughed. "But you lads are nutty! You might have dropped me!"

"You, Moira?" One of the men answered. "Never!"

Baxter turned to Skinny. "Thanks, but I coulda helped carry her, you know?"

Skinny looked Baxter up and down. "Couldn't risk it," he finally answered. "You have the smoothest hands I've ever seen fer a man. Not sure heavy lifting is yer strong suit."

Baxter's face became flushed. He was about to retort when he realized Skinny wasn't being purposefully unkind. He was just unabashedly honest.

"Hey, Moira," one of the men tried again. "What happened

to ya?" Before he could say anything more, it was Skinny's turn to jab an elbow into someone's ribs. The man fell silent, confused.

"Thank you, again, gentlemen," Moira praised. To Baxter, she said, "Shall we go and see what the fuss is all about?"

"Excellent idea, Miss Dodd," Baxter agreed, once again regaining control of the handles behind the chair and guiding his date toward what he assumed was the main area. "Oh," he paused, "your hair clip." He pulled the clip out of his pocket and attempted to fluff the flower back into its original shape.

"Nah," Moira shook her head. "You keep it. Probably look better on you," she teased.

Baxter grinned, mischievously, as he clipped the small red flower to the side of his blonde locks. Moira lifted a hand to her mouth to stifle a laugh, but it was no use. "I was...right!" Tears of laughter streamed down her face. "Better on...you," she breathed heavily.

"I doubt that," Baxter laughed. "But now I've committed to it, there's no turning back."

They crossed the threshold, hesitantly. Inside, it was a struggle to squeeze through the crowd without the footrests of Moira's chair nearly clipping people's ankles at every turn. But eventually, they found a spot catty-corner to the stage. The place was packed to the gills with every chair or booth filled. Baxter didn't mind, he leaned against a pole and rested his hands on Moira's shoulders as they gazed with anticipation at the stage. It was a bold move, he realized, but Moira didn't seem to mind.

Moments later, without introductions, the band launched into their rendition of 'Whiskey in the Jar.' Applause erupted.

"Is that—" Baxter began, stunned.

"The same," Moira answered confidently.

"But they're famous!" Baxter protested. "What are they doing in a dive bar in a small corner of Dublin playing for a handful of people and making crap money in the process?"

"You think too much, Mr. Baker," Moira chastised, peering at him from over her shoulder. "Here, look." She pointed as solo singer-songwriters and members from at least one other world-traveled band joined the first. No one bothered to warm up, as each performer was ready with his or her instruments, they just joined in...keyboard, guitar, bass, drums, fiddles, vocals.

Baxter listened with appreciation and awe as the music soon morphed into a version of 'Dreams.' The music grew louder, drowning out the voices of the crowd. Baxter could feel his heartbeat pulsing in his head, seemingly to the rhythm of the music, and despite the body heat and limited elbow room, this was the most exciting time he could remember...and he had experienced a lot.

Moments later, Skinny pushed his way through the crowd, sloshing two pints of Guinness along the way. "Here ya go, lass," he handed one to Moira and offered the second to Baxter. "On the house, just promise not to stay away so long next time, okay, Moira?" He winked and disappeared into the crowd.

"Never been here before, you say?" Baxter leaned close to her ear. His breath on her neck gave her the chills.

"Well," she answered mischievously, "never with you. That's fer sure." She sipped her Guinness.

How odd, Baxter thought to himself. *And she's obviously never been here while in a wheelchair before. Her friends all seemed surprised to see her that way, and she was visibly shaken when they carried her up the steps.* The best that he could tell was that whatever happened to her, happened somewhat recently, but she didn't want to talk about it.

At that moment, Moira did the most surprising thing, she bent her Guinness-free arm and rested her left hand over his, clasping it over her shoulder.

Baxter's luck was turning around. He could feel it.

Baxter and Moira waited until most of the club had cleared out before they attempted the staircase a second time. Fortunately, with an assist from Skinny's men, the descent was easier. Except this time, Baxter insisted on helping, and so it was Skinny's turn to stand guard, always keeping two steps ahead, treading carefully backward while holding the rail, just in case Moira took a topple.

At last, they reached the bottom, and they welcomed a cold blast of fresh air after the stuffiness of what had become a smoke-filled room. It was so heavy; they could still smell the cigarette smoke on their clothes. Baxter's eyes were a little red and his nose stuffy, but he didn't care.

"Good seeing ya, Moira," Skinny offered.

"Don't stay away so long next time," another friend added, glancing at her chair, but saying nothing.

"Will do," she nodded. "Gotta make sure you lads aren't getting up to no good!"

"You're a fine one to talk, lass," he wagged a finger, good-naturedly.

To Baxter, Skinny warned, "You be good to her, ya hear me? Otherwise, you'll have to deal with Skinny." He pointed a thumb at himself as if it needed clarification.

"I plan on it," Baxter answered, attempting to run his fingers through his hair in what he hoped would be a suave moment. Only, he connected with the flower he'd forgotten about. His sleeve got stuck on it, and for a moment, his wrist was trapped to his head lest he accidentally pull his hair out.

The men laughed, shutting the door behind them. The sound of several locks being latched could be heard from the outside.

"Would you look at you?" Moira teased. "Here, lean over."

Baxter obeyed as Moira reached up and untangled his sleeve

from his hair. She retrieved her hair clip and stuck it lopsidedly on her head. She didn't care and neither did Baxter. He grinned sheepishly.

"You hungry?" he asked. While the bar was great on drinks and peanuts, it was sadly lacking food.

"Yeah," she answered. "And I gotta find a loo," she confessed. "It was too crowded to move in that place."

"Know of any place open at this hour?" he asked.

"Not at this hour," she confessed. "We could always—" But she stopped herself. *Go back to her place? Nah,* she thought. *Too risky.*

"Yes?" he answered, hopefully.

"Go back to the office," she suggested. "I always keep a couple of extra frozen dinners in the break room in case I get stuck working late or can't make it out to lunch."

Baxter took the handles on the back of her chair and aimed them toward the office. "We need to talk to that arse boss of yours about your hours," he joked. Really, he had no idea she put in that kind of time. But how could he? He was always late to arrive and early to leave.

Moira chuckled. "Quite."

"So why do you suppose famous people hang out in little dive bars like that one?" Baxter was perplexed. "There's no money in it."

"Did it ever occur to you that it's not all about the money," Moira suggested. "Maybe they want to practice their craft among friends, to feel normal again by stepping out of the public eye. To play music just for the music's sake."

"Why, Moira," Baxter commented, "I had no idea you were such a poet." He pushed her chair carefully across the cobblestones. "I suppose you are right."

Chapter 18
Betrothed

"What's this?" Jax found Midge draped across his couch wearing nothing but a silk robe opened at the front, yet strategically covering all the intimate places of her body. Her hair was washed from a fresh shower and wrapped in a cotton towel.

"I have a present for you," she smirked.

"I can see that," Jax made his way over to her.

"Not me," she stuck her bare foot out and pressed it into his chest, stopping him. The robe slipped away, revealing the bottom half of her torso. He paused to admire her, grinning back at her, seductively. "Over there," she gestured toward the coffee table. On it, sat a little white box wrapped in a red ribbon.

"What do we have here?" Jax asked, curiously, venturing over to the table. He held the box up to his ear, playfully. "It's not ticking, so it's not a watch or a bomb," he joked. "Shall I shake it, or is it fragile?"

"Not anymore, it's not," Midge retorted. "But it used to be when it was alive."

"You don't mean?" Jax was taken aback.

"Proof of my commitment to you," Midge explained, an uncustomary tear forming in the corner of her eye.

"Are you crying?" Jax asked, more surprised than concerned.

"Let's just say, it wasn't easy murdering my bestie," Midge answered. "So open it, you lug. Then maybe you'll be convinced that I fully intend to marry you...tomorrow, if you like."

Jax picked up the box and pulled at the ribbon until it unraveled. Lifting the lid, he peered inside. There, he found a tuft of hair and what appeared to be the tip of a human finger, both carefully sealed in tiny clear bags, the kind someone uses when they don't want their silver jewelry to tarnish. He lifted the finger out, hesitantly. "You don't mean—"

"Extracted from Rue's corpse after I killed her," Midge explained.

"How did you do it?" Jax was intrigued.

"My, you are morbid," Midge answered. "Single gunshot wound to the head. I removed the tip of her finger and cut a lock of her hair, then rolled her body off the cliff."

"Which finger? What cliff?" Jax asked, suspiciously.

"What difference does it make? Don't you believe me?" Midge asked, indignantly. "Fine." She rolled her eyes. "Pinky finger and a remote area of the Causeway at night. Are you happy now?"

"Not much blood." He turned the bag with the finger over. "Other than a little smeared bit on the bag here," he noticed.

"It was making a mess everywhere, so I cauterized it and cleaned it up," Midge explained.

Jax moved on to the hair. "I thought hers was more a mousy brown. This appears darker with a bit of gray in it."

"Maybe you misremembered." Midge became agitated. "And

even I have a few early gray strands. I just dye mine. Listen, I didn't have to do that. I did it to prove my love and devotion for you, but if that's not enough—"

"Take it easy, my pet." Jax put the box on the table, concerned. "Of course I believe you. I guess I was just surprised, given how much I know Rue Brennan meant to you." Even now, he had trouble saying Rue's name. It dripped off his tongue with jealous disdain.

Midge sniffed back a few more tears. "I did it for you...us." She slipped the robe off her shoulders, revealing her breasts. She lifted her chest to give Jax a better view.

Jax lunged at her, dragging her to her feet and pulling her close to him.

As he kissed her neck, she asked, "You did say we were cleared to marry, didn't you?"

"I applied for the license months ago. We're in the clear, but we should do it soon before anyone finds out that I'm marrying an escaped convict."

"Do you think anyone in Ireland would care what I did in America?" Midge unbuttoned the top of Jax's shirt with her fingers. "Correction...what *we* did?"

"I'd just as soon not take any chances," Jax answered. "I've got big plans for us," he boasted. "Let's head to the local registry in the morning."

Jax was unusually cheerful when he arrived at the factory early Monday morning.

"Good morning, Mr. Liebling," Moira greeted Jax as he made his way past her desk and to his private office.

Most times, Jax grunted at her or waved a hand by way of acknowledgment. But today, to her surprise, he stopped to smile at her. She flinched a little. It was as if the Devil himself were baring his teeth. "Good morning, Ms. Dodd," he greeted. "Did you have a nice weekend?"

Moira thought back to the Temple Bar and the evenings that followed, all with Baxter Baker...all innocent, of course. She refused to let him lift her out of her chair, even when he asked, claiming that she wasn't ready for him to see 'down there' just yet. She was referring to her legs, but his mind went elsewhere. The most they'd shared were a few kisses at the end of each date. In a way, Moira thought it was better this way. She had to be sure.

"Yes," Moira smiled dreamily, "a very nice weekend, indeed." It was an extended weekend, actually, as Baxter convinced her to call in sick before the week was out. As an afterthought, she added, "And you? Good weekend?"

"Yes," Jax answered, tucking the Irish Times Moira had left out for him under one arm. "As a matter of fact, I got married."

"Oh," Moira was surprised. "Well, congratulations, Mr. Liebling."

"Thanks," he unlocked his office door before gazing around the room. "No Mr. Baker?"

"Not yet," she sighed. In her head, all those 'rational' thoughts began flooding in. *If he can't even be bothered to run his own company, how can I trust that he'll be responsible in other areas of his life? Can I even count on him to be there for me if I need him to?* She flushed those thoughts from her mind. After all, it was just the beginning. Nothing said she had to commit to anything, just yet. Still, she was beginning to regret following his suggestion to call in sick Friday so that they could spend a little more time together. It was careless of her.

"Well, when he does, can you have him pull the quarterly sales numbers for me?" Jax brought her out of her thoughts.

"Of course...but, er, I can do that for you now, if you like?"

"You?" Frankly, Jax hadn't really thought of Moira as

anything more than a convenient pretty face. "Well, that would be fine...thank you." He closed the door of his office behind him.

Had Moira not have been clenching her teeth so forcefully, her jaw might have dropped. While it boggled the mind at who might want to marry Jax Liebling, she was most astounded that he asked how her weekend was and even said, 'thank you.' *Perhaps marriage agrees with him,* she thought.

She clicked on the keypad of the Apple Powerbook Baxter had purchased for her, amazed at how small and portable it was compared to the large and clunky desktop PC she was accustomed to. After entering her password, she navigated to the financial folders and printed out the reports she knew Jax would want to see, balance sheets, income statements, and the like. She retrieved them from the office printer, but before dropping them into a manilla folder to deliver to Jax, she snuck a peek at the numbers.

Aside from the fact that she felt Baxter's pay, which far exceeded her own, should be swapped for her salary, given that she was doing the work for the both of them, something else caught her eye...two 'something else-s' in fact. First, Jax Liebling appeared to take no salary at all. *How can that be?* Second, the company appeared to have taken a substantial hit this last quarter. She flipped through the pages of the profit and loss statement. From what she could tell, almost none of the Church of Infinite Love campuses bought any of their health bars in the last quarter. Most sales were to smaller grocery chains, herbal shops and organic food stores.

She heard a shuffling in Jax's office and quickly closed the folder, papers inside, just as he threw the door open. "Ah," she spun her wheelchair around, handing him the folder. "I was just about to bring this to you."

He took the folder from her. "You didn't happen to look through any of this, did you?" Jax eyed her suspiciously.

"No," Moira lied. "Of course not. I wouldn't know what I was reading even if I did...which I didn't, of course."

After a long pause, Jax nodded, mumbling under his breath as he turned his back on Moira, "Who's pulling the strings now, Jersey Girl?" He retreated back into his office and closed the door, just as Baxter finally arrived for work.

"Hello, gorgeous," Baxter stroked the side of Moira's hair and leaned in to kiss her on the cheek.

"Not here," she whispered back, gesturing her head toward Jax's office. "Let's keep it professional, shall we?"

"Right," Baxter agreed, sitting on the edge of her desk with one leg on the floor and the other dangling in midair. "Anything interesting happening today?"

Just then, Jax's door flew open. His face was hot with anger as he blew past Moira and Baxter without so much as a word. He was so livid, he went right for the stairwell instead of the elevator, using the descent to flush out some of his pent-up energy.

"What was that all about?" Baxter asked.

"He asked to see the quarterly reports," Moira answered.

"I take that to mean they weren't good?"

"No, they weren't," she confirmed. "But you didn't hear it from me. I'm just the secretary, got it?" She winked.

Baxter caught on and winked back. He wasn't worried. He certainly took little time to bother about the numbers, so he was grateful to have someone working for him who did.

Just then, there was a knock at the open door as an older woman wearing a gray uniform peered around the corner. It was the floor manager, Orla.

"Are ye feeling any bett-ah?" Orla asked.

"Am I—" Moira seemed confused until Baxter nudged her chair with his foot. "Oh, right," she smiled, remembering. "Yes, much better. Thank you for asking. Hope everything went okay while I was gone."

"Oh, fine," Orla answered. "I run a tight ship."

"Well, good," Moira seemed relieved.

"I've jest got a question about a box of bar wrappers we received," Orla crinkled her forehead, confused.

"What about them?" Moira asked.

"Well...here." She reached into her pocket and pulled out the pink wrapper cover and handed it to Moira.

Baxter peered over Moira's shoulder as they took a closer look. Instead of the standard Vandenberg Nutraceutical logo, it had been replaced with a cartoon-like image of Jax himself, the side of his face prominent like a Victorian cameo.

"Did you know anything about this?" Moira asked Baxter.

Baxter's eyes grew wide as he tilted his head as if to say, *not in front of the help*.

She fell silent.

"Well, of course I did!" Baxter stood, speaking with much more bravado than he felt. "A little rebranding we're doing."

"Oh," Orla nodded, uncertainly. "Will you be wantin' us to use these new ones from now on then?"

"Er," Baxter thought a moment, eyeing Moira for help.

"How many of the old wrappers do you have for the, er...*Love*, bar?"

"Not many," Orla laughed. "They are the first to sell out because everyone hopes the ingredients will help add spice to the bedroom, if you know what I mean." Orla blushed at Baxter.

"Not with that man's face on it, they won't," Moira mumbled under her breath.

Orla and Moira shared a chuckle while Baxter tried to find a way to bide some time.

"Hmm," Baxter thought a moment. "Why don't you use the old stock first, and I'll be sure to check in with our marketing team to see when the official rollout is."

"Yes, Mr. Baker," Orla blushed, feeling a little guilty about laughing at Moira's joke.

"Thank you, Orla," Baxter smiled, escorting Orla out of the office and closing the door behind her.

Turning to Moira, he asked, "Did you know anything about this?"

"No," Moira answered. "I'm as surprised as you are."

"There's something fishy going on here," Baxter said.

"Several somethings, if you ask me," Moira confessed.

"What do you mean?" Baxter was confused.

Moira reached into her desk and pulled out a second copy of the Irish Times. "Turn to page three," she instructed.

Baxter unfolded the newspaper and turned the pages. There was his picture, a closeup of him on a Vandenberg company yacht standing next to, none other than Erasmus Vandenberg, with the headline, 'Getting Away with Murder.' Baxter's face dropped. In it, an 'unnamed source' accused Baxter of being the real mastermind behind Erasmus Vandenberg's death, and how he'd planned all along to take over as their new CEO.

Baxter bunched up the paper, angrily, and tossed it on the floor.

"It's just tabloid gossip," Moira reasoned. "I wouldn't take it too seriously."

"No, the *Irish Mirror* is celebrity gossip, this is a legit newspaper," Baxter complained. "I think someone in my own family has been after my head since the skeletons in the Vandenberg closet have surfaced."

Moira treaded carefully. "Wanna talk about it?" she asked gently.

Baxter held her gaze for a moment, trying not to get distracted by the flecks of gold in her bright green eyes. *Well, if I can't trust Moira, who can I trust?*

Chapter 19
Fuming

Jax Liebling was quiet, calculated, and seemingly calm as a cucumber as he entered the old poorhouse in Belfast, the same one that Bernie Forger was repurposing into COIL's new Young Ambassador Academy. He'd had time to get ahold of his anger before it got away with him on his journey from Dublin.

Bernie was busy going through plans with one of the contractors hired to help renovate the thirty-five rooms on the premises, into dormitories with boys on one side and girls on the other. On each end, were sleeping quarters for several of the soon-to-be headmasters and lead instructors. At the center, were plans for a dining hall and main classrooms.

"Will you be wantin' a quote on the flooring and paint as well?" the contractor asked, making large squiggly marks on a legal-sized clipboard with notepad. He used the edge of the pen to slide under his hard hat and give the itchy side of his head a scratch.

"Not necessary," Bernie answered. "The students will take care of that."

The contractor appeared confused for a moment, but decided it was best not to ask.

It was then that Bernie noticed Jax Liebling standing there, fists balled. "Mr. Liebling," Bernie turned toward the smaller man in surprise, clearing his throat awkwardly. *Slithery fellow,* he thought to himself, *I didn't even hear him come in.* "I had no idea you had an interest in our school. What brings you to Belfast?"

"You know very well why I'm here," Jax's bottom lip quivered as he struggled to remain calm.

The contractor eyed the scene, uncomfortably. They had already been working late and certainly didn't want any more delays. "Eh, me men are going to knock off now, but will crack on again first thing in the mornin."

"Er, right," Bernie acknowledged as the contractor rounded up the few men still at work, even though it was past dinner time. "Appreciate the extra time!" he called after them.

To Jax, he said, "I'm afraid you've lost me." Bernie shrugged his shoulders.

"At least 39% of the revenue generated at Vandenberg Nutraceuticals...soon to be known as the Jax Corporation...came from the Church of Infinite Love."

"Is that so?" Bernie feigned ignorance. "I had no idea."

"You had every idea," Jax accused. "With church membership dwindling, I took a risk in buying you out, but I was promised my partnership with the church would continue, and even grow during the rebranding period."

"So, what's the problem?" Bernie asked. "We're still partners."

"Purchases from the church have come to a startling halt, even though we've been fully operational for several months now. Mind telling me why?"

"You'll have to speak to Mr. Lundy about that, I—"

"I'm asking you!" Jax sucked in a deep breath and forced himself to exhale slowly through his mouth. He regained his composure.

"Look," Bernie explained. "We have limited funding at the moment, and I've been putting everything into getting this school underway. Plus, I've always said the factory should be relocated somewhere out of the Westport family's turf." The corner of Bernie's lips turned up in a smirk. "On the plus side, you can't pay a tithe if there's no money, can you?"

"So what was your plan?" Jax demanded, ignoring the comment. "To put me out of business and then set up a new nutraceutical factory in Belfast? Or, just leave Baxter Baker and I hanging out to dry?"

Bernie paused dramatically, staring into space. *I wish Lundy were here,* he thought. *He's much better at these confrontations.*

"I assure you that I have no intention of harming Vandenberg...Er...Jax Corporation. It's just that the timing is off."

"But I'm investing everything—" Jax caught himself. "I am investing a very large sum of money in your school to support the church. Lundy just had me sign an agreement. Had I known you were going to stop promoting our products in favor of selling members books and school admission, I might have done things differently."

"Don't you understand?" Bernie questioned, solemnly. "The faith-healing business isn't what it used to be, and there's more money to be had in selling parents on prestigious, religious-based education. They'll drop a year's tuition and room and board if it means their son, *or daughter,* we allow girls in our school too, can climb the ranks to Ambassadors, Deacons and Deaconesses, Ministers and Elders of the church. And, what better way to recruit prospective members than by sending our young army out with meaningful pamphlets and pocket-books that explain our faith in simple terms?"

"Well, why not just print a few quotes from the Bible on the inside of our health bars? I would argue people would be more inclined to enjoy a tasty snack than to actually take the time and read," Jax argued.

"Not a bad idea," Bernie answered. "You should run with it."

"You and Lundy are screwing me over," Jax argued. "Keep it up and I may have to rethink my investments in your academy."

"Well, then you'd be making a huge mistake," Bernie replied. "Besides, you just said yourself, you've already signed the agreement." Bernie may have been arrogant and shortsighted, but brave he was not. He saw the color rise on Jax's face. Jax looked like a tea kettle ready to boil over. "Look," he tried again. "We all stand to get rich off this school...not that it's about the money, of course." His eyes shot upward toward heaven.

"How do you figure?" Jax eyed the walls of the old building, noting that the air felt clammy and damp. "This place could only hold a small number of students, at best."

"Well, that's the brilliant thing," Bernie's eyes lit up. "Walk with me, Jax. And, I'll show you around."

Against his better judgment, Jax fell into step beside Bernie who took two steps to Jax's one given their height disparity. Upon noticing that, Bernie walked faster. He seemed to be enjoying Jax's struggle to keep up.

"If we put in bunk beds and have the benches in the dining hall also serve as a study area, why, we can stuff about four students in each room." Bernie led the way down the corridor, stopping at one of the rooms in question. There was one tiny square window to the outside world. It had bars on it, but no window panes. A cold draft could be felt as it blew through the room. Jax shuddered a little. The room resembled an ancient prison cell, and he couldn't imagine four young kids fitting in there comfortably. He didn't particularly care, either way. It was just an observation.

Bernie led the way to a more spacious room, a good three times the one they were just in. This room already had a desk and chair, a modest bookshelf, and a very large window with a view overlooking the grounds. In the corner was a full-sized bed. This room even came equipped with a small fireplace.

"The headmaster's suite," Bernie explained. "I imagine I shall live here in the interim, until we can find a suitable replacement."

Given Jax's recent conversation with Lundy, he could easily see himself there. But that wasn't to be shared with Bernie...at least, not yet. Jax eyed a half-eaten muffin on a plate, and a soiled coffee cup beside it on the desk. If he didn't know better, he'd have guessed Bernie had already taken up residence.

"But there's more," Bernie added, "much more. This way, please."

Bernie led Jax down another very long and dark hallway that had a damp, musty aroma mixed with bleach. Jax choked a little on the repugnant mix of smells. The walls, he noticed, were stone whereas the front of the school was a mix of brick, wood and concrete.

Bernie read his mind. "You can see where we've already made some additions. And this building is at the forefront of fifty acres of property, seventy-five if we're able to buy out the modest widget factory next door." He motioned toward the wall as if pointing to the neighboring factory on the opposite end of the property line. "The poor ingrate has yet to figure out that wooden toys and plastic dollies are dying products that no one wants anymore. Lundy made him a nice offer...more than what anyone else would ever offer."

"With my money," Jax retorted. "So, your plan is expansion, then?" His eyes suddenly grew wide as they reached the end of the hall where an open-air window revealed a vast landscape that overlooked what appeared to be a very large concrete pit, at least the length of tennis court. On the horizon, a soft orange hue signified the setting sun. It would be dark soon. "What is that supposed to be?"

Bernie cleared his throat uncomfortably. "While we have every intention of building out more dormitories that will allow us to house more students and offer degree programs in sought-after topics other than religious studies, degrees like business administration, retail management, marketing and such, we have to first address the elephant in the room, so to speak.

"And what elephant would that be?" Jax asked.

Bernie clasped his hands behind his back in a professorial manner, shaking his head, solemnly.

"The reason the Church of Infinite Love came under so much scrutiny was not because of our healing practices or the ingredients in our food products," Bernie explained.

"It wasn't?" Jax played along, but not without a hint of sarcasm in his voice. "Then pray tell, what was it?"

"The problem was a few bad seeds ruining the church's otherwise stellar reputation," Bernie explained.

Jax's eyes lit up in recognition. "Oh, I see," he nodded, "you mean the incidents that hit the newsstands claiming the church was responsible for the death of several young women."

"Wretched girls, if you ask me." Bernie pursed his lips as if he just tasted something sour.

"I suppose it didn't help that one of your Ambassadors saw fit to take out Erasmus Vandenberg and anyone else who stood in the church's way?" Jax reminded Bernie. "Isn't that what really blew the lid on everything, causing you to have to rebrand in the first place?"

Bernie was stuck on a thought that he couldn't seem to let go of. Instead, he answered, "If the children were taught to behave properly from the get go, none of this would have happened."

Jax found Bernie's blinders to the truth somewhat fascinating. "But then, dear old Erasmus would still be alive and you wouldn't be in charge, now would you?"

A hint of a smile crossed Bernie's lips as he glanced in Jax's direction. He could tell that Jax was beginning to understand his perspective…finally. The smaller man's face had returned to a normal shade and he appeared decidedly less aggravated.

"True," Bernie answered. "But I attribute that to God stepping in and showing everyone who's boss."

"Do you really believe that God would kill a man to continue the church's work? Why not just use his powers to change people's minds?"

"God gave us free will, so he neither killed Erasmus nor did he prevent him from being killed. Rather, through his teachings, I was led to recognize that he was calling me to take my divine place as the leader of this flock."

The shear narcissism, Jax thought, vehemently. *Where does this idiot get off thinking himself the likes of Jesus, the Pope, Gandhi, or even…me, for example.* Jax may not have been religious, but he definitely saw himself as vastly smarter, more accomplished and more worthy than Bernie, and yet God hadn't bothered to reach out to *him*. This reaffirmed Jax's belief that there was no God, and if there ever *had* been a God, he was now dead.

"So, about the pit?" Jax reminded him.

"We're establishing a building here where the more troublesome students will reside. These will be the ones sent here not just for religious education, but for behavioral reform."

"I see," Jax nodded. "But what's the purpose of such a large concave hole? The base of it looks like solid concrete." His face twitched a little, gleefully almost.

"There will be a basement with several secluded rooms

where the unrepentant can be left alone to pray and learn the error of their ways."

"Solitary confinement?" Jax was aghast. "Prison cells?" It's not that Jax cared one way or another, he was just surprised that a 'man of God' would go to such extreme measures.

"We like to think of them as private prayer rooms," Bernie answered simply. After a long pause, he turned to Jax. "Well, it's getting dark. I suppose we should be locking up for the evening. But I hope I've eased your mind about a few things. I know things with the factory are a bit tricky right now, but once the school gets up and running, we'll be expanding our programs, and...I almost forgot," Bernie's eyes lit up, "as I mentioned, we want to procure the property next door. Instead of outsourcing for our printed materials, we can do them all in house and have the students run it...sort of like a work-study program."

Even Jax had to admit this was a pretty good idea. As Bernie motioned for Jax to follow him back through the hallway to the main entrance, Jax felt something growing in the center of his chest. It gnawed at his insides like an angry scavenger bird eating its prey. *What was this feeling?* he asked himself. Then he realized it...*envy, disgust, and anger.*

Jax took a deep breath and commented pleasantly, "I see where you and Mr. Lundy are going with this, but I will have a talk with him about the financial aspects, to see what else we might do to keep the factory afloat in the meantime."

"That's the spirit!" Bernie encouraged. "And who knows? After we've filled these halls with lots of hungry students, maybe your snack bars will be part of the dining program here."

Jax nodded, thoughtfully, before asking, "But do me a favor, would you?"

"What's that?" Bernie hesitated.

"Before it gets much darker, could we walk a bit of the grounds, just so I can see more of your...vision?"

Bernie tugged at the collar of his shirt, uncomfortably. "Perhaps the morning would be better—"

"I'm busy in the morning," Jax interrupted. "It's the start of a long week at Jax Corporation. Just another ten minutes or so." He felt Bernie's reluctance. "That way, I can feel more confident in our joint venture and speak more competently with Lundy. If I had been a smarter man, I would have asked to see the grounds before signing anything. But, I realize I can be a little...impulsive." Jax smiled, eyes boring into Bernie as if willing the taller man to change his mind.

It worked.

"I suppose a few extra minutes won't hurt. I'll just grab a flashlight from the headmaster's room, just in case." Bernie paused to snatch a small light and hung its chord around his wrist. He also pulled out the desk drawer and retrieved a set of keys. Jax noted that Bernie seemed to know where all the supplies were in a place that he supposedly had yet to occupy.

Finally, they had reached the main hall. As they stepped out into the night air, a cold chill passed through them. The temperature had dropped considerably since Jax's arrival a short while earlier. The contractors were gone and save for the sound of an owl in the distance, it was silent.

"Are we the only ones here?" Jax asked, surprised.

"For now," Bernie answered, leading the way down a dirt path that passed the pit that would become the 'private prayer rooms.' "The workers should be back at first light though, but until school is in session, nights are like a graveyard around here." Bernie circled around the pit. "Watch your step," he warned Jax. "The edges are unstable and the ground can give way. Wouldn't want either of us to fall in," he laughed nervously. "Once we pass that circle of trees up ahead, you'll see where we've cleared some of the wooded area to create space for additional dormitories and classrooms. It's—"

Bernie felt something on the back of his heel, as if his shoe got caught and started to slip off, causing him to feel unsteady. His eyes grew wide as he lifted his arms out to the side to regain balance. Bernie's jerky movements caused him to drop the keys into the pit. As they tumbled in the dirt, rolling toward the concrete block at the bottom, Bernie reached out in vain to attempt to grab them, leaning his body forward, bending his knees slightly to remain upright. Just then, Bernie felt a swift thrust as Jax's boot connected with Bernie's bottom, sending him topping head-first into the pit. The drop was at least two stories.

Bernie screamed, not entirely certain what bumped him and caused his fall. And yet, the man had just enough of his wits about him to spin his body mid-air in an attempt to land on his feet, bending at the knees. When his body impacted the concrete, he let out a yell in agony. For a moment, it was silent save for the wind in the trees. The bottom of the pit was dark, Bernie's body barely visible in the shadows. Eventually, the sound of heavy breathing could be heard from the floor of the pit, followed by a mild whimpering.

In the commotion, Bernie also managed to drop the flashlight, now lying in the dirt at Jax's feet. Jax picked it up and shined it into Bernie's eyes. Bernie's leg was contorted to one side and there was a large red blood splatter around his head.

"My leg is broken!" Bernie whined as the reality of what caused his fall finally sank in. "And, you nearly killed me!"

"Oh, don't be so melodramatic," Jax answered. "As you said, the crew will be here in the morning and can fish you out."

"The morning?!" Bernie's eyes grew wide. "You're nuts! It's freezing out and my head is bleeding. I could die out here if left alone! Call for help!"

"I think a little time in the private prayer pit will do you a world of good, don't you? Here," Jax rolled a bottle of water down the side of the hill that eventually landed at Bernie's broken leg.

He followed it with a wrapped snack. "Have some water and a Jax Corporation nutrition bar. That ought to keep you until morning."

Jax turned to walk away.

"You can't leave me here!" Bernie screamed. "Jax! Come back here! You and Lundy can't run this place without me! If I die, it's all over!"

Jax grinned to himself. *What a self-absorbed prick,* he thought. At that moment, he had no idea whether or not Bernie could survive the night or not. He probably could, he reasoned. Might even be able to climb out, even with a broken leg. *Oh well,* he thought to himself. *Guess we'll find out come morning.*

"The Peelers are here, boss." A young contractor tapped on the superintendent's shoulder at the site where Bernie had taken his fall. Now a shade of blue, the body still lay untouched at the bottom of the prayer pit. Even from a great height, a decent pair of binoculars could tell you that the leader of the Church of Infinite Love was dead.

The superintendent nodded as members of the Royal Ulster Constabulary arrived on the scene. One of the officers twitched nervously. "What have we got here?" he asked. It was too soon after the Troubles and any suspected foul play was met with tension.

"That down there is Bernie Forger," the superintendent explained. "He's the one who hired us fer work on the property. He was plenty alive when we last saw him yesterday. But today he's...well, see fer yerself."

"Can your men help us safely get down there?" the officer asked.

"Uh, yeah, sure," the superintendent looked around. "Bobby,

get the men to bring round the aerial ladder and harnesses, would ya?" The contractor nodded and ran off. In a matter of minutes, the ladder was stationed near the pit which in the light of day, looked more like a giant sinkhole.

It took little time for the RUCs to make their assessment to the chief constable. Bernie Forger could have died from head and internal injuries as a result of his fall, hypothermia, or at the notice of one of Vandenberg's half-eaten old nutraceutical bars near Bernie's corpse, poison or allergies. There were a few odd boot and shoe prints on the grounds, but they could have belonged to any of the contractors traipsing through there. Bernie's own shoes had slipped off in the fall, and while they could determine the location where he fell by the displaced soil and grass, it was unclear whether he jumped, was pushed or slipped due to dislodged soil. Since he obviously had a bit of the munchies, it was assumed that he likely fell, and given his physical state, was unable to climb out. By the time the contractors discovered his body the next morning, he'd been dead for about seven hours. One contractor noted seeing a man arrive at the academy just as they were leaving late the evening prior, but couldn't be sure they'd recognize him if they saw him again.

"Found this too," an officer handed a bagged item to the constable.

"What's this?" he asked.

"It's a cufflink, sir," the officer answered. "Gold plated with a Waterford crystal piece in the center. Me missus got me the same kind for Christmas last year from Westport Jewelers."

"You mean the same Westports suspected of small to medium-sized grifts in County Dublin?"

"The same, sir."

"Christ," the Chief Constable stood over the body, befuddled. "It could take weeks for a full autopsy report to figure out if it was foul play, and if it was, who the suspects are...the West-ports...the Vandenbergs...someone else?"

"Poor fella," one of the officers commented, sympathetically. "If he had time to eat a bite, it meant that he couldn't have died on impact. Musta been rough at the end."

"Yeah, well at least his troubles are over," the constable answered, brashly. "Ours are just beginning."

Chapter 20
Affairs of the Heartless

"How are you holding up, Edwina?" Lundy asked, sympathetically, over the crackle of the static from a long-distance call over an outdated landline.

"As well as you might expect from a woman whose father left his family in ruins after sinking his own corporate battleship and leaving his money to harlots with no breeding," Edwina spat, bitterly.

"Not well, it sounds," Lundy answered quietly. "Well, perhaps I can cheer you up?"

"Really?" Edwina sat up. "Tell me you have good news."

"I have *potentially* good news," he replied. "I convinced Jax Liebling to invest in the academy."

"After everything he's already spent on the factories?" Edwina as surprised. "Where did he get the money? The Vandenberg family has been well connected to the who's who in the industry for nearly a century...the Rockefellers, Carnegies, you name it. But I've never heard of him."

"I couldn't say, exactly," Lundy answered. "However, I don't care where his money comes from as long as it gets us where we want to go."

"And so, he's investing. What good does this do me, exactly?" Edwina was not about to mince words.

"It will do you plenty good when you become the headmistress of the academy."

"You can't be serious!" Edwina answered.

"What?" Lundy questioned. "Are you opposed to acting as headmistress to a school in Ireland purpose-built to forward the work of the Church of Infinite Love?"

"Not at all," Edwina answered. "I would relish it, but according to church law, I'm as high in the ranks as a woman is allowed."

"But the man who made the rules is dead," Lundy answered, curtly. Erasmus Vandenberg, Edwina Vandenberg's late father, had lots of rules around the 'dos and don'ts' of the sexes. Most times, the 'dos' applied to the men and the 'don'ts' to the women.

"Bernie will never agree to that," Edwina clucked.

"Why don't you let me worry about Bernie."

"Well, what am I supposed to do in the meantime?"

"Be patient, my love," Lundy answered, affectionately. "I told you before, I'm playing the long game."

"Is it the long game that resulted in me getting cut out of my father's will?" Edwina sulked.

"Now, pet," Lundy replied, sympathetically, "you know I did my best to talk Erasmus out of that, but if I pushed too hard, he'd would have been on to us. And I might have lost my job. Then where would we be today?"

"Hmm," Edwina remained unconvinced. "Not sure I like where *we* ended up."

"Give me some time, Edwina," Lundy pleaded in a show of emotion that was uncharacteristic of him. "Once Vandenberg

Nutraceuticals goes under with Jax and Baxter at the helm, we can swoop in and buy it back for a song."

"If he's as rich as you say, why on Earth do you think it might go under?" Edwina asked, reasonably. "Seems good with money."

"Perhaps so," Lundy agreed. "But I appealed to his ego, of which he has in plenty. If he's tying up resources in the academy and future publishing house, what recourse will he have once he realizes the church has stopped buying products from him?"

"What?" Edwina was surprised. "Stop buying? When did this happen? Why did the church stop purchasing from Vandenberg Nutraceuticals?"

"The new branding of the church," Lundy reminded her. "No more faith healing for a while. It draws too much attention. The money is now in education."

"So, without the church's partnership, he'll suffer?" Edwina asked. She had a little twinge in her heart, the last remnant of a conscience. She sucked in a deep breath and brushed the feeling aside.

"Yes, and Bernie will get the...err...credit."

"He'll murder him," Edwina was convinced. "Liebling has a questionable past. If Bernie takes the fall for screwing him over, I pity what Jax will do to him."

"But with Bernie out of the way, guess who gets to be the new head mistress...and head of the church?" Lundy dangled that carrot, confidence seeping into his voice.

"And what makes you think the church will allow it, given that I am a mere woman?" Edwina's voice dripped of disdain.

"Ah," Lundy replied, "what if the Church of Infinite Love finally stepped into the 20th century? We can make that happen, you and I."

"You and I?" Edwina gave it some thought. She knew Lundy cared for her, as much as any lawyer could care for anybody, but she never thought of him as a potential life partner, let alone a life partner *and* a business partner."

"Yes," Lundy affirmed. "What do you think?"

"I think my father must be turning in his grave." she answered, curtly.

"Probably," Lundy agreed. "He only liked me slightly better than you, and probably only because I protected his money." There was an agonizingly long pause across the phone line. "Edwina," he coaxed, "you still haven't answered my question."

"I think you're a crazy bastard," Edwina laughed. "But you're my kind of crazy."

"I'll take that as a 'yes,'" Lundy smiled. Not much brought Lundy joy, but somehow, the thought of running an empire with he and Edwina reigning supreme was enough to send a pleasant chill up his spine. He hung up the phone moments later, whistling to himself as he sorted the last of the contracts he'd drafted for Jax Liebling...the most important of which was the one where Jax confirmed that should anything happen to him, everything he'd invested in the Church became theirs to use the money as they see fit because Jax agreed to escheat his accounts. Lundy clicked his briefcase, closed and snapped the small desk lamp that hovered over the tiny table in his hotel room, and the room went dark.

The next evening Lundy's room phone rang just as he was stepping out of the shower, a good hour before Edwina usually rang him up.

"Miss me already?" he asked Edwina, sweetly. It sounded strange coming from Lundy.

"Looks like I was right," Edwina barked. "Turn on the news."

"What happened?" Lundy snapped on the small television in

his room and twisted the squeaky knob until it tuned into the Raidió Teilifís Éireann nightly news. "What am I looking for?"

He didn't have long to wait. The news ticker at the bottom of the telly read, "Leader of the Church of Infinite Love found dead in Belfast." In the scene, the area behind the academy where the prayer pit was located, was blocked off with yellow tape and a swarm of RUCS were on scene.

"Bernie's dead," Edwina answered sourly. "I told you Jax was a loose cannon, didn't I?"

"Relax, my love," Lundy reassured her. "We don't know that. And, even if he did it, as I told you last night, we move on without him."

"I don't feel good about this, Lundy."

Lundy could feel her sour expression across the phone line. "Don't tell me you're suddenly developing a conscience, my love," he answered, playfully.

"I'm not sure how to take that, Lunds."

Lundy raised an eyebrow. Edwina always resorted to calling him 'Lunds' as a pet name when she was about to do something manipulative. "I just mean that we can't take responsibility for what one man chooses to do to another, can we? Might as well make the best of it," Lundy reminded her.

Just then, there was a loud banging at the door. "Hang on, pet." Lundy put the phone down and eyed the keyhole at the front door...Jax. Lundy left the chain on the door as he opened it just slightly, peering an eye out. Jax stood there, beside himself.

"How did you get up here?" Lundy demanded. "No one but guests are permitted past the lobby. And you, most certainly, are not a guest."

"Never mind that," Jax whispered. "We've got more important things to discuss. I know you murdered Bernie!"

"Me?" Lundy was confused. "I did nothing of the sort."

"Have you seen the news?" Jax tried again.

"Just now," Lundy answered. "Give me ten minutes and I'll meet you in the lobby downstairs. We'll find an empty conference room or someplace quiet to chat."

Jax ran a hand through his hair and nodded, anxiously. "Good plan. I don't much care to be alone with a killer," he whispered. "It's best to be in a more public space."

Lundy closed the door and picked up the receiver. "That was Jax, coming here to accuse me of killing Bernie."

"He's accusing you?!" Edwina was flabbergasted. "But that's preposterous!"

"I know, but I'm meeting him downstairs. I've got to know what he's up to."

"Be careful, Lunds," Edwina pouted. "I couldn't bear it if anything happened to you."

"I will, my darling. I promise to phone you as soon as I'm back upstairs."

Lundy hung up the phone, and within minutes, found Jax in the hotel bar gulping down a scotch.

"I told them to charge it to your room," Jax told Lundy when he arrived.

"That's fine," Lundy sucked in a breath. He considered himself a patient man, but he was beginning to unravel the longer he had to deal with Jax Liebling. "But what's all this about..." he paused to make sure no one else was in earshot, "well, you know."

"I know it was you who took out Bernie," Jax leaned in and whispered.

"What are you talking about?" Lundy whispered back. "I only just heard the news moments before you arrived. And from the looks of it, it was an accident...no foul play."

"Right, well, between the church's lack of support for the factory and this, I'm afraid I'm rethinking my business investments. I've changed my mind about the school."

Lundy coughed. "You're upset, I can see that. Why don't you

have another scotch and let me put this whole thing to rest, alright?"

Jax nodded and motioned the bartender for a refill. While his voice was shaky, Lundy couldn't help but notice that his hands were steady...odd.

After Jax's fresh drink arrived, Lundy continued, "I'm just as shocked to learn about Bernie's death as you, and what's this you say about a 'lack of support for the factory?'"

"Sales are down 39% since the church stopped buying product from us, something of which I have only just learned, by the way. Between that and the bad press, I'm barely getting by as it is."

"Well now, I didn't know that, else I would have had a talk with Bernie." Lundy feigned a look of pain, touching his fist to his lips in a moment of grief. He recovered in the blink of an eye.

"You're his lawyer and closely associated with his accountants," Jax spat. "How could you not know?"

"Look, Jax, I promise I'll talk to my associate, Mr. Adani. I'm sure there's been a misunderstanding."

Jax said nothing, his lip twitching as he stared blankly at the bar.

"But since Bernie isn't here anymore," Lundy offered, "perhaps you might consider taking his place?"

"Of the church, you mean?" Jax's eyes widened, turning his head to face the lawyer.

"Well, yes," Lundy answered. "We already talked about your role at the school. And if you assume a leadership role, then you and I can figure out the budget, together. How does that sound?"

Jax stared at Lundy for several seconds as if at the end of a tight chess match. Finally, he answered, "The investigation into Bernie's death might shut down construction of the academy for months. So for now, why don't we focus on Jax Corporation and how to make it work for us?"

Lundy was beginning to put the pieces together, though he didn't like to think he might be outmatched by this irritating little man with a very large ego. "It's been a long day for the both of us, and I'm still torn up over Bernie's death," Lundy lied. He wasn't the slightest bit concerned, but he put on a good front. "Why don't we chat in the next day or two and see what we can come up with?"

Jax slid off the stool and grabbed the jacket he had strewn on the pub chair beside him. "Certainly," he turned to leave before remembering, "oh, and about that clause we spoke about in the event anything happened to me?"

"Yes," Lundy answered, biting the inside of his lip, nervously. "What about it?"

"Turns out, I just got married the other day. There's a new beneficiary to my money. So, don't think about murdering me, as well, as it will hurt your cause, not help it."

Jax bounded out of the lobby as if late to catch a train, leaving Lundy speechless and with yet another expensive bar tab.

When he phoned Edwina back later that evening, he said, "Jax Liebling is turning out to be a bigger problem than I thought."

Chapter 21
Phone Call

Against his better judgment, Ortega followed Midge's orders and reported Rue missing the morning after their call. The Guard asked uncomfortable questions that Ortega did his best to answer. *What was your relationship to Rue Brennan? What was she wearing when you saw her last? Do you have a recent photo of her? When and where did you see her last?*

He couldn't let on that they were here on an investigation that he really had no business investigating, with a woman he once suspected of murder. He had no photos of Rue, and the last time he saw her was before he, Shep and Penelope left for the factory, leaving Rue with grocery duty. He thought he was protecting her by having her stay behind. In hindsight, perhaps the only reason she agreed to it was because she already had plans to meet up with Midge. Or maybe Midge kidnapped her? He really couldn't be certain.

The only thing he had going for him at this moment was his

keen observation skills. "She is about five-foot-three or four with brown hair and hazel eyes, thin and generally travels with a small denim backpack instead of a purse. The last time I saw her, she wore a red hoodie sweatshirt with blue jeans and black sneakers."

"Any distinguishing features?" an officer asked. The name tag on his uniform read, 'Doherty.'

"Other than a few freckles on her nose and a round face with chubby cheeks, not much."

"You seem to remember quite a bit about her, Mr. Ortega. How did you say you know her, again?" Doherty asked, suspiciously.

"I'm a retired detective," Ortega explained, tiredly. "She and her boyfriend run their own private investigation company. We crossed paths at work."

"Hmmm." Doherty asked, "And how is it that you 'crossed paths' again in County Dublin?" He rested his arms on his desk, one on top of the other, and leaned in with interest.

"It was a social trip," Ortega lied. "Me and my fiancé...Penelope...were planning a destination wedding. The girls are friends, you see."

"I see," the officer nodded. "And why isn't Penelope here with you as well?"

"Because she's busy picking up our other friend from the hospital...burst appendix."

"And if we contact the hospital, they can confirm this?" Doherty squinted his eyes at Ortega.

"Of course—" Ortega began before catching himself. "I'm sorry, but is there any reason why you are acting as if I'm a suspect in the missing person I'm reporting?"

"Just doing my job," Doherty explained. "I'll see what I can find out. Just leave your contact info with the desk clerk on your way out." Doherty reached into his desk and pulled out a carbon copy form with two duplicate yellow and pink layers under the white top sheet. He then popped the cap off a stick pen and pressed hard into the form, lowering his head in a way that suggested to Ortega that the conversation was over.

Ortega was about to offer some passive-aggressive quip, but then thought better of it. After all, that was in no way going to help Rue's case. And second, as he peered at Doherty hunched over his desk with burnt out aggression, he saw something...himself.

"Oh, and just one more thing," Doherty remembered, looking up. "Don't even think about investigating this yourself, detective...enjoy your retirement."

Outside the Garda's offices, Ortega reached into his pocket to phone Penelope with an update, and to see how she was getting on with Shep who was just released from the hospital.

Nothing.

He rifled through his pockets, then looked around him in vain, as if he'd dropped it. No...in his frazzled state, he'd left his cell phone behind.

Back at their rental, Shep lumbered slowly through the front door with Penelope standing guard, just in case he toppled.

"I'm okay," he reassured her, wincing a little as he walked. "Just gonna rest in this chair for a minute." He settled into a small kitchen chair that creaked beneath his weight.

"Can I get you anything?" Penelope offered. "Something to eat, perhaps?"

"You know what?" Shep eyed her with amusement.

"What?" she asked, concerned.

"I'm not hungry!" he bellowed and then winced again, grabbing his side. Shep did his best to stifle a laugh as a few tears formed in his eyes. Finally, he said, "Maybe I should lie down for a bit."

Penelope rushed to his side, putting his arm around her shoulders and bending her knees to help him stand. He did his best not to put too much pressure on her, while she remembered to exhale on the lift like she was lifting weights at the gym. Still, he was a bit heavy for her slight frame.

The two staggered to the bedroom he and Ortega shared. "Tell Ortega I'm sorry, but I'm gonna have to take the bottom bunk tonight."

Penelope bit her lip. She wasn't sure Jose was going to be in that room at all, but they'd figure that out this evening.

After depositing a recovering Shep to his room, Penelope closed the door.

Just then, a cell phone rang...Ortega's cell phone. She hadn't even realized it was sitting on a side table by the front door. It seemed to get even more insistent with each ring. She glanced down at the number...Darwin.

Her heart sank. Maybe Ortega could ignore his calls, but she couldn't.

"Hello, Mr. Fennec," Penelope answered quietly. A frantic Darwin rambled incessantly, asking where Rue was, but not waiting for the answer. He went in circles ranting about how Ortega hadn't called him back. What was happening over there? Was everyone okay? Finally, he ran out of steam. After a moment of silence, Penelope replied. "For Rue's safety, we were told not to ask any questions and not to look for her."

"What?!" Darwin could be heard yelling into the phone above the sound of airplanes taking off and descending, followed by loud announcements over an intercom with the bustle of hundreds of people chattering in the distance. "What do you mean, you—"

"Mr. Fennec? Are you at the airport?" Penelope demanded. He ignored her, cycling back to his combination of ranting while demanding information. Penelope couldn't stay on the line. She knew it wasn't safe...not for Rue and not for them. "Goodbye, Darwin. Please be careful." She hung up the phone and broke into a sob. She could feel Darwin's desperation. She knew it all too well in her own life, but there was nothing she could do for him, save for her failed attempt to at least let him know that Rue was alright...probably.

The call came in from Officer Doherty not twenty-four hours later. He got a lead from the County Londonderry police after a pub owner called in a couple of suspicious women who climbed into one woman's dark hatchback while leaving the other's rental behind. The rental car was in Rue Brennan's name, and they were calling to have it brought in for evidence. Not far from the scene, another report came in of a body discovered by a bicyclist the next morning during one of his early-morning rides. The body was thought to be that of a woman.

"The corpse had been charred so badly that it could take weeks to make a positive identification," Doherty explained to Ortega over the phone. "There were a few traces of blood at the scene. We're having it analyzed now."

Ortega coughed, fighting off the queasiness in his stomach. His face went pale, and the room began to swirl.

"Did you hear what I said, Mr. Ortega?" Doherty spoke a little louder into the phone.

"I did," Ortega sucked in a deep breath. "Just...processing."

After a long pause, Doherty continued, "Consider this a courtesy call...I looked you up, detective. Seems you had an excellent reputation while you were on the beat...even solved a number of high-profile cases that were deemed unsolvable."

If ever a time when Ortega found enlightenment, this would have been the equivalent of Newton's apple landing on his head, or what some spiritualists would call an 'awakening.' He'd spent his life solving the unsolvable cases, but where did it get him? He neglected his friends, his family, his health, and his sanity, and for what? The pursuit of social justice? No, he decided. It was all ego. What began as a noble effort in making the world a safer place spiraled into an obsession. But no matter how many of the bad guys he put away, a fresh breed always seemed to crop up. Even worse were the rich crime families like the Vandenbergs and the Westports, the cults like the Church of Infinite Love, and the oligarchs who didn't care who they murdered if someone got in the way of their best interests.

"You still there?" Doherty finally asked.

"Yes, sorry." Ortega rubbed his forehead. "What can I do to help?"

"Nothing!" Doherty snapped into the phone, before catching himself. "Under normal circumstances, I'd be bringing you and your lady friend in for questioning...I still might have to. But given your reputation, I'll just ask politely that you don't leave the country any time soon. You get me?"

Ortega smirked and shook his head. *He sounds just like I did two decades ago, the poor sap.* "Don't worry," he reassured him, "I have no intention of going anywhere. Not until I find out what happened to Ms. Brennan. Thank you, officer."

"Was that about Rue?" Penelope asked, concerned, once he'd ended the call. Then she saw the look on Ortega's face. "What happened?" her voice trembled.

Ortega gently took Penelope's arm. "I think you had better sit down."

Chapter 22
Rescue

Baxter arrived at the factory at his usual time...a good hour and fifteen minutes past the time he promised to be there. He could hear a loud beeping from the parking lot, and as he neared the entrance, he saw it.

There, along the side of the building a large yellow crane was hoisting what appeared to be a golden-lettered sign and aligning it against the building. On the ground, were pieces of the company's old sign as if it had been ripped down like old wallpaper. Baxter could make out a "V", an "EN", and a "TI." That was what was left of the Vandenberg Nutraceuticals signage. As he watched with mounting anger, the new name became clear...JAX.

Baxter spotted Jax near one of the crew members installing the sign, wearing a hardhat, his arms crossed like some sort of a god. Jax nodded with approval.

"What the hell is this?" Baxter demanded.

"This," Jax answered simply, "is the dawn of a new day."

"You're one crazy fella. You know that? Completely—"

Baxter's rant was cut short suddenly, as a potato sack was slung over his head, plunging him into darkness and making it difficult to breathe. Someone bound his arms while another grabbed his feet. He could hear the sound of heavy boots on the ground and the squeal of tires screeching to a halt. A heavy door slid open, and the next thing that Baxter knew, he was being thrown onto a hard metal floor, his head banging against the edge of what he assumed was the opposite wall of a van. He heard muffled sounds outside, followed by a "let's go!"

The van slammed shut with Baxter and his assailants inside.

Jax smiled, approvingly, and returned to witness his new name being plastered on the side of the factory wall. Somehow, the contractors missed the kidnapping. Or, it's possible that they simply didn't care.

Inside the van, several men could be heard congratulating one another on a job well done. One of the men leaned over and shouted in Baxter's ear, "How do you feel about swimming with the fishes in the Irish Sea, my boy?!"

He jolted at the noise erupting in his ear. Then, something occurred to Baxter. The man spoke with an American accent, a Northern one.

"That'll teach him to bring the Devil into a house of God," another chimed in. Baxter couldn't be sure, but from the shuffling, he suspecting there were at least three men in the van with him, maybe more.

They traveled across bumpy roads for what seemed like an eternity, some loud with heavy traffic, and others with jagged hills and twists and turns that sent Baxter sliding uncomfortably across the floor. At one point, the van jolted so hard he was certain that his head was going to smash into the side again, but at the last minute, something intervened...a hand.

"Still alive in there?" a lilting voice asked.

"Moira?" Baxter muffled.

"Shhh," Moira whispered, smiling devilishly at the three men in the van with her. Unlike the others who sat on bench seats, Moira had a fixed place in her wheelchair, clumsily strapped in with a large belt that ran shoulder to hip. Across her lap was a wool blanket. It was fairly warm that day, but she complained about always feeling a bit cold. She blamed it on mild anemia.

The three men laughed, two had large builds and bellies that suggested a fixed diet of beer and lots of all-you-can-eat dinners. The other, by contrast, was a bit taller and leaner, but lacked any muscle definition. His shirt had 'Leo' embroidered on it, a clear indication that he had no idea how a secret kidnapping was supposed to work. And yet, all three acted as though they were part of some covert military operation.

The van made one final drive down a steep incline before stopping abruptly on a flat section of asphalt. The largest of the men stepped over Baxter's feet and slid the side door open until it clunked into place. "Out with ya!" He grabbed Baxter's legs and began sliding him out of the van, his head and shoulders about to smack the ground when Moira intervened.

"Hang on, boys," she said. "Do the lass a favor and get me out into the fresh sea air so I can have a chin wag with him first, yeah?"

The man stopped and smiled, elbowing his other large friend in the ribs. He blushed slightly.

"Anything for you, sweetheart," he agreed. "Milton, go help the lovely lady out."

"Thank you, Tom," she winked at him. "Just sit the heathen upright so I can look him in the eyes."

Tom relented, grabbing Baxter by his arms and hoisting him to a standing position just long enough for the men to lower the wheelchair lift and help Moira out.

"Thank you, gentlemen." She positioned her chair several

feet from Baxter. "Now, if you don't mind, sit him up and pull that sack off his head."

"You sure that's a good idea? I mean, our orders were to—" the thinner man intervened.

"Feed him to the fishes, I know, Leo," Moira nodded. "But I'll have you know this bastard put the moves on me. Me, a lame woman. Let me at least say my peace, won't you, loves?"

"Alright, Moira. I suppose that would be okay."

"What's all the racket back there?" the driver called from the front seat. Until now, nobody had given any thought to him.

"Give us a minute," the large man called.

The driver merely tapped his fingers on the side of the open window, impatiently, but said no more. He took a moment to adjust his rearview mirror to see what was happening behind him.

The man tugged the sack off of Baxter's head, purposefully grabbing a tuft of hair along the way.

"Ow!" Baxter yelled. A small patch of blood could be seen on the side of his head where it had made contact with the van wall. Baxter sucked in the sea air, finally able to breathe fully. His eyes darted around his location. Behind him was a small, deserted stretch of beach with the cliffs surrounding them on both sides. He could only catch a glimpse of the water from his periphery view. In front of him, a steep paved access road led to the spot where they currently sat. While not a public spot, it wasn't likely for any strangers to stumble upon them anytime soon, but he hoped for the best, nonetheless.

"Can someone please explain what this is all about?" Baxter caught how frantic his high-pitched voice sounded and took in another breath to calm his nerves. He returned with a different voice, a soft-spoken, charming one. "Gentlemen," he began, "there must be some misunderstanding."

"Oh, there's no misunderstanding, son," the man spat, leaning his face just a few inches from Baxter's nose. "We know who's responsible for the death of all those innocent girls, not to mention some of our church leadership. It was you and your Satanic ways all along!"

"Satanic—" Baxter was confused. It took a moment, but suddenly all the links came together. They were blaming him for every death related to the Church of Infinite Love and Vandenberg Nutraceuticals, no matter how unlikely. Up until now, he thought his own family was responsible for this. Suddenly, it became clear...he was the scapegoat, and Jax had set him up. He looked at Moira, betrayed. "But you?" His heart sank.

Moira paused long enough to survey the scene, as if making calculations. Satisfied, she grinned mischievously, and then in one swift moment she yanked the blanket from her legs, revealing a sawed-off shotgun. She cocked it and took aim at the large man. "Back away from the van," she commanded.

"What?" The man was confused. Then he smiled down at her, taking a step toward her chair. "Listen, little lady. I know you probably got what they call...Stockholm...whatever. But you're safe now from this bastard's advances."

Moira took a warning shot at his feet. He squealed and shifted back and forth, lifting his feet as if standing on hot coals.

"Over by your friend," she pointed the barrel at him, motioning toward the other large man, who was now hiding around the back of the van. "But come out so I can see you both. Hands up and behind your heads!"

In a show of braveness, the thinner man charged her from the side, lunging for Moira's shotgun.

"Not so fast," the young driver appeared in a flash, grabbing the back of Leo's shirt, pulling him backward and holding a small knife to his neck. Leo winced, making a feeble attempt to grab the driver's arm, but the driver was quick, shoving him forward.

Moira stuck out a leg and tripped him. He fell, face first onto the asphalt, managing to break his fall with his hands. "Ow," he wailed. "My wrist!" He rolled on the ground nursing his wrist, his one foot still hooked to the footrest on the wheelchair. Moira kicked his foot out of her way, taking a moment to lean over and lift the footrest up so her legs were clear. With shotgun still in one arm, she stood, tossing her blanket on the chair behind her.

"Over by the other two," she commanded. To the driver, she said, "Thanks, Scratch."

Scratch merely nodded, standing dutifully beside her.

Leo clambered to his feet and stood by Tom and Milton, all with hands behind their heads.

"My arms are getting tired," Milton complained to Tom.

"Shut it!" Moira threatened, taking a moment to shake out each leg from the long journey she spent sitting. After shifting from side to side, she finally settled with both feet firmly planted on the ground.

"What in the hell is going on, Moira?" Tom demanded. "I thought you were on our side?"

She glanced at a stunned Baxter who merely whispered, "You can walk?"

"Course I can, Sweet Face," she laughed. "And dance and hike the Cliffs of Moher."

"Scratch, wanna free the handsome bloke so he can help you tie these boys up?"

"I don't—" Tom's face grew red.

"No, you don't," Moira finished for him. "Shut it, or it's you who will be swimming with fishes. But don't worry, I'm sure there's a heavenly afterlife waiting just for you."

The waves from the sea started rolling in faster now. Moira looked for a place to tie her hostages, but couldn't find a suitable source.

"Guess we coulda planned this out a bit better, huh, Scratch?"

"We could ditch the van and have Quid pick us up?" Scratch cut the ties binding Baxter's arms.

"Thanks," Baxter rubbed his wrists, gratefully. He winced a little where the ropes had dug into his flesh. His wrists now had raw, red and deeply imprinted marks on them.

"Looks like that's our best option," Moira agreed. "Get the ropes out."

"Run!" Tom yelled, and the three men darted, two to the left and one to the right.

Moira took aim and shot Tom in the leg. He screamed as he fell onto the sand. Then, she recalibrated her sights on Milton and Leo. She fired a shot in the sand beside Leo's foot.

"Stop," she ordered. They did. "I'm doing my best not to shoot you dumb arses, but you don't seem to be gettin' the message."

"You shot me in the leg, Moira!" Tom yelled.

"Nothing but a flesh wound," Moira countered. "You'll live."

Moira stood guard while Scratch, with the help of Baxter, secured the men to the seats in the van. Not wanting to chance a dead man on her hands, they took a few moments to tie a makeshift tourniquet on Tom's injury from a piece of the potato sack that had once covered Baxter's head.

"Here's how this is gonna go down, boys," Moira addressed them. "The three of us are going to get a safe distance. Now, you can yell for help all you want. That's fine. But when the good detective gets here, you're going to let him in on exactly what it was you had planned for poor Baxter here. And if you don't—" she paused.

"If we don't," Tom spat, angrily. He wasn't sure what was worse, the fact that they failed in their mission, or that he was outsmarted by a woman.

"Well then, the Westport family won't be as kind to you as I have been just now. You'll be safer if you just confess."

Scratch slammed the door of the van shut before Tom could respond.

"It's gonna be a warm day," Moira noticed. "Crack a window on the passenger side before you lock up, would ya?" Scratch nodded.

Baxter, now standing beside Moira for the first time, turned to look her in the eyes. Even standing, she was still a good five or six inches shorter than he was. "I—" he fought to find the right words as they shared a moment.

"Oh," she seemed to remember something, "one second." Moira pulled a knife from underneath her skirt and systematically dug it into the two front tires of the vehicle. "Just in case." To Scratch, she asked, "Got the keys?"

"Yup," he answered, as the three trudged up the concrete ramp.

"What about your chair?" Baxter asked.

"Think my covers blown now, don't you?" she laughed.

"Aren't you worried they'll tell 'em you were involved? How are we going to explain them being tied up?"

"Good thinking, Sweet Face," she agreed, "help me out."

Baxter followed Moira back to the beach, where they procured her chair. Baxter folded it up and dragged it behind them as the three headed back to the road.

"Not gonna get much of a signal out here, I'm afraid," Scratch said.

"Not to worry," Moira answered. "There's a little coffee shop about a mile away that most people don't know about. We can use their pay phone to call for Quid to come pick us up."

"A mile?" Baxter cringed, touching the side of his head which he just realized was hurting and was matted with a dried-out blood stain."

"Yeah," she smirked, "looks like we're taking that hike after all."

Chapter 23
Moira and Constantine

Flashback: Two Weeks Ago

Moira found her uncle playing bocce ball in a designated court on the grounds behind his mansion. Too large a man to bend and pick up the balls, he'd spent years having one of his servants retrieve the weighted balls for him and line them up on a cart so that all he had to do was merely throw them when the time came. Whomever he was playing also knew better than to beat him. Well, everyone except Moira.

"Hello, Uncle." She arrived wearing jeans and a green blouse.

"Moira!" Constantine greeted his niece, gleefully. With both Moira's parents gone, and having lost his own daughter, Molly, at such a young age, Moira had become like a daughter to him. "What brings you here today?"

"Do I need a reason to visit my favorite uncle?" she answered.

Constantine knew her too well. "Cut the bull crap, Moira. You and I are cut from the same mold, and you know it."

"Fair enough," she answered, planting a kiss on his cheek. "I have found myself in a predicament and I need your help."

"What kind of a...predicament?" he eyed her belly, instinctively.

"Not *that* kind!" she chastised. "I need to ask you, what do you know about a man name Jax Liebling?

"The toilet guy?"

Moira scrunched her nose. "What? Never mind," she continued, picking up a bocce ball. The attendant who had been playing politely bowed out, but not before gathering and restocking the balls on the cart. "I'm talking about the man who is the silent partner attempting to help Baxter Baker buy out the Vandenberg factories."

"And how is it that you know Baxter Baker?" Constantine asked, once again eyeing her belly.

"Again, it's not about that!" she whined, putting her hand on her belly, protectively. "I know Baxter Baker...and not in the Biblical sense, I might add...because when I was looking for a job, Jax Liebling hired me."

"Why would you be looking for a job when you are working for me?"

"No offense, Uncle, but I'm old enough to make my own way in the world. No more handouts."

"Handouts? You're the best associate I've got."

"I applied to become a receptionist two months ago," Moira explained.

"Receptionist?" Constantine was incredulous. "I didn't spend years training you to perform the most intricate grifts in the country to resort to some low-paying job that—"

"It's a respectable job, and I stand to be promoted to executive assistant if I do well over the next three months."

Constantine pursed his lips. "My statement stands."

"I can't go on doing petty jobs conning tourists to purchase funny traveler's checks or pay me cash settlements for fender benders anymore. And sometimes, during those slip and falls," Moira's voice went up in pitch, "I actually fall...and hurt myself!"

"You're as bad as your mother," Constantine complained. "She had a conscience and look where it got her."

"You'll kindly leave my mum out of it." Moira's nose grew red, the only feature on her face that let on that she was becoming angry. "She died honorably."

"Honorably," Constantine agreed, "but penniless. Why she ran off with that musician fellow, I'll never know."

"It's called love, Uncle. You should look it up."

Constantine shook his head. He missed his sister. Following a messy divorce, she ran off with a man who played the local music circuit. For years, the man dreamed of going on tour and traveling the world. Finally, his chance arrived. They got as far as Iceland before the plane went down in a freak accident. Moira was only ten years old at the time.

"The point is," Moira took the ball Constantine was holding and tossed it on the field, drawing him out of his daydream, "it started off like a normal interview and then got weird."

"What do you mean, weird? Did Baxter—"

"No!"

"Did Jax—"

"No, would you listen?"

"Sorry," Constantine apologized, "continue."

"At the end of the interview, Mr. Liebling said that the job was mine on one condition."

"Why, that little—"

"No!" Moira patted his arm. "He asked me to promise to come to work in a wheelchair. He'd rent one for me."

"A wheelchair? Why?" Constantine took a ball from the cart and flung it. It landed next to Moira's, tapping her ball slightly.

"He said that Baxter has a thing for the ladies, and wanted to ensure he wouldn't make a pass at me."

"And he thought a chair would do it?" Constantine was surprised. "Not only is he an idiot, but he must be blind. Has he even looked at you?"

"I wish him being shallow were the worst of it," she explained.

"What do you mean?"

"I mean, I don't think Jax Liebling is on the up and up."

"Men in high places rarely are."

"No, worse than that," Moira shook her head. "I did a little digging. You remember the blowup in the news that uncovered the fraudulent faith healing that led to deaths at the Church of Infinite Love...the ones traced back to the Vandenberg family?

"Of course, I do." Constantine furrowed his brows. "Why do you think I've been hired to protect that dolt playboy, Baxter Baker, in the first place? He was the one who sold his family out. I should have tossed him out on his ear. He's the reason the Dublin factory is up and running again."

"No, he isn't," Moira explained, "this was all Jax Liebling's idea."

"What are you getting at, Moira?"

"What I'm getting at is that I think Jax knows very well who my famous uncle is. I think it's a trap...a well-laid plan so that Jax can make Baxter the fall guy for all the bad that happened in the family. And, I think he plans to take out Baxter and pin the blame on the Westports."

"He wouldn't dare!" Constantine's face turned to rage.

"Jax Liebling *would* dare. He's a sociopath with an overinflated ego who will take out anyone who gets in his way."

"Well, then you've gotta get out of there."

"I've got a better idea," Moira offered. "One that will protect Baxter...er, Mr. Baker, and keep the family name out of it."

"I don't want you in any danger." Constantine shook his head.

"It's too late for that, Uncle," she replied. "I've been brought into the fold, so to speak."

"What does that mean, exactly?"

"I've convinced Jax that I'm on board with the church's new direction and that Baxter is clearly the anti-Christ and needs to be stopped."

Constantine's face dropped. "Are you being serious right now? You mean that boy really *is* in danger?"

"Yes," Moira's lip quivered a little. "They're going to kill him if we don't stop it."

"Correction," Constantine replied, leaning a hand on the cart for support, "*you* have nothing to do with this. Leave it to me to protect him. After all, it's *me* he's paying for security."

"Uncle Constantine," Moira was serious, "I can lead you right to the men who are going to try and take him out."

"No."

"You have to let me help," Moira pleaded.

"Why?" Constantine looked at her belly again.

"For the thousandth time, I'm not pregnant. I haven't even kissed the man!" she nearly yelled. "But I'll gladly pretend I am, if it will mean you'll help me!" A few tears were forming in the corners of her eyes.

Constantine put out a meaty thumb and wiped one away. "You really like that boy, don't you?"

Moira nodded.

"Why him?" he was confused.

"I dunno," Moira shrugged, "I just do."

"Okay, Moira. Okay," Constantine promised. "Let's come up with a plan, together."

It Had to Be You

Moira left her uncle's house nearly three hours later, after they'd devised a plan to prevent the untimely demise of Baxter Baker. She climbed into one of Constantine's limos so that Dough could drive her back to her small flat in Dublin. Dough tried to open the door for her, out of habit, but she waved him away. She was having none of it. All this pretend chivalry was starting to get to her. As she slammed the door shut on the front passenger's side, Dough climbed in beside her on the driver's side. He looked at her, questioningly, as the Westport family usually rode in the back seat, not side-by-side with the 'help.' But Dough thought better than to say anything.

"Wouldja like ta hear some music?" he offered, reaching toward the radio and snapping it on. U2's "The Sweetest Thing" came through the speakers, gravelley at first, but then clearer as Dough adjusted the dial for better reception.

Moira didn't answer. Instead, she leaned on one hand, peering out the window, a weighted feeling of regret in her belly, mixed with an odd sense of relief. On the one hand, she was glad that Baxter was going to be safe. On the other, she didn't feel right about her current grift. She had convinced herself that her deal with Jax was the last one she'd be a part of, and now, she was falling in the footsteps of her cousin Bristol and his friend Darwin Fennec. They had to flee to the States to avoid Constantine's wrath. What made her think this one would be different? She was about to pull one final grift...on Uncle Constantine.

"Can I get you anything else, sir?" Iris asked Constantine gently after Moira had gone.

Constantine had since relocated to his favorite chair where

he and Moira had hatched a plan to prevent bad things from happening to Baxter Baker. There was something about the whole situation that didn't sit right with him. For example, if Moira was so concerned about Baxter's safety, why not warn him before they kidnapped him? Why even let it get that far? Furthermore, if Jax Liebling was set on pinning this on the Westport family, why on Earth would he bring a member of the family into his plan? No, he thought to himself. Something didn't add up.

Iris stood patiently, waiting on Constantine's answer.

"Uh, no, thank you, Iris." Iris turned to leave before he stopped her for a moment. "Just one more thing, Iris," he added. "How is our unexpected house guest doing?"

"Oh, fine, sir. As a matter of fact—" Iris began before Constantine held up a hand to stop her. "That's alright, Iris. The less said, the better."

"Of course, sir," Iris nodded.

Moira's surprise visit almost revealed that Constantine had a secret of his own. Hidden away in a lesser-traveled area of his mansion, an American was being kept out of the public eye. He still hadn't put all the pieces together yet, but he knew one thing for certain, Jax Liebling was becoming a royal thorn in his side.

Chapter 24
Convergence

Present Day

Quid was a bit shorter and rounder than Scratch, but had a friendly round face that somehow inspired trust. He picked up Moira, Scratch and Baxter at the small, out-of-the-way coffee shop that, for whatever reason, was closed that day. And so the three stood out front, with little but a thin awning to protect them from the rain. Thanks to the wind, it didn't work and the three were a soggy mess by the time he arrived.

"Want me to turn the heat on?" he offered when they had settled into a white Ford transit van. It had two black racing stripes down the hood, but outside of that, it was pretty unremarkable.

But perfect for flying under the radar, Baxter thought.

"Nah," Scratch answered. "We can dry off proper when we get to Constantine's."

"Constantine?" Baxter sat up, surprised. "You mean, it's Constantine Westport I have to thank for saving me?"

"No, Sweet Face," Moira answered. "You may have paid my uncle for protection, but were it not for me, he'd have had no idea this was going down."

"Your...uncle?" Baxter instinctively touched his head again before sitting back in the seat, his head still throbbing.

Moira took Baxter's hand supportively, weaving her fingers with his and whispering, "We'll get that bruise on your noggin' fixed up in no time," she promised.

He looked down at their intertwined hands, more confused than ever.

Some time passed, but eventually, they arrived. Once at the main Westport mansion, they pulled into what appeared to be a series of horse stalls, except once past the initial entrance, it turned into a private parking garage. One side was lined with utility and transportation vehicles, such as the one they were in, and on the other were stretch limos and black sedans and smaller compact cars.

"You should see Uncle's personal sporty collection." She flashed her green eyes at him as they exited the vehicle.

Baxter merely nodded, following Moira and Scratch through a secret tunnel that led from the garage to the main house.

Once inside the main room, Constantine Westport's primary housekeeper, Iris, quickly attended to them. "I'm sure you'll be wanting to dry off," she said, sympathetically. "Give me a few moments to tend to the jacks, and you can go freshen up there."

A boisterous laugh erupted from the corner of the room, as Constantine Westport lumbered his way to his favorite leather chair situated at the helm of the main sitting area. As soon as he sat, an attendant handed him a whiskey, neat.

"Thank you, Siobhan," he acknowledged.

For the first time in his life, Baxter was speechless.

Moira interrupted the silence by running and giving her uncle a soggy hug to him in his chair.

"What are you doing, silly lass? You're getting rainwater all over me and my good chair!" But he laughed in a way that very few got to hear.

Moira was a force to be reckoned with. She stood back and shook her head from side to side flinging droplets of rainwater from her soaking-wet fiery red hair all over him and his precious chair.

Constantine bellowed louder, "Cheeky. You've got the same attitude as my Molly had." He laughed so hard he had to fight back a tear.

Moira touched his shoulder, sympathetically. "Aye," she answered. "But even she would have had better sense than to get mixed up with the likes of him, now wouldn't she?" Moira motioned to Baxter who felt suddenly conspicuous, and for once, humble. He was used to controlling the room. This new dynamic left him feeling extraordinarily uncomfortable.

"Where is he?!" A voice erupted from the hallway.

"Who the hell is that?" Constantine demanded.

The doors flung open, and a crazed Darwin Fennec rushed into the room, red-eyed as if he hadn't slept in a week. He probably hadn't.

"Finn?" Constantine lurched forward in surprise.

"Why did you do it, Constantine?" he yelled as Scratch and Quid grabbed him and pulled him backward. He was fit to be tied.

"Do what?" Constantine was confused.

"You murdered Rue! You did it to get back at me for Molly!"

Baxter had never formally met Darwin Fennec nor Rue Brennan, but he'd learned about them after Emma Post had begun investigating the death of his uncle, Erasmus Vandenberg. They were the ones who helped solve the murders of two of

Emma's close friends and blown the cover of the Vandenberg's criminal dealings. *But why was he here, now?*

"Just hold your tongue, Finn." Constantine waved a hand at him. "Just listen."

"I'm not going to—" Darwin fought against the arms that held him back.

"Darwin," a female voice called.

There, from the shadows, stood Rue Brennan, wearing a flowing red summer dress with ruffles at the ends that flared just around her knees.

Darwin stopped struggling. Moira eyed the scene, confused. *What the heck is going on, and who is this strange woman?*

Constantine motioned for the two men to release him. Darwin sailed toward Rue and hugged her so hard that the two of them buckled to their knees.

"Darwin," Rue huffed. "Loosen up so I can breathe," she smiled, tears pouring down her face. She hugged him close, wrapping the back of his head with her hand and pulled him toward her shoulder, where they sat on their heels, crumpled together on the floor in a tight embrace.

If there were other people in the room, Darwin and Rue were not aware of them.

"But I thought you were—" Darwin began.

Rue shook her head. "No," she explained, "Midge set it up to protect me from Jax Liebling."

Baxter's eyes widened at Jax's name. He couldn't yet connect the dots between Rue, Darwin and Jax since he wasn't around during that particular drama, but it occurred to him rather late that Jax was likely the instigator behind his kidnapping. Perhaps he had gotten Bernie to convince a few members to get involved. He couldn't be sure...

"Well," Rue continued, "first I was bait, and then—never

mind. I'll tell you more later. What's important is that Mr. Westport has been letting me stay here to keep me safe."

Darwin eyed Constantine, questioningly. Constantine merely shrugged his shoulders.

"But I thought you wanted me dead after what happened to Molly." Darwin was confused. Molly had been Constantine's daughter and Darwin's first love. She got into both drugs and the wrong gang, leading to her early demise. Constantine threatened to kill both his son, Molly's brother Bristol, along with his best friend, Darwin. Or as Constantine had always known him, *Finn*.

"For a long time, I did," Constantine confessed. "But then I realized that I was misplacing my anger."

Darwin stood, helping Rue to her feet and wrapping an arm around her, unwilling to let her go again.

Constantine took a sip of his whiskey. "See, I was really angry with myself and how I led my daughter into a life of addiction and crime, but I channeled that grief and anger and directed it at you, Finn. But I know now that you were only trying to help my daughter." After a long sigh, he added, "I'm sorry."

Darwin eyed Constantine with disbelief, waiting for the punchline or the other shoe to drop...a shoe that involved him being dragged away and his dead body dumped in a river somewhere. Confused, he asked, "You're...sorry?"

"Yes," Constantine answered.

Channeled grief and anger? Darwin thought. *An apology?* None of that sounded a bit like the hard man Darwin knew as a young lad.

"And you don't want to kill me...or Rue?" Darwin asked for confirmation.

"I do not." A long silence ensued before Constantine added, "I can see you're confused. But after years of therapy, I have learned a healthier way to process my emotions and not cast blame on others. I'm taking responsibility for my life," Constantine finished, proudly.

Moira gave her uncle a supportive pat on the shoulder. Darwin stood, jaw dropped in disbelief. Moira was finally starting to put the pieces together of who these two new visitors were and why they were here.

"Tell me, Finn," Constantine asked, "how is Bristol?"

"Bristol?" Darwin answered, scratching his head nervously. "Uh, fine. He's fine."

"And his wife and kids? How are they?" Constantine leaned forward, eyes blazing directly into Darwin's eyes.

"They are, uh, fine," he stammered. Suddenly, it was as if he were a teenager again, meeting Constantine after he'd gotten caught in a grift gone wrong. "How did you—"

"I got friends everywhere," Constantine explained. For a man angry at his son, it was clear that in his heart, he wanted nothing but the best for Bristol and his family.

"Darwin," Rue suddenly realized. "How did you find me? Midge stole my phone and threw it into traffic and—" Suddenly, a lightbulb went off in her head. "You tracked me through my phone, didn't you?" She wrinkled her nose at him. Then, she remembered. "But how? There's no way the signal would reach—"

"No," Darwin explained. "I couldn't track you in the US, and since Ortega and Penelope weren't giving me any answers, I hopped on the first available flight from New York. Once here, I traced your phone as far as Derry."

"I'm surprised there was anything left to track," Rue remembered Midge wrestling the phone from her and watching with anger as her friend sent it bouncing on the road.

"Well, I guess I got lucky," Darwin explained. "Once I was in the area, it was just a question of figuring out where you'd be. If Midge were involved, I reasoned, a pub."

"Good guess," Rue snorted.

"I hit the only one with a rental car abandoned out front. Turns out, the woman who owned the bar is a sleuth herself. She remembered two women leaving the bar, one seemingly very drunk—"

"Or very drugged—" Rue pursed her lips, annoyed.

"Indeed," Darwin paused to shake his head. "But she also remembered the license plate, make and model of the car that Midge was driving."

"Wow, maybe we should hire her." Rue was impressed.

"She then went on to complain that the rental company she called was taking forever to pick up their 'feckin car,' claiming it wasn't theirs. She was aggravated that it was taking up space in her 'feckin parkin lot.' She finally called the Garda out of aggravation."

Darwin smiled before turning to Constantine. "They eventually tracked the rental to Rue Brennan, but the other car, the one Midge and Rue drove off in, was unregistered. However, it was easy enough to tie the vehicle to you, Mr. Westport. It was one of the many brands you've always used, even back in the day... manufactured by Opel."

"If only everyone had the same brand loyalty as I do," Constantine chortled. "Impressive, Finn."

Iris, who had been waiting in the wings, finally felt it safe to return to the room.

"If you would care to freshen up, Mr. Baker, you can follow me this way, please."

Both Darwin and Rue looked over their shoulder in surprise.

"Baker?" Rue said. "As in Baxter Baker?"

"The same," he cringed, "sorry to meet under such extreme circumstances."

Darwin offered a hand. "No, not the best circumstances, I'll agree. But if I understand it, you helped Emma uncover a cult scheme that had previously led to the death of several people, and nearly took a bullet in the process."

"Er, not nearly," Baxter pulled up his wet shirt to reveal a scar where he was shot trying to protect Emma Post.

There was a slight gasp from Iris and several attendants. Moira's eyes perked up, not at the fact that Baxter's torso was undeniably toned, but that he had been brave enough to actually risk his life for someone. His stock just rose in her book.

"I'm starting to feel like I'm running a sanctuary," Constantine complained. "First her," he pointed to Rue, "and now him," he motioned to Baxter.

Moira kissed the top of Constantine's balding head. "You did good, Uncle," she said. "Alright," Moira announced, noticing her uncle's fatigue and taking charge. "Iris, can you help see to it that our guests are looked after? Everyone, get some rest and we can all discuss this further over dinner."

"But what about—" Baxter sidled up to her and whispered.

"I'll put in an anonymous call to Detective Ortega. He was working with Emma, no?"

"That's right," Baxter agreed. "So they'll check in on our friends by the sea?" He was, of course, referring to the men who had tried to kidnap him and drown him in the ocean not hours earlier.

"What friends?" Moira asked, winking.

"Emma who?" Baxter played along.

"That's better," she smiled. "And you, Sweet Face, are coming with me."

With that, Moira led a willing Baxter out of the room. From the hallway, he could be heard whispering, "How is it that you stumbled on Detective Ortega's number, exactly?"

"Shhh," Moira whispered. "You ask far too many questions, Sweet Face." She guided Baxter to the end of the hall, making a left toward yet another long hallway.

"C'mon," Rue took Darwin by the arm. "You need some rest after the shock you've had."

"I'm afraid if I let myself go to sleep, I'll awake and discover this was all a dream, and that you're really gone," he lamented. Darwin was still convinced he must be hallucinating.

Rue stood on her toes and planted a soft kiss on Darwin's lips.

"I'm not gone," she promised. "And I swear, I'll never leave you again."

Moira had a private guest room at Constantine's house. It was her home away from home. Compared to the rest of the estate, her room was simple. From the doorway to his right, Baxter noticed a queen-sized white canopy bed with a ruffled top. On the left side of the bed, there was a small end table with a lamp and a white rotary phone and what appeared to be a bathroom door. On the bed's right, stood a tall ash armoire. Directly across from him, bright sunlight beamed through a double-paneled window with French shutters that were currently open. Under the window sat a small writing table and chair. And against the wall opposite the bed was a matching ash dresser and a tall rocking chair in the corner, facing the window.

"What?" Moira questioned Baxter's expression.

"Nothing," he answered. "This room feels like you only...softer." He smiled.

"Hmmph," she answered. "Sit."

He sat at the writing table while Moira disappeared into the bathroom. She appeared moments later with cotton balls and hydrogen peroxide.

"Thank you, Nurse Moira," he joked. He lifted his chin and grinned, closing his eyes as he waited for her to apply the antiseptic to his bruised head. He braced himself for the pain and was determined to put on a brave face.

"Here," she clunked the bottle on the table and dropped the bag of cotton balls. "I've got that call to make, remember?"

She spun on her heels and headed to the phone where she dialed Ortega's cell phone number, apparently from memory.

Disappointed, Baxter soaked a cotton ball. Oddly enough, there was no mirror in the room. He noticed a long, silver letter opener on the desk, squinting to see his reflection in it as he applied the antiseptic to his head. He couldn't really see the injury well at that angle, but the stinging let him know he had reached the right area. He winced, then quickly darted a glance in Moira's direction to make sure she hadn't noticed. She had her back to him.

Moira was busy dialing in a code to block her number to outgoing calls. She wasn't taking any chances on being traced. Baxter also noticed she screwed something over the mouthpiece...*to disguise her voice?*

"That's right, detective," she said, moments later. "Probably best to get there soon before the tide comes in." Detective Ortega could be heard asking a question, but Baxter couldn't hear exactly what. Moira hung up while he was still talking. She returned, eyed Baxter sitting there, a soggy, bloody cotton ball in his hand.

"You are hopeless, Sweet Face. You know that?" She smiled at him, holding up a wastepaper basket just next to the desk. He hadn't noticed it before now. He tossed the cotton away. "Aww," she wrinkled her lips. "You missed a spot." Moira grabbed a fresh cotton ball, tipped the bottle of hydrogen peroxide just enough to soak it, and then reapplied it liberally over the wound.

"Ouch!" he complained.

She smiled, wickedly.

"You're enjoying this, aren't you?" Baxter complained.

"A bit," she confessed. "If I hadn't seen that bullet wound with my own eyes, I woulda thought you'd never gotten your pretty little head bruised or your hands calloused."

"What's that supposed to mean?" Baxter was indignant.

"It means that you're a wee bit more genteel than what I'm used to."

"Well," Baxter grimaced at her, "You're rough and tumble enough for the both of us."

"You've got that right," Moira smiled seductively as she walked backward toward the bedroom door, bending her knee and kicking it closed with her boot, locking the two of them inside.

Chapter 25
No Witnesses

Penelope, Ortega and Shep approached the van cautiously. It was exactly where the anonymous caller said it would be, except that now, it was turned on its side with tidewaters flowing in and out around it. It was still shallow this time of day, but suspiciously quiet.

Ortega thought he recognized the caller's speech patterns as someone he had met, but the voice was distorted, and there was such a sense of urgency that he wasted no time in getting to the scene once they had hung up.

Meanwhile, Shep, having been newly released from the hospital, still winced every three steps. The doctor had ordered bed rest, but Shep was on a mission and simply wouldn't listen.

Suddenly, Shep grabbed Ortega's arm as he stepped onto a dry part of the beach, a mere four feet from the van. Penelope paused behind them. Much smaller than the large man, she struggled to peer around him. Shep pointed a silent finger that traced a line marking the van...a line of machine gun holes.

Ortega nodded, carefully motioning for Shep to go one way while he went the other, circling the van. Ortega paused long enough to roll his pants up, but his socks and shoes were soon to be sloshing on mucky sand with sea water lapping around his heels. In the States, both men would be armed, but here, they only had batons as weapons.

Shep eyed the driver's seat through the only available window. The glass was smashed in with fragments scattered over the steering wheel and seat, most of it settling on top of the passenger window, now steeped in the sand but largely intact. At first glance, there was no evidence to suggest the driver side door had been tampered with, nor any blood stains to indicate that someone up front had been shot.

Penelope sucked in a nervous breath as Ortega struggled to climb over the side of the van and tug at the side door. Finally, the heavy door slid open and clambered to a stop.

"Holy shit," Shep muttered as he and Ortega witnessed what was inside. Ortega gagged a little as he turned his head. Penelope took a step toward him but he waved an arm and shook his head.

Inside, the three men who attempted to kidnap and kill Baxter Baker were not only still tied up from when he, Scratch and Moira left them, but each had multiple gunshot wounds to the chest. Whomever shot them wasn't taking any chances because, in addition to the peppered shots to the van, they must have opened it long enough to distribute single gunshot wounds to each of their heads: Tom, Milton and Leo. The bodies lay in a heap at the bottom of the overturned vehicle.

It's not as if Ortega hadn't witnessed gruesome scenes before. But most times, he was expecting it. After some time off in retirement, coupled with a call from a woman that clearly indicated there were three men, all of whom were alive and waiting for him...he didn't expect this.

Penelope, however, recognized the look on Ortega's face. It's the one he got when he was both overwhelmed and somehow blaming himself for an invisible failure of which only he was aware of.

"Jose," Penelope said calmly, "whatever it is, I can help."

She was, after all, a forensic scientist by profession. Although, thanks to her involvement in her former boss's cases, she was now and ex-one. But she had been the best in the business and despite her kind heart, when it came to gruesome scenes, she had nerves of steel and a stomach to match.

Ortega composed himself, climbing down as there wasn't much space alongside the open van for two people. "Okay," he relented as he and Shep backed away from the scene. "Just brace yourself. Looks like there are three men inside, as promised, but all have been shot to death." Ortega put out a hand to help Penelope up onto the side of the van. She handed her camera bag and forensic accessory duffle bag to Shep who dutifully held them until she was safely up.

She sat on the edge of the open door, her legs dangling inside the cargo space. "Hand me the hazard gear first...shoe covers, gloves, jacket." She announced. "Thanks," she replied as Shep handed them up to her, piece by piece. "Camera next." She ordered. Shep handed her the camera bag and waited as she unzipped it and procured her Nikon. After several minutes she said, "Hang on. I'm goin' in."

Ortega and Shep awaited further instruction, until Penelope finally declared in a muffled voice from within, "Need my flashlight!"

Shep scrambled to comply, hanging a long arm over the edge.

"Thanks" she accepted it.

"How'd she know she'd need her equipment?" Shep asked.

"Dr. Washburn always plans on a crime scene," Ortega explained. "Even if the men had been alive, we would have wanted to collect photos of the scene for evidence, anyway."

Shep nodded. "That makes sense."

Just then, the team heard sirens in the distance…An Garda Síochána.

"How did they—" Shep began to ask.

"Don't know," Ortega answered, "but it's not great for us to be caught here uninvited."

"Hey there!" A gruff voice called as a larger older man clambered down the steep slope, struggling in what appeared to be a bullet proof vest. Just then, Penelope popped her head out from the van. The man's eyes shot them a glare. "Inspector Clover, don't move!"

Ortega's eyes lit up. His look of dread turned to one of relief. Maybe this wasn't such a bad thing at all…

When the Inspector reached the sand, he squinted at Ortega, "What in the feckin' hell are yew grinnin' at?" Then, his eyes grew wide. "Detective Jose Ortega?"

"The same," Ortega grinned. "Nice to see you again, Ian."

"Well, as I live and breathe," Inspector Clover laughed. "I heard you retired."

"I did," Ortega nodded. "Or, so I thought."

Penelope and Shep shot each other questioning looks before Shep interceded, "I hate to be the one to state the obvious here, but we've got a triple homicide on our hands."

Clover eyed Shep up and down before darting a look from Penelope, who was still in the van, and Ortega on the ground. He smirked. "Still together, I see," he whispered, jabbing Ortega in the ribs.

By then, two of Clover's officers were on hand, awaiting Inspector Clover's instructions.

"Dr. Washburn," Inspector Clover addressed Penelope. "Nice to see yew again. But wouldja mind tellin' me what yer doin' messin' with the evidence of a crime scene in a country where yew have no place messin'?"

Penelope eyed Ortega who knowingly nodded.

"Oh, I wasn't messin'," she began. "Er, messing." The two guards helped her climb out of the van, but not before she'd handed Shep her camera case and a few evidence bags. Once on the ground, Penelope looked mournfully at her rain boots, now covered in mud. She could feel the cold water soaking her socks. Somehow, she hadn't thought to bring waterproof rain boots in her haste to pack. She adjusted the camera, now hanging from a strap around her neck. "We received an anonymous call that there were three people of interest tied up and waiting for us here, ones that could shed light on the Vandenberg case."

"I'm afraid yew've lost me, lass." Clover lifted his cap and scratched his head, before leaning back and speaking quietly to Ortega, "Care to catch me up on what in the feckin' hell is goin' on?"

"Inspector," one of the guards called. "You really need to see this."

Inspector Clover pushed past Penelope and Ortega and looked down into the van.

"I can assure you, the three of us had nothing to do with this," Shep explained.

"Oh, can yew now?" Clover tilted a head up at the excessively tall and large Shep. What Clover lacked in height, not that he was small by any means, he made up for in girth and attitude.

"It has to do with a case we were on in Florida involving the Vandenberg family and the Church of Infinite Love," Ortega explained. "We expect they are trying to cover their tracks in the States and re-open operations in Ireland."

Clover eyed the dead men in the van distastefully. "Any idea who these men are?"

"Not yet," Ortega answered. "We only arrived moments before you did, expecting to find three very alive men."

"Well, we got wind when several calls came in about civilians hearing what sounded like machine gun fire, but, for obvious reasons, no one wanted to get close to it to see what was going on," Clover explained. "I haven't even had time to call anyone else in yet." He turned to Penelope. "Seeing as you're already here, what have you got fer me?"

"Well," Penelope explained. "I can't tell for certain without access to a lab, but the bodies are still relatively fresh. And given you just got the call, I'd say that adds up."

"What else?" Clover waved his hand.

"One of the men had his passport on him," Penelope motioned for Shep to bring over the evidence bags. He obliged, handing it over to the Guards. "He's American, and given their shoes and clothing, I suspect they all are."

"Three persons of interest gunned down during daylight hours with a machine gun?" Clover clarified.

"AR-15," Penelope confirmed. "So, they either smuggled them in themselves and were shot with their own weapons or—"

"Mob hit?" Clover finished.

"Maybe," Penelope shrugged.

"Feckin' hell," Clover removed his hat and scratched his head again. A flaky red bald patch at the top of his scalp seemed to glow angrily at the abuse.

"There's one more odd bit," Shep offered. "Look," he pointed at some of the track marks just at the edge of the dry part of the beach where the sand met the ramp that led to higher ground. "Most of it is washed away, but they appear to have come from a wheelchair."

Penelope's eyes lit up as she turned to Inspective Clover, hopefully. "If you can give me just a little more time to scour the van. I can see if there are tread marks inside and any other pieces of evidence."

"How am I going to explain this to my superintendent?"

Clover asked Ortega. "You're not even supposed to be here. And, you're retired!"

"I'm not," Shep explained. "I'm currently active with the Sheriff's department in Tampa, Special Investigations. We regularly work with contractors in situations like this one. And since these men are likely American and tied to a case I was already investigating—"

Shep paused to let Inspector Clover connect the dots any way he saw fit, leaving out the part about the fact that he wasn't, technically, assigned to this case, either. He merely took a temporary leave of absence citing health issues. But he didn't feel the need to tell Clover that.

"Inspector!" one of the Guards called. "Look at this!" The officer reached a gloved hand down and pulled out a small broach that was wedged between one of the victim's feet and the edge of the floor.

"What is it?" Clover asked.

"A ladies pin of some sort."

"Lemme see that," Penelope ordered, before eyeing Ortega and Clover and adding, "please." She put her plastic gloves back on and eyed the broach, tumbling it over in her hand. It was gold with a cleanly polished Connemara stone at the center. She sighed, loudly.

"What is it, Penelope?" Ortega asked.

"If I didn't know any better, I'd say this custom ditty is a creation from Westport Jewelers," Penelope said. "My mother was mad about this stuff back in the day."

"The Westport Grifters are in on this?" Inspector Clover replied. "Feckin' hell!" He motioned toward his guards. "Men, we're going ta have ta pay a visit to Constantine Westport's home."

"Wait," Ortega intervened. "Ian, how's it gonna look with the Guard barging in there without all the evidence? Let Dr. Washburn finish scouring the scene for clues, and we'll report anything we find."

"He's right," Shep added. "They know you, but not us. They see you anywhere near the property and who knows how the family will react? Why not let us have a talk with them first?"

Inspector Clover thought a moment, before letting out a forced cough. "Come to think of it," he coughed again. "I think I'm...Tá mé tinn. Think I'll take the rest of the day off to recover." He leaned in and whispered quietly to Ortega and Shep, "I'll have my men block off the crime scene. You leave Dr. Washburn here to finish up her report while you pay the Westports a visit. I can stall until tomorrow morning, but then I need to send my men in to start investigating. Understood?"

"Understood," Ortega nodded. "Thank you, Ian."

Inspector Clover shook his head as he walked over to the two Guards assisting him, muttering under his breath, "Feckin' hell."

Ortega's phone buzzed just moments after he'd left Penelope and Shep at the crime scene commandeering their rental vehicle for investigative purposes. Penelope was tasked with finishing up on collecting evidence and Shep on documenting what they found. It hadn't escaped Penelope's attention that she only knew of one person, potentially, involved in this case who used a wheelchair... Moira Dodd. *But how is she involved in this? If she is involved?*

Inspector Clover left one officer behind to oversee the crime scene, ensuring that evidence didn't disappear and to see to it that the two returned safely to their temporary residence. It wasn't so much that Clover suspected them of anything, but he still had to cover his ass with his superiors.

Ortega eyed his phone...an encrypted message. That could only be from one person—Darwin Fennec. *But how did the signal reach him overseas? Hell, he couldn't even get good reception a block from his house.* A sudden flash of heat crossed his face. *Darwin must be in Ireland.* He feared what his occasional colleague and sometimes friend would do, as he was convinced that it was Constantine Westport who was responsible for Rue Brennan's death. *I hope he doesn't do anything stupid,* Ortega thought.

Then he decoded the message. It read: *Rue is alive. Westport is innocent.*

That was it. *Guess he's not in a place where he can share more,* Ortega reasoned. But given this new information, all signs still pointed to Constantine Westport's involvement in this. He just wasn't entirely sure what it was.

Time to find out, Ortega muttered to himself.

Chapter 26
The Visit

"He can talk to me first or he can talk to Inspector Clover," Ortega's voice could be heard in the hall. "Mr. Westport stands a better chance with me because I actually wanna believe he's innocent."

Dough, Mr. Westport's front-line security guard blocked Ortega from entering the premises. With a name like Dough, one might have expected the guard to be on the softer, lumpier side and more than a little overweight. Instead, he was a small, thin man with lean muscles and a spring in his step that suggested years in the boxing rink. There was something in his eyes that Ortega used to recognize in himself in his younger years—fearlessness.

Dough signaled Scratch to remain with Ortega as he went to see Constantine. A few minutes later, Dough returned and Ortega was ushered into a small library, just off to the side of the main living room where people usually gathered. Scratch remained guarding the front door while Dough, after Ortega was seated across from Constantine at his desk, slid the panel of the library door closed. He stood at the door, directly behind the retired detective, watching his every move. Meanwhile, Constantine sat stuffed behind the desk, his large frame struggling to fit in the space provided. His chair squeaked painfully under his weight.

Ortega and Constantine eyed each other in silence for what seemed like an eternity before Constantine finally asked, "Do I know you?"

Ortega opened his mouth and let out a puff of air, as if he were a balloon that had suddenly been popped. "No, Mr. Westport, you have no reason to know me. However, I believe Moira does," Ortega treaded carefully.

"My niece?" Constantine was surprised. "What does Moira have to do with anything?"

"I got a call from someone on my private cell phone not two hours ago. The voice was disguised, but we have reason to believe it was her." He thought back to the factory visit and wheelchair track marks in the sand at the crime scene. It was a long shot, but his spidey sense, along with Penelope's findings, left him confident that he was on the right track. "Don't know how she got my number, but that's not what's important."

"What *is* important, Detective Ortega?" Constantine tried to lean in, formidably, but his belly got in the way. *Gotta go on a diet,* he thought to himself and sat back.

"She alerted me to the fact that three men who'd botched a kidnapping were tied up with a neat little bow and waiting for me to pick them up, and to get there before high tide so they didn't drown."

"Is that so?" Constantine feigned ignorance. "What's that gotta do with me?"

"Do you know where your niece is at the moment, Mr. Westport? She is your niece, isn't she?" Ortega confirmed.

"Wait a minute," Constantine wagged a finger at Ortega. "I thought you were here to question *me* for something. Every time anything interesting happens in this town, officers are banging down my door, assuming I was involved in some way."

"We'll get to you in a minute," Ortega tried again. "But first, where's Moira Dodd?"

Constantine thought carefully before answering simply, "Dunno. Haven't seen her," he lied.

Ortega considered his options. He could drag this out and see if Constantine slipped, giving him information about the crime that he shouldn't have known, or be direct. He decided on the latter.

"Mr. Westport, we did find three men exactly where Miss Dodd said they'd be."

"Well, there you go," Constantine bellowed.

"They were dead," Ortega finished. Constantine's face dropped in surprise. "Shot to death. I'd like to know why and by whom."

"As I said, I haven't seen Moira in days. And I know nothing about these men you found."

"They found a broach at the crime scene with the family logo on it, one from the Westport jewelry line," Ortega added.

"So?" Constantine mocked. "That don't mean nothin'."

Ortega twitched uncomfortably. He could fish for the next few minutes, or do what generally worked in these situations. He picked the latter...and lied. "They also found a few red hairs at the scene, belonging to a woman, and DNA samples that will no doubt be traced back to Moira Dodd." In truth, Ortega couldn't confirm that any human hair was found at the scene that didn't belong to the deceased, nor would DNA test results be available that quickly. He was taking a gamble. "Since Moira is a known member of the Westport family, how long do you think it'll be before Inspector Clover comes banging down your door asking about your involvement?"

"I'm not saying nothin' else without my lawyer present—"

Just then, there was a knock at the door. "Uncle, let me in!" It was Moira.

"Oh, geez," Constantine rubbed his forehead with a meaty hand. "You gotta be kidding me."

Dough backed away as Moira bolted through the door.

Moira seemed frazzled, having only just now realized that Ortega was on the property. "Are you Detective Ortega?" she asked.

"I am," he answered.

"And did you receive an anonymous call about three men tied up on the beach?"

"I did," he replied.

"And did they confess to trying to kidnap and murder Baxter Baker, CEO of Vandenberg Nutraceuticals?"

"Confess," Ortega scratched his head. "No, they didn't confess."

"How is that possible?" Moira was incredulous, eyeing Ortega and Constantine back and forth.

"Because they're dead, Moira," Constantine finished.

"What?!" Moira's face dropped. "That's not possible. When I left —er—"

"Not another word," Constantine cut her off. "Keep your mouth shut until we talk to the lawyers."

"Mr. Westport—" Ortega began.

"Out!" Constantine stood, pressing his palms into the desk for support. "I want you out!" Dough grabbed Ortega by the arm. Instinctively, Ortega tried to shrug him off, but Dough had the grip of a pitbull.

"I'm here in an unofficial capacity," Ortega raised his voice.

"But tomorrow, you can expect a swarm of Guards at your door who won't be as understanding as I am. Let me help you."

"Let him go, Dough," Moira commanded. To her uncle, she said, "Let Mr. Baker and I talk to him. We can sort this out."

"Baxter Baker...is here?" Ortega was surprised.

"He's not the only one," a voice at the door called. Ortega turned to see Darwin standing there, Rue at his side.

"Oh sure," Constantine complained. "Let's let everyone in here, shall we?" To Dough he said, "There's not enough therapy in the world for this shit!"

Ortega's eyes fell to Rue. At one time, he didn't think much of Ms. Brennan. In fact, when she was a suspect in a case, he wasn't very nice to her at all. But she'd come to earn his respect over time, and his opinion of her softened. He felt a little lurch in his heart. His lip quivered. Rue caught his expression for just a moment, surprised that it was filled with such sentiment. She hadn't known him to be compassionate.

"It's nice to see you again, Ms. Brennan," he greeted her cordially, fighting back a few tears and a lump in his throat. "I'm glad you're not...dead."

Rue grinned, "Oh, stop. You old softie," she teased.

Ortega cleared his throat as his eyes darted from Rue, to Darwin, to Moira, Constantine and Dough. "Someone wanna fill me in on what's going on here?"

"I was hoping to speak with you in private," Moira confessed. "I mean, Mr. Baker and me."

"Actually, Moira," Baxter crept into the doorway when no one was looking, peering around Darwin. "Since Mr. Fennec and Ms. Brennan are here too, I think we should have a larger conversation to include them. We're all connected in ways of which I'm not even sure yet."

A look of fear crossed her face as Moira eyed her uncle, and

Constantine caught it. "What have you been up to, lass?" he questioned.

Moira replied, hesitantly, "Uncle, remember the conversation we had a couple of weeks ago about Mr. Baker?"

"Where you thought he was in danger. Of course. Isn't that what today was about?"

"Yes, but there's more." She turned to Ortega. "Perhaps I should start there and fill you in..."

Chapter 27
Secrets

Moira finished telling Ortega about her conversation with Constantine surrounding Baxter Baker's safety and her concerns about Jax Liebling.

"So, you did like me all this time!" Baxter declared, triumphantly, missing the point entirely.

Moira punched him in the arm. "Now's not the time for that," she whispered.

At Constantine's suggestion, Baxter, Moira, Darwin and Rue joined him in the living room where he could sit comfortably in the chair that was quickly becoming his throne, with each couple sitting on either side of him. Ortega opted to stand. This time, Dough and Scratch stood at each end of the room, like two Fu Dogs guarding their master.

"So," Ortega offered, "you knew Jax Liebling was up to something and went to your uncle for help. And so, it was you who intercepted today's unfortunate kidnapping with Mr. Baker."

"Yes," Moira admitted, shooting an apologetic glance toward her uncle.

"And you, Mr. Westport," Ortega addressed Constantine, "were less than honest when you said you knew nothing about the men we found on the beach under the cliffs today. Is that correct?"

Constantine shrugged before adding, "But I had nothing to do with their deaths. Alls I did was provide transportation to rescue pretty boy over there because Moira was so concerned about him. Had no reason to suspect anything might happen to them."

"But," Baxter thought a moment, ignoring the 'pretty boy' reference altogether. "Moira," he turned to her, "if you suspected that I was in danger, why did you let it get this far? Why didn't you warn me?"

"Well," Moira thought quickly. "I didn't want to worry you —" Even as she said it, she knew how unconvincing that sounded.

"Moira," Baxter adopted a sullen voice. "I may be a cad and am not everyone's cup of tea, but I never pretend to be something I'm not. And more importantly, I've always been honest with you about...everything." He took her hand. Constantine's eyes shot up. Baxter released her hand and let out a cough.

"What's going on?" Constantine demanded?

Moira's eyes darted from Baxter to Constantine, uncomfortably. Darwin and Rue watched the scene with fascination, not entirely sure how all of this pieced together.

"Uncle," she confessed, fighting back tears. "I messed up."

Iris, who stood silently in the corner of the room, rushed to Moira's side with a tissue.

"Thank you," Moira accepted it. Iris merely nodded and went back to her corner. To the group, she said, "Jax Liebling called me into his office one day—"

"Why that—" Constantine's face became flushed.

"That's not it!" Moira squealed. "He had been putting feelers out there for weeks seeing my whole opinion of the Church of Infinite Love, and Mr. Baker, and my work at the factory as an assistant, and even you, Uncle Constantine. It was like he was testing the waters."

"For what?" Ortega asked.

"For my loyalties, I think," she confessed. "Once he realized that I wasn't interested in religion any more than I was interested in the family business, he offered me a way out."

"What kind of way out?" Ortega coaxed.

"Well," Moira looked apologetically at Constantine and Baxter. "He said he had a plan that would give me the freedom to forge my own path, and one that would get him the money he needed to buy out the Vandenberg family and run the factories his own way."

"Factories?" Ortega questioned. "As in — plural?"

Moira nodded. "I'll bet if you dig a little deeper into who really purchased the Florida factory, you'll find that Jax Liebling was involved."

"But what does this have to do with my kidnapping—" Suddenly, Baxter was hit with clarity. "Oh, I was to be ransom."

Moira nodded.

"Wait, though," Baxter added. "They were planning to kill me! Did you know about that?!"

"No!" Moira cried. "I most certainly didn't know about that! That's just what I told Uncle Constantine to get him on board with the plan."

"What? You lied to me...and you used me?" Constantine was wounded. He darted an angry glance at Darwin, as if this were somehow his fault. Darwin held his hands up and shook his head. He had no idea what this was about.

"What was the plan, Moira?" Ortega redirected the conversation.

"The plan was to have some of Bernie Forger's uber-devoted followers kidnap Baxter out of some religious commitment."

"Bernie Forger," Rue confirmed. "The new Elder of the church following Erasmus Vandenberg's murder?"

"Yes, exactly," Moira confirmed. "I was to intercept and redirect Baxter safely here, where he'd hole up thinking it was unsafe to return to work."

"And then Jax would send a ransom note to the Vandenberg family…and the matriarch, Edwina Vandenberg, would get her lawyer, Mr. Lundy, to give them what they asked." Ortega put the pieces together. "And you and he would split the profits."

Moira nodded.

"You used me?" Baxter's betrayal could be heard in his voice. "But I…I really liked you. And furthermore, my family is furious with me. Why would they pay the ransom instead of saying, 'good riddance'?"

"Because they needed you to be the scapegoat for both the church's and Vandenberg Nutraceutical's bad deeds. Let you take the blame, and after some time passes, it's business as usual," Ortega realized.

"For the record," Moira tried to explain. "I do like you, an awful lot." Baxter shook his head, disgusted. "The plan was for me to take my share of the ransom and get you to run away with me," Moira confessed.

"What?" Baxter uncrossed his arms and recrossed them.

"Well, your family hates you—"

"I wouldn't say hate," Baxter defended.

"They were trying to put the blame on you," Moira answered fervently. "And if the Vandenberg and Church of Infinite Love collective empire fell, or even if it didn't, I wanted you to be free from all that."

"You did?" Baxter's voice softened. When she put it like that, it was rather touching. He took her hands in his, staring into her bright green eyes.

"But then I realized those men were going to kill ya," she finished.

And the romantic bubble was burst.

"How did you know that, Moira?" Ortega asked.

"The way they were talking," she confessed. "They kept saying how proud Bernie would be to see them carry out justice, and the favor God would have on them...amour of God and all that."

"Not to mention them telling me I was going to swim with the fishes," Baxter added.

"At first, I thought they were just a little overly enthusiastic," Moira offered, brushing a wisp of red hair behind her ear. "But the closer we got to the destination, the more convinced I was that they were serious. Scratch heard it too."

At the mention of his name, Scratch (one of the Fu dogs), nodded. "Aye," he agreed. "They sounded pretty serious ta me."

"So, how did they end up dead?" Ortega asked.

"I dunno," Moira answered. "When I phoned you, we had just gotten here after Quid picked us up. I told 'em to confess, fully expecting them to try to pin some of the blame on me. What I didn't expect was someone to kill 'em."

Ortega turned his attention to Constantine. "As of right now, the Guard assumes Moira and the Westport family are involved. So, if there's anything in this story that's missing, I suggest you fill it in for me now."

"I had nothing to do with any of this," Constantine complained. "I mean, other than providing transportation when Moira needed it...and now you know why I hate that the Vanden-berg family business returned to Ireland. They leave a wake wherever they go and give the respectable work of grifting a bad name." Constantine shook his head.

"Honor among thieves, is that it?" Ortega asked.

"Something like that," Constantine nodded. "An art form, at the very least."

"Jax is trying to frame me and the family," Moira was convinced.

"How can you be sure?" Ortega asked.

"I heard you telling Uncle about that broach."

"And?"

"And, I make it a point to never wear jewelry, nail polish, makeup, nothing that can obviously be traced back to me if accidentally left behind. If they found something that belonged to me, it was planted."

"By?"

"The same man who tried to murder me," Rue chimed in. "Jax Liebling. He's had it in for me ever since I helped put his girlfriend away for murder."

"Speaking of his girlfriend," Ortega added. "Have we heard from Ms. Pasternak recently? Because where she goes, death seems to follow."

"Does this Ms. Pasternak have a pretty thick New Jersey or New York accent, by chance?" Moira asked. "I'm not great with American accents, but that's what it sounded like to me."

"Yes, why?" Ortega raised an eyebrow.

"Because I received an anonymous call from a private number the night before the kidnapping," Moira answered. "The woman was trying to put on a passable Irish accent, but it was *really* bad." Moira chuckled.

"And what did she say?" Ortega asked.

"She said, 'if things go south tomorrow, call Detective Ortega.' Then she added, 'I'm only gonna say this once, so you'd better commit this to memory.' She rattled off your number and hung up."

"Good memory," Baxter commented.

"It's part of the job description," Moira answered. "But that's what caused me to get my guard up. In either plan, Baxter ended up here, under my protection—"

Constantine loudly cleared his throat.

"Under Uncle's protection," she corrected. "I just decided it might be best to plan for the worst, just in case."

"Why would you trust an anonymous voice on the phone, anyway?" Baxter was curious.

"Because I remembered something peculiar that Mr. Liebling said under his breath one day at work," Moira's eyes darted away as if triggering a memory. "He said, 'who's pulling the strings now, Jersey Girl?'"

"Midge said I was bait," Rue told Ortega, after she and Darwin had requested a private meeting with the retired inspector. "I thought I was supposed to help unravel the workings of the church and help you take them down for good, but I suspect she had other plans."

"Do you think she's working for Jax?" Ortega asked. "Maybe that it's all a ruse but they're actually working together?"

"I don't think so," Rue answered, thoughtfully. "I know that's a naive thing to say, but I really suspect that she's afraid of him. And she has this strange 'friend code.' Do I think she used me for her purposes? Yes. Do I think she put me recklessly in danger? Absolutely. Do I think she cares about me and doesn't want to see me dead? Yes...in her own twisted way."

"So, she helped you fake your murder," Ortega confirmed.

"Yes," Rue nodded. "She let Jax think he'd won."

"But, how did she get Constantine to offer to keep you in hiding?"

Suddenly, a disembodied voice chimed in. "She dropped Rue

off on the lawn near my front doorstep. Told my guys that Jax Liebling was trying to pin the blame of her death on the West-ports in a turf war," Constantine's voice may have been muffled, but it was definitely him. "And that Finn was sweet on her. My boys were so confused to find a girl, nearly dead, lying on the lawn. Or, at least one that appeared drunk or strung out on drugs, possibly an overdose, that they didn't notice that the bearer of such news had vanished...with one of our vehicles, I might add! Do you know how hard it is to spot a woman with dark green hair wearing all black in the middle of the night? It wasn't until they noticed the headlights in the distance that they caught on that she was getting away."

Darwin searched under the desk in the library where they spoke and in the fake plant on top, smiling at his discovery of both a tiny termite bug and a speaker. He glanced around the room before waving at a porcelain bust that sat on one of the shelves. He had discovered the hidden camera as well.

"Since we're clearly not getting any privacy, would you care to join us?" Ortega invited.

"No, you carry on. Forget I'm even here," Constantine bellowed before the sound dropped off with a bout of noisy static.

"None of this explains why she insisted you come to Ireland, Rue," Ortega commented.

"Maybe it was my super sleuthing on the last case we worked on?" Rue suggested, hopefully.

Darwin and Ortega sent her a questioning look.

"No," she relented. "You're right. While I understand a good bit about how a Church of Infinite Love campus operates, I'm a little out of my element here. Come to think of it, there's the factory. But are there even any church campuses out here?"

"Don't know," Ortega confessed. "We got distracted by you and the murders; we haven't had a chance to look. All that's come to light recently is the school that Bernie Forger recently broke ground on."

"But either way, you anger Jax," Darwin cut in, deep in thought.

"What?" Rue asked.

"He was angry enough to try and kill you. And what is bait after all, but a distraction?" Darwin added.

"So, what was Midge trying to distract Jax from?"

"And what makes him so angry?"

"Well, you did help put Midge behind bars," Darwin suggested. "Not to mention having a big role in uncovering the church's and the Vandenberg family's shady dealings."

"That's not it," Rue was convinced. "If anything, that would lead Jax to convince the Vandenberg family how much they really needed his help."

"No, I agree." Darwin all but read her mind, nodding.

"What am I missing?" Ortega's glance darted back and forth between the two of them.

"He's jealous of me," Rue answered.

"How so?" Ortega asked.

"I'm Midge's 'bestie'—her words. The only thing he can't control is how she feels about me. And that angers him to no end."

"What would dangling you out as bait do for Midge? What's her end game?" Darwin asked.

"I'm really not sure," Rue answered. "Midge wouldn't tell me, other than she was trying to clear up tensions between you and Constantine Westport, and help take down the church, but I find it hard to believe her intentions are honorable."

"Well," Ortega interjected. "Here's what I *do* know...both of you are on the next flight out of here back to the States, even if we have to use Darwin's resources to get you a fake I.D."

"Already taken care of," Darwin tapped the side of his pocket. To Ortega he added, "Don't ask."

"But wait," Rue complained. "I still wanna help."

"The best way you can help, honey, is to be safe." Darwin took her shoulders. "I can't lose you again." Rue nodded, wrapping her arms around his waist for a prolonged hug—just long enough to make Ortega, who was standing right in front of them, feel a little uncomfortable.

"That's right," Ortega confirmed, "I want you both out of this investigation. Do you understand?"

The two nodded, somewhat reluctantly.

"I think we're done here for now," Ortega spoke directly into the planted bug. In the distance, they could hear Constantine's deep breathing, but he still pretended not to be there.

As they were leaving, Darwin turned to Ortega. "Oh," he whispered, handing him a tiny flash drive. "Something I thought you could use."

"What is it?" Ortega whispered back, palming the small device.

"Thumb drive," Darwin explained. "Not on the market yet, but will be soon. You'll find some beta data mining tools on there."

"Data mining?" Ortega asked.

"Yeah," Darwin nodded. "I can fill you in when Rue and I are safely back in the States. Essentially, it'll help you cross-examine the data from different crime scenes, including the people involved, and formulate the relationships between them."

"So, essentially what I do," Ortega smiled. "I'll be out of a job soon."

"Hardly," Darwin answered. "But it can help you work faster and more efficiently."

"At my age," Ortega reasoned. "I'll take all the help I can get."

Darwin laughed. "Don't sell yourself short, Ortega. You've got a lot of fight left in you."

Ortega slapped Darwin on the back. "Thanks, Mr. Fennec. As always, you are just full of surprises."

Darwin gently knocked on Constantine's bedroom door in the early hours of the morning. It was Quid's turn at overnight duty. He opened it hesitantly.

"We're heading to the airport," Darwin whispered. "You'll let Constantine know?"

"You can tell him yerself," Quid answered, opening the door wide. "He's been waiting for you for the last hour."

"Come in, me boy," Constantine's tired voice could be heard from the bed. "Pardon my indiscretion, but you are leaving rather early." Across Constantine's lap was a custom-built breakfast tray large enough to fit over his frame. On it were eggs, bacon, blood pudding, baked beans, tomatoes, toast and...yogurt. Darwin eyed the yogurt, amused. "What?" Constantine defended. "I'm trying to eat healthier."

Darwin smirked. "I can see that."

"Ah, screw you, Finn," Constantine laughed. It turned abruptly into a phlegmy cough. "See what happens when I eat dairy?" he complained. "That's the yogurt."

Darwin bit his lip. "Just wanted to let you know that we're off...and I wanted to thank you for looking after Rue."

"Of course," Constantine answered. "Despite what you might think, I still consider you family."

"Well, I appreciate that," Darwin answered, uncomfortably. He was still trying to shake the notion he'd had that Constantine was out to get him for all these years. He still wasn't completely convinced.

"Thank you, Mr. Westport," Rue added. "I am very grateful for your protection."

"And that goes on even after you've gotten back to the States," Constantine added. "I've got my connections. You're under the protection of Constantine Westport now."

Rue wasn't entirely sure what to make of that, as the last people who tried to 'protect her' were her cult family. She simply nodded, appreciatively. Wasn't worth causing a fuss that close to their departure.

"Well," Darwin added. "We'll be off then."

Just as they'd reached the door, Constantine stopped him. "Tell my son that I welcome a phone call."

"I will let him know," Darwin answered, simply, before closing the door behind them.

Baxter Baker and Moira Dodd were on the next available flight out of Shannon airport. They'd slipped out shortly after their conversation with Ortega. At best, Moira would have been accused of attempted kidnapping. At worst, she could be facing murder or attempted murder charges.

"I can't believe I ended up doing to Uncle Constantine what Finn did all those years ago," Moira's face contorted, miserably. To add insult to injury, the two had 'borrowed' a service vehicle from Constantine's garage.

"Well, look on the bright side," Baxter explained. "You see how he forgave Darwin, right?"

"Yeah, after Bristol and Finn ran to the states over a decade ago!" Moira whined.

"Yeah, but this time no one he cared about got killed...I'm still here."

"I guess," Moira shrugged, sinking into her airplane seat.

"Not sure how much Uncle Constantine cares about you, though...if I'm being honest. And I'm sure he's not thrilled about being tied to a triple homicide."

"Well, no matter...at least, I forgive you," Baxter added with a hint of a whine. "You did try to kidnap me for ransom and almost got me killed."

"Trust me, Sweet Face," Moira smirked, "given your gunshot wound, I'd say there are lots of people who've got it in for ya."

"Hey now," Baxter's whine increased in volume. "You know as well as I do that that bullet wasn't meant for me."

"Hmm, all I know is you must have a guardian angel to have escaped death twice now."

Baxter took her hand in his and kissed it. "Angel is right."

"Oh, cut that out," Moira blushed. "Your charms don't work on me."

"And yet, here we are on a lovely adventure together."

"Yeah, if you had your way, we would have taken a flight out of Dublin to Manhattan and been picked up as soon as we landed," Moira mocked. "Guardian Angel is right. Just leave the planning to me."

"Alright, my dear," Baxter leaned back in his chair and let out a happy sigh. While he had some money in reserve, he didn't have a lot of it. So, things might be tight for a bit. For the first time, he didn't care. He felt this odd sense of relief sitting next to his green-eyed beauty. It was as if he was home for the first time in his life. "I'll leave it to you." Moments later, he added, "Although, I hear Cambodia is rather nice this time of year."

Chapter 28
Penelope's Revelation

Ortega returned to the flat just in time to see Shep wheeling a piece of luggage into their small living room, the same one he'd had at the start of their trip. He was dressed in black traveling slacks and a sweater with a wool coat draped over his arm, looking enormous next to his tiny bag.

Penelope stood beside him, tiredly, wearing a bulky bathrobe, her hair wet, and no makeup.

Ortega was enamored, but tried not to show it. *She looks even more beautiful without makeup, having her hair done or wearing fancy clothes*, he thought. *How is that possible? In fact, how is it possible that she becomes even more beautiful every time I see her?*

"What's going on?" Ortega finally asked, bringing himself back to the situation at hand. "Is everything okay?"

"Yeah," Shep nodded. "For the most part. My wife called at the tail-end of our investigation today. Just found out my littlest has to have his tonsils out. I need to be there to support the missus...four kids is a lot for one woman to handle on a good day, let alone when one has to go in for surgery."

"Married?" Ortega echoed. "Four kids?"

"You're looking at me with as much shock as she did," Shep motioned toward Penelope. "Why is it so hard to believe that someone chose to marry and procreate with me?" Shep seemed almost hurt. Though, he could have been joking. With Shep, it was difficult to tell.

"Not hard to believe at all," Ortega tugged at his shirt collar, awkwardly. "It's just that you never mentioned them, is all."

"For security reasons," Shep explained. "Given my line of work, I think it's best that people don't know everything about me."

Ortega nodded, trying to understand. After all, up until their recent case, the one they'd dragged him into, he wasn't certain that Shep's work was all that dangerous. But, what did he know? Maybe he was wrong.

"Do you need a lift to the airport?" Ortega offered. In truth, he was dead on his feet, and he wanted nothing more than to take a hot shower and climb into bed, preferably with Penelope...in both places, the shower and the bed.

A car horn could be heard honking outside.

"Nah," Shep answered. "That's my taxi. Thanks, though. Oh, Dr. Washburn can fill you in," he motioned to Penelope. "But while I was stuck in the hospital, they kept replaying this broadcast about Bernie Forger and his new plans for the church, before he was found dead—"

"Bernie's dead?" Ortega was surprised. This was news to him.

The car horn honked again.

Penelope touched Ortega's arm while saying to Shep, "You get home safe. I'll fill the good detective in."

Shep nodded, eyeing the two of them quizzically—as if he'd

only now just figured something out—and made his way to the cab outside.

After Shep's cab had driven away, Ortega closed the door and eyed Penelope. "It's very hard to concentrate with you in that robe," he commented, flatly.

"Would you rather I took it off?" Penelope grinned, seductively.

"You know I would, but—"

"But you wanna know about Bernie's broadcast?" Penelope pinched her lips together, fighting back a smile.

"Curiosity has gotten the better of me," Ortega admitted.

"First things first," Penelope answered. "Rue is—"

"Rue's fine. So is Darwin."

"He's here too?" Penelope remembered the sounds she heard on her last call with Darwin, ones that sounded suspiciously like an airport.

"Not for long," Ortega answered. "I sent them packing on the first plane out this coming morning."

"About Mr. Fennec—" Penelope began, biting her lip, awkwardly.

"I know about the phone call," he finished for her.

"You did? But how?" Penelope had been riddled with guilt since answering Ortega's phone just a few nights ago without him realizing. Only, apparently, he *had* realized.

"It registered in my cell phone call log," Ortega said. "Unless you specifically delete it, I can see that a call came in, and was answered, and lasted about a minute and a half."

"I'm sorry," Penelope sulked. "But it was killing me to see Mr. Fennec suffering like that!"

Ortega took her shoulders and gave her a kiss on the forehead. "You're a compassionate soul. I would have expected nothing less from you. I understand."

Penelope was surprised. *No criticism? No, 'Well, you should have...'* She was growing fond of this new and improved, and emotionally intelligent Ortega. She just wished they'd both gotten to this point a hell of a lot sooner.

"So, what's this about Bernie Forger?"

"While we were focused on Baxter Baker and Jax Liebling, Bernie was busy announcing a new direction for the church, one that includes a new training academy and publishing house near Belfast."

"They don't waste any time, do they?" Ortega grumbled, angry that he hadn't caught on to this sooner.

"It was all hush-hush until that broadcast," Penelope explained. "But now, Bernie's dead, and they haven't ruled out homicide yet."

"I'm starting to think we should bow out of this whole mess while we still can. Rue and Darwin are safe. Baxter is safe—"

"What happened to Baxter?" Penelope asked.

"Let's just say, he's created his own witness protection program with Moira."

"I see." Penelope wiggled her eyebrows and rolled a shoulder, suggestively.

"The point is," Ortega finished. "Why not let the Garda do their job and we go back to minding our own business, like we should have done from the beginning?"

"That doesn't sound like you," Penelope pointed out.

"Well, maybe I've had a change of heart," Ortega answered, unconvincingly.

Penelope was quiet as if wrestling with some bit of news that she dreaded sharing.

"I know that look," Ortega accused.

"What look?" Penelope asked, innocently.

"That look that suggests you're afraid to tell me something... either because you think it will make me angry or you think it will send me like a rabid dog after the next big lead."

Penelope bit her lip. "Probably the latter."

"Penelope," Ortega took her shoulders and peered into her eyes. "If you don't tell me, you'll be riddled with guilt and regret it. Transparency is always the best policy...learned that the hard way with Nancy and her affair."

Penelope sighed, "It seems that a press release went out announcing Edwina Vandenberg as the new head of the Church of Infinite Love," Penelope relented.

"I assumed it would have been Jax Liebling." Ortega was shocked, releasing her shoulders. He began making small circles around the room as he thought.

"I'm pretty sure he did too," Penelope sighed. "Nothing but a bunch of terrible people doing terrible things to one another in the name of religion."

Ortega slumped his shoulders. "Not everyone," he answered.

"What do you mean?" Penelope asked, quizzically.

"I seem to remember Elsbeth Ions being innocent in all of this. I mean, she pretended to have a developmental disorder to protect herself from getting involved with the family, but I look at that as self-preservation," Ortega reasoned.

"And, Emma Post seemed quite fond of the girl, taking her under her wing and all."

"I tell you what," Ortega decided. "What if I pay a visit to Elsbeth at her Uncle Edgar's estate, just to fill her in and make sure she's okay. Maybe ask a few questions about her mother, Edwina, and pass on whatever we discover to my buddy Inspector Clover. Then, we can leave with a clear conscience."

"What makes you think she'll talk to us?" Penelope asked.

"Hmm," Ortega thought a moment. "I'll contact Ms. Post in the morning. See if she can't put a call in to Elsbeth and see if she'd be willing to chat with us."

"Good thinking, Jose." Penelope touched the side of his face, lovingly. "But for now, we should get some rest."

Ortega yawned, nodding in agreement. He knew he should be phoning Doherty to let him in on Rue's re-appearance, but there was a part of him that needed to know she was safely back in the States first. Though, in the back of his mind, he knew he was lying to himself. *Let sleeping dogs lie,* he thought. *Why not let the trail end and give Darwin and Rue the chance to go back to their lives as usual, without having to answer uncomfortable questions from the Irish police?*

"Jose?" Penelope brought him out of his thoughts. "You're drifting again. Come back to me." She took his hand and led him into the bedroom.

Chapter 29
Elsbeth

Elsbeth's Uncle Edgar, Edwina Vandenberg's brother, greeted Ortega and Penelope at the door of his estate.

Not having met him before, Ortega assumed he must be one of the servants. "We're here to see Edgar Vandenberg," Ortega announced. "Jose Ortega and Dr. Penelope Washburn. He's expecting us."

Edgar paused for a moment before letting out a chuckle. "I dare say he is. Please come in." Ortega and Penelope entered the main hall and couldn't help but admire the high ceilings and grandeur of Edgar's home.

Edgar closed the door behind them. "May I take your coats?" he asked, eyeing Ortega's windbreaker and Penelope's light rain jacket.

"That won't be necessary," Ortega answered. "We won't be staying long."

"Tea, perhaps? Biscuits?" Edgar offered.

"Er, no, if you could just tell—"

"Uncle Edgar, you're not funny," Elsbeth appeared suddenly at the bottom of a grand staircase. She was so swift and silent that no one heard her enter the room.

Edgar stuck his tongue out at Elsbeth, like a small child. She did the same, in return, before the two started laughing at their inside joke.

"I beg your pardon," Edgar explained. "My companion, Isaac, is running errands today for Elsbeth's last supper before returning home...my, that sounded ominous as soon as I said it, didn't it?" He eyed Elsbeth, amused.

"So, you're Edgar Vandenberg?" Ortega confirmed.

"You're a quick study," Elsbeth retorted.

Ortega eyed her, questioningly. According to Emma's description, Elsbeth was a timid girl who stumbled over her words and kept to the shadows. While this young woman, on the other hand, was—in Ortega's mind—mouthy.

"Now, Elsbeth," Edgar chastised, "don't be cheeky." To Ortega, he said, "I apologize for my little ruse there. There's so little fun to be had for this old man, that I like to have my little gaffs now and again. I'm Edgar, nice to meet you." He offered a hand to Ortega. Ortega shook it, somewhat puzzled. After all, while Edgar gave the appearance of being much older than he was, Ortega was fairly convinced that they were both about the same age.

"Nice to meet you," Ortega offered.

"And you, my dear," Edgar cupped Penelope's hand with both of his own. "Aren't you lovely? I'm allowed to say that, aren't I?" Edgar asked. "I mean, at my age."

"Uncle Edgar, don't be gross," Elsbeth wrinkled her nose. "Besides, she's not much younger than you, anyhow."

Penelope stiffened, the smile on her face dropping momentarily before she recovered. Elsbeth caught that micro expression across Dr. Washburn's face, and smiled to herself.

"Cheeky is right," Penelope whispered to Ortega.

Edgar released Penelope's hand. "I don't suppose either of you would care to see my collection, would you?" Edgar offered.

"I think they're here to see me, Uncle," Elsbeth answered, somewhat impatiently. Edgar caught Elsbeth's eye for a moment, before she turned her gaze to the floor. It was the briefest of exchanges, where, for the first time, Edgar saw something in Elsbeth's manner that he didn't like...Edwina. Elsbeth shuddered, as if she could read his mind. "But we could talk *and* see your collection at the same time?" she suggested, brightly.

"Collection?" Ortega asked.

"Yes," Edgar explained. "An eccentric habit, I'll admit. But I have one collection of rare reptiles, amphibians and insects, all dead now and well-preserved under glass, but all *deadly* when they were alive."

"I don't think—" Ortega began.

"I would love to see it," Penelope gushed. Ortega was surprised. "What? I'm a forensic scientist. What's not to love about a deadly collection?"

Ortega furrowed his brows at her, confused.

"I also have an ancient bodies collection too." Edgar winked. "Isn't *that* exciting? I've even got a few shrunken heads."

"Well, now you're just sweet talkin' me," Penelope said, accenting her Southern drawl.

What is she doing? Ortega wondered.

Edgar took Penelope's arm. "Allow me," he said as he escorted her to his lab with Elsbeth and Ortega following awkwardly behind.

"Emma said you wanted to talk to me," Elsbeth said to Ortega, quietly.

"Yes," Ortega answered. "She's worried about you...so are we."

"Why?" Elsbeth asked.

"Because we got wind of Bernie Forger's death. Do you know who he is?"

"No, should I?" Elsbeth's eye twitched, just a little. Ortega had spent far too long on the force to not know what that twitch meant...Elsbeth was lying.

"Not necessarily," he played along. "He took over when your grandfather...er...passed."

"You can say 'died,'" Elsbeth retorted. "Saying 'passed' doesn't really make it any gentler now, does it?"

"No," Ortega shook his head. "I suppose it doesn't."

By now, they had reached the lab. Edgar had cleared out a small corner that once housed a plethora of insects, redistributing them under a glass counter by adding a few more shelves to accommodate them. Now, the exhibit featured a decayed body with strands of long hair behind a glass case. Adjacent to the body, were, as promised, what looked like a few shrunken heads, an assortment of teeth, some miscellaneous bones and hair samples, and even a few cloth remnants of ancient clothing and some pottery.

"I've got two more bodies that I haven't figured out how to display yet." Edgar's eyes gleamed. "Would you like to see one of them?" he asked Penelope.

"What do you think?" She grinned.

Ortega just shook his head.

"Excuse me," Edgar reached past Ortega, unlocked a long drawer and slid it out from under the exhibit. On it lay a body, probably belonging to a man, rather small-boned and frail.

Penelope squealed with delight. "How did you procure such a find?" she gushed.

"Last visit to Ecuador," Edgar explained. "If you have the financial resources for such a purchase, people rarely ask questions."

"You devil," Penelope teased.

"For you, I could be," Edgar flirted.

This was a side of Penelope that Ortega had never seen, and he wasn't quite sure what to make of it.

"Could I take a picture?" Penelope asked. "With my cell phone, I mean."

"Phones can take pictures now?" Edgar was surprised. "When did this happen?" Edgar asked.

"While you were hanging out with dead bodies," Elsbeth retorted.

To Penelope, Edgar said, "By all means...but," he added, "this is just for your personal use, yes? No publicizing this, okay?"

"I wouldn't dream of it," Penelope answered, while snapping some of the body along with the other body and items on display. "I just find all of this completely fascinating."

"Well, you must return more often," Edgar grinned, putting an arm around her waist.

"Isaac will be home soon," Elsbeth reminded him.

"What does Isaac have to—" He caught Elsbeth's expression. "Oh, right—"

Ortega wasn't clear on Edgar's relationships with Isaac, his companion, but apparently it didn't include Penelope in the mix.

"Wanna see the other one?" Edgar reached for the next drawer over, and fumbled with the lock as he tugged at the drawer's handle. "Must be stuck," he frowned as he fought with it.

"Listen," Ortega said to Elsbeth. "Before I head back to the States, I made a promise to Emma that I'd keep you safe." This time, Ortega's eyes twitched a little, but Elsbeth didn't catch it. While he did speak with Emma the night before, he had made no such promise. "We learned that your mother is about to take Bernie's place, just as he had taken your grandfather's place."

"What does any of this have to do with me?" Elsbeth asked. "I came here to get away from all that," she explained.

"Well, if Edwina...sorry, your mother...accepts the position, then she will likely also move to Ireland and assume the role of headmaster of the church's new school."

"New school?" Elsbeth feigned surprised. *There was that twitch again.*

"So, you didn't know anything about it?" Ortega pressed her.

"Of course not. My mother doesn't share anything with me. Not even the fact that she's been boinking her lawyer, Lundy, for years now without anybody knowing. Anytime he was over at the house, Mother kept referring to him as 'Uncle Lundy.' What a joke."

Ortega's eyes widened. Elsbeth realized she had inadvertently given the detective information that he didn't already have.

"May I ask you one more question, Elsbeth?"

"I guess," she answered, reluctantly.

"In your heart of hearts, do you think your mother, Edwina, is capable of murder?"

Elsbeth gave this a moment's thought before answering, "I believe my m-m-mother is capable of anything." Elsbeth was frustrated, and Ortega knew it...the stutter was real.

"Are you going to be okay?" Ortega asked Elsbeth, as they turned their attention back to Edgar, Penelope and his odd collection. Edgar was making apologies about being unable to show her the other body. She reassured him that it was fine. She had seen more than enough, anyway. He insisted they move on to his snake collection.

"Of course," Elsbeth answered. "I'm leaving here tomorrow. With any luck, the New York estate will soon be turned over to me, and my mother can do whatever she likes."

"Won't the family bother you or try to recruit you into the church?"

"I'm an embarrassment to my family," Elsbeth answered. "They would just as soon forget me as I them."

With that, Edgar looked up from a viper he was showing Penelope. In his eyes, he appeared hurt.

"Present company excluded," Elsbeth reassured him. To Ortega, she said, "Aside from Uncle Edgar and Cousin Baxter, the lot of them can go to hell."

"Excuse me, sir," Isaac appeared in the doorway. Edgar jumped, stepping a few inches away from Penelope, as if he had been doing something untoward.

"Yes, Isaac," Edgar answered, "what is it?"

"Would you like me to clear the field for clay shooting this afternoon?"

Edgar eyed Elsbeth who merely shook her head. "No, thank you, Isaac," he answered. Then, turning to Penelope, "Unless you would fancy a shooting lesson?"

"Perhaps some other time," Penelope declined.

"I'm a sporting man," Ortega answered. "Mind showing me the field?"

"Not at all," Edgar answered. "This way."

"Satisfied?" Penelope asked as she and Ortega returned to their flat.

"Almost," he answered, reaching into his pocket to retrieve the thumb drive Darwin had given him. "You brought your laptop with you, right?"

"Yes," Penelope giggled. "One of us has to be up on the times. Why?" She eyed the small plastic drive Ortega had pinched between his fingers.

"A present from Darwin before he left. Some kind of 'data mining' tool," he explained. "What say we have a look at it?"

Penelope brought out her laptop and opened it on the kitchen table. After restarting her computer, Ortega intuitively plugged the drive into the side of it.

Nothing happened. Ortega and Penelope gazed at the screen.

"Do we need to tell it to do something?" Penelope suggested.

"Good thinking!" Ortega explained. He sifted through the Rolodex in his mind to something Darwin had shown him a while back and used a Finder to track down the location of the drive's content and open it.

Within moments, the tool was launched, but most of the navigation was foreign to Ortega. "Here," Penelope offered. "Mind if I poke around a bit?"

"Poke away," he agreed.

It took about fifteen minutes of 'What does this button do?' before she figured it out. "Oh, I get it," she explained. "We have to feed it info and tell it to sort it out. Here—" She pulled out her phone. "If I can send my phone images to my computer and upload it here...voila!" The images of Edgar's odd collection popped up on the screen.

"Not sure I follow," Ortega confessed.

"I think you just have to tell it what you know of the case so far, and let it sift through the data and draw its own conclusions."

"Hmmm, worth a try," Ortega conceded. "You may have to help me, though."

Penelope grinned at him. "You know, you're pretty sexy when you're helpless."

"Well, then," Ortega leaned over and planted a kiss on her lips, "you must find me sexy all the time because I am helpless around you."

Penelope paused. "Not as much when you're being corny." Ortega pinched her bottom. "Hey, now!" She jumped.

The two were suddenly distracted by a strange whirring sound. The fan on the computer powered on as if it were working very hard.

"Think it's okay?" Penelope asked.

"Not sure," Ortega confessed. "Why don't we let it sit overnight. Assuming the laptop doesn't blow up, we'll check it again in the morning."

"Sounds like a plan." Penelope wriggled her eyes at him. "I need a shower. Wash my back?"

"Your back, your front...in between," he joked.

"Corny!" she said again.

"You love it," Ortega laughed, following her into the shower.

The next morning, Penelope was fixing herself a cup of tea when she saw it.

"Jose!" she called. "I think you better come out here!"

"What is it?" he asked, groggily.

She pointed to the laptop. A collection of images and text flashed across the screen. The program had come to some conclusions.

"Shit! Shit! Shit!" Ortega exclaimed, "How could I have been so blind? I've gotta call Clover."

Chapter 30
New Bestie

"Want to tell me what's going on here?" Jax eyed Midge lining up her suitcases outside the front door of Jax's apartment, Elsbeth beside her wearing a wool coat, cap and gloves.

"I'm afraid there has been a change of plans," Midge explained.

Jax eyed the two of them, suspiciously. "What are you up to?"

"I'm leaving you, Jax," Midge answered. "For good this time."

"Is that so?" he answered. His voice was calm, but his balled fists suggested he was doing his best to keep his temper under control. "May I ask why, after you and I just married? We were going to rule the new Jax nutraceutical empire together, not to mention my stock in the new Church of Infinite Love college and publishing house. Are you opposed to being rich?"

"No," Midge sighed. "But I am opposed to you."

Jax tilted his head and tucked his chin, uncomfortably.

"What changed?" His eyes rose to meet Elsbeth's, who despite her rigid disposition, lowered her eyes, uncomfortably.

"It has nothing to do with her," Midge explained. "And you know, for the briefest of moments, I thought it might work. But—"

"But?" Jax encouraged.

Midge hugged herself and let out a laugh. "For the longest time, I thought you were the smartest of them all, but it turns out that you're not."

"I'm not?" Jax raised an eyebrow.

"No," Midge shook her head. "Granted it took me a while to put all the pieces together before I could start moving them. Would you like a quick summary?"

"Please," Jax answered. "Would you care to come back inside and sit down?"

Just then, a man wearing a wool jacket with the lapel pulled up, hands in pockets, reached the top of the stairwell that was situated down the hall.

"Just for a moment," Midge agreed. "I promise, this won't take long."

To Elsbeth, she asked, "I hate to leave the heavy lifting to you, but could you be a dear and get our driver to load up our bags?" Elsbeth nodded, summoning the large man to assist her.

"Heavy lifting, indeed," Elsbeth grinned as she did little more than point to the bags.

He grabbed them, wordlessly, pausing to give a sideways glance at Jax, who merely glared back at him.

"Shall we?" Midge pointed to the door. Jax obliged, pushing it open and following behind her inside. She shuddered a moment as he closed the door behind them.

"How can you leave, when I can still give you the chills, even after all this time?" he grinned, hopefully.

"That's fear, Jax," Midge answered honestly. "And I'm tired of being afraid. Please open the door."

"But you're the only person I've ever loved," Jax protested. "You have nothing to fear from me."

Midge eyed the door, and so Jax relented and opened it just wide enough that the outside hallway was visible from where they stood.

"I know you *think* you love me," Midge answered. "But I've come to understand with time and wisdom that what you feel for me is obsession. And the day you stop being obsessed with me, is the day it's all over for me."

Jax paused to frame his words carefully. "You were going to tell me what pieces you have put together?" he reminded her.

"Oh, of course," Midge remembered. She swiftly and succinctly explained everything she had discovered, beginning with how Jax planned on taking control of everything, the newly rebranded nutraceutical company (conveniently now in his name), the Church of Infinite Love, and even the soon-to-be established church academy and publishing house. He was even presumptuous enough to think he could oust the Westport grift family from Dublin and assume the territory, establishing a new order with his own people in place.

It was Jax who convinced Bernie to rile up several of his followers to kidnap Baxter, with no intention of letting Baxter live. It would be far easier to make Baxter a scapegoat for the church's and Vandenberg Nutraceutical's past wrong doings if he wasn't around to explain himself in the long-term.

Jax wanted Moira Dodd involved so that he could point to the Westports as the ones to blame for Baxter's death, only his plans went awry when he arrived at the scene and discovered that the three kidnappers had been murdered. He quickly left the broach and other evidence intended to frame the Westports and vanished, later pretending he knew nothing about it.

Meanwhile, Bernie wanted to cut all ties from Jax's nutraceutical company, believing that the new college and published works would bring in money more quickly. He wanted to re-establish the old ways, and if there was to be a new faith-healing practice, it would be in Belfast, not Dublin, and out from under the Westports's watchful eyes and 'insurance policies.'

Once Lundy let Jax in on Bernie's plans for the school, suggesting that Jax would be a better fit at running it and convincing Jax to make a sizable investment to secure his place with the budding nonprofit, it was Lundy who put the idea in Jax's head that Bernie was too much of a hothead to properly run the church and the school. This was reinforced by the discovery of the three dead men, who Lundy likely blamed on Bernie (even though he didn't entirely believe he was responsible). Jax took it upon himself to stage Bernie's unfortunate accident, though Lundy might have inadvertently put the suggestion in his head... or at the very least, incited violence. Once again, Jax took the opportunity to try to pin it on Constantine Westport, and his not receiving a tithe for Bernie's practices on his turf. Despite the fact that the school was setting up shop in Belfast, Bernie was still broadcasting to his members all over Ireland, including the Westport turf. And Constantine Westport had no way of knowing that Bernie was beginning to sever ties from Vandenberg Nutraceuticals.

"What you didn't realize, my sweet," Midge finished, "was that Lundy had no intention of putting you in charge of everything. It was just your ego getting in the way, once again."

Jax stood upright, lifting his chin, defiantly. "What are you talking about? What do you know?" he demanded.

"He wanted your money, that was all," Midge confided. "Once you purchased the remaining shares of the former Vandenberg Nutraceutical company and helped fund the school, he was done with you. Lundy only needed your backing to cover the trail of old crimes in the States and put a new head in place of the rebranded Church of Infinite Love, or COIL, as they like to call it now."

"A new leader? What are you talking about?" Jax's face began twitching, agitatedly. "You don't mean...you?!"

Midge snorted. "No, dummy. Not me! Though, they could do worse. I'm talking about Edwina Vandenberg."

"Edwina? What does she have to do with anything?" Jax was incredulous.

"Lundy and Edwina have been playing bouncy-bouncy for quite some time now. Edwina was denied the right to take her father's place at the helm because she was a woman, but under the new code, one that she and Lundy were busy cooking up, there would be no such rule in place."

"Then how did they plan on getting rid of me?" Jax's brow broke out in a sweat. "Were they going to murder me like they did the men who kidnapped Baxter?"

"Oh, Jax. My poor, stupid husband." Midge shook her head. Jax lunged at Midge who revealed her trusty .32 Beretta and he jumped back. She pointed it at his chest. "Don't make me shoot you. It's bad enough you convinced me to murder all those girls back in New York." Jax backed away and Midge lowered her gun. "But that's your MO, isn't it? Getting other people to do your dirty work? They, nor a member of the church, weren't the ones who shot those men."

"Then who?" Jax asked.

"Me," Elsbeth answered timidly from the doorway. Jax's energy unnerved her.

"You?" Jax was astounded.

"They were going to kill Cousin Baxter. Aside from Uncle Edgar, he's the only family member I actually give a rat's ass about," Elsbeth explained.

"Final question," Jax asked Midge. "Why did you marry me if

you had no intention of staying?" If Midge didn't know any better, she'd say that Jax's voice cracked, just a little, in sorrow.

"Because I wanted my name tied to your bank account should anything happen to you. But more importantly, I wanted you to know that you can't control me anymore."

A lightbulb went off in Jax's head. "You little minx," he smiled. "That's not it at all." He pointed a finger at her. "You just wanted to prove you were smarter than me."

"It wasn't hard," Midge grinned.

"Are you the one planning to kill me so Lundy and Edwina can have me out of the way?" Jax asked. "Did you have some arrangement with them?"

"Are you kidding me?" Midge squinted at him, annoyed. "To this day, they don't know anything about me."

"Then exactly how do you plan to get rid of me and take my money?" Jax asked. "And might I remind you, you're a fugitive. How do you plan to cash in?"

"I'm going to give you an out clause, Jax," Midge offered. "This is your one chance to keep your cash, and your head, before Elsbeth and I head to the Netherlands. Not sure you're aware of this, but they are the first country expected to approve same-sex marriage...very progressive, don't you think?"

Jax looked back and forth between Midge and Elsbeth. "You mean?" He connected the dots in his head.

"Between her inheritance and mine, we stand to have quite a little nest egg. But again, it doesn't have to be like that. I don't want to take your money. You can pull up shocks and disappear, and we never have to see one another again."

Jax took a step toward her. "Is that what you really want?"

"Yes, Jax," Midge answered. "It's what I really want. I told you; I'm leaving you, forever."

She and Elsbeth turned to leave, hand in hand.

"I'll come after you," Jax promised. "I'll never let you go."

Midge sighed. "I was afraid you'd say that...goodbye, Jax."

As Midge walked out of Jax's life for the last time with Elsbeth at her heels, the man who was presumably their driver walked in. The two women quickly found their vehicle waiting for them outside. Midge slid behind the wheel and started the engine. "Unless you prefer to drive?" she asked Elsbeth.

"Who are you kidding?" Elsbeth teased. "I've never driven a car in my life."

"Spoiled brat," Midge joked.

Elsbeth merely laughed, sinking back into her seat, feeling a sense of relief for the first time in her life, soon to be rid of her family for good. She was sad that she'd likely never see Baxter or Edgar again. That was unfortunate. She rested a hand on Midge's knee. But the tradeoff was worth it, she decided.

Meanwhile, inside Jax's apartment, the man in the wool coat closed the door behind him and stared directly into Jax's deep-set eyes as if studying him.

"Did Lundy send you?" Jax asked. "I know my Midge talks a big game, but she wouldn't have the heart to hurt me. I know she loves me, in her own way."

"Don't know any-ting 'bout what yer woman would or wouldn't do, mate," he answered.

"Whatever Lundy offered you, I can double it," Jax offered.

"Who the feck is Lundy?" The large man eyed Jax, tilting his head like a confused puppy.

"If Mr. Lundy didn't send you to kill me, then who did?" Jax was more confused than scared. He still had unwarranted faith in his powers of persuasion.

"It seems that Constantine Westport is tired of getting blamed for crimes he didn't commit. Thanks to you, the inspector keeps poking his nose around, asking questions about Bernie Forger's death and his three henchman who tried to take out

Baxter Baker. To add insult to injury, ya never paid yer tithe, neither."

"So, you've come to collect, have you?" Jax smiled.

"In a manner of speaking," the man retrieved a large wire with leather loops at each end. "He jest feels that if he's gonna git blamed for some-ting, he might as well have it be for some-ting he was actually responsible fahr."

Jax's eyes grew wide as he realized that negotiations were useless. Midge tried to give him one last out, but he didn't take it. And now, it was too late.

In less than a minute, Jax Liebling was dead.

Chapter 31
Giant's Causeway

Penelope Washburn stood on the basalt rocks overlooking Giant's Causeway, letting out a shiver as the wind picked up. Jose Ortega wrapped his arms around her. She clung to his arms in front of her belly and leaned into his chest. In the past, Ortega would have been a little uncomfortable with the fact that Penelope was a bit taller than he, and that he was caught showing a public display of affection. But these days, none of that seemed very important. What *was* important, was that the two of them were together.

"It's been a pretty wild turn of events, hasn't it?" she sniffed, trying not to let emotions get the better of her.

"I'll say," Ortega agreed, hugging her more tightly.

They watched as the waves crashed against the coastline, blinking occasionally as wind and sea spray stung their faces... they didn't care.

The two thought back to what Darwin's beta program spit out. There, clear as day, was one image of Elsbeth Ions along with all the data points connecting her to the death of the three Americans. It also predicted with 93% certainty that Midge was somehow involved, and that there was reasonable probability that Rue Brennan's kidnapping was a distraction...though, the beta mining tool was better about sorting and predicting data than it was about understanding human thought patterns.

"What will happen to Elsbeth and Midge?" Penelope asked.

"Don't know," Ortega answered. "If I know Clover and this Doherty fellow, I suspect they'll join forces and swarm all roads leading to all airports in the vicinity, large and small."

"Too bad the program didn't predict where they'd go next," Penelope offered. "Any chance they'll hide somewhere in Ireland?"

"Doubtful," Ortega answered. "It's too risky for them, not only because they are both wanted for murder but they racked up quite a few enemies in the short time they were here."

The two began walking the Causeway's paved path, hand in hand, while a crowded tourist bus drove past. A few hikers steamrolled past them, but neither Ortega nor Penelope were in any hurry.

Penelope took a deep breath of fresh air and smiled, blissfully. "Under normal circumstances...paradise."

"Would you live here?" Ortega asked, curiously.

"What? In Ireland?" Penelope asked, thinking a moment. "I suppose I might. Hard to say, I've been a New Yorker for so long. Though, I don't really have a job to go back to now, do I?"

"I'm sorry about that," Ortega grimaced, knowing he was at least partially responsible for her dismissal, given that she'd pulled one too many favors to support Ortega on crimes neither one of them had any business investigating.

"It's alright," she answered. "Probably time for a change, anyway."

"What kind of change did you have in mind?" Ortega asked.

"I don't know," Penelope replied, thoughtfully. "Work that's rewarding but doesn't involve crimes of passion and dead bodies."

Ortega nodded as they rounded the bend. The wind picked up a little while the clouds rolled in, threatening rain.

"What about you?" Penelope asked. "We still don't know who killed Bernie Forger and Jax Liebling. Was it Midge, members of the church, the Vandenbergs, or the Westports? Someone else?"

"You know what, Penelope," he squeezed her hand, "I really don't care."

"You? Not care? How is that possible?" Penelope's mouth dropped.

"I almost lost the woman of my dreams thanks to this damn job. I've risked my life and those I've cared about, and I'm done. Leave it the young Dohertys of the world to pick up where I left off. I'm through sacrificing my life for criminals that keep cropping up and festering like termites and roaches."

"You mean, you're going to stay retired?" Penelope was doubtful.

"No," Ortega confessed. "But maybe something along the lines of what Darwin Fennec does…a little consulting, but nothing involving the Vandenbergs and Westports in a turf war… more like, finding someone's missing cat…or something."

"Not sure there's a career in that," Penelope teased. "But I support whatever you decide." She stopped, turned toward him, and leaned in for a kiss.

Ortega kissed her back, before his mind wandered, blissfully. He stared out over the ocean, lost in thought.

"What is it?" Penelope asked.

"Time for a complete change of scenery. Somewhere where I don't have to get caught up in the day-to-day drama."

"Like where?" Penelope asked.

"I dunno," he answered. "Where would you consider moving to with me? Unless, of course, you're opposed to that idea."

Penelope beamed, looping her arm through his as they stared off into the distance. "You couldn't keep me away if you tried."

"So, where do two reunited lovers go for a fresh start?"

Penelope thought on this. "Portugal," she finally announced.

Ortega was surprised at her definitive answer. "Okay," he agreed, "Portugal it is."

About the Author

Danielle Palli is a multi-genre author, Board Certified Positive Psychology & Mindfulness coach, and a multimedia content creator & book coach. She lives in Florida with her husband and a plethora of pets. She finds joy in nature, travel, music, theater and the arts, and is known for singing and dancing around the living room at any hour of the day or night. As a free-spirited outlier enamored with life, she finds that life is more exciting when you color outside the lines. Learn more: www.DaniellePalli.com.